DRAGON GEM

Dragon Gem

VENAS AND THE CAVES OF NOTTINGHAM THE SPECTRUM DIA

Vanessa Xu

Copyright © 2021 by Vanessa Xu

Cover, text and illustrations Copyright © by Vanessa Xu

The moral right of the author has been asserted

All rights reserved.
No part of this book may be reproduced in any manner whatsoever without written permission to the publisher except in the case of brief quotations embodied in critical articles and reviews.

First Printing, 2021

Thank you, everyone who supported me during the production of volume two

I thank my Mum
Pablo F.
Karla B.
Tommy B. J.
Cyril D.
Isabel
Maja

And thank you for choosing this book :)

OUR ADVENTURE CONTINUES

WELCOME BACK TO THE WORLD OF MARTIAL ARTS AND MAGIC

Map of the Warring States of China

Contents

Dedication ... ix

Prologue
A Frozen Midnight ... 1

Flame 1
Ninchanted Academy ... 6

Flame 2
Jade of Health ... 22

Flame 3
The First Day ... 38

Flame 4
Midnight Wander ... 64

Flame 5
Home ... 89

Flame 6
Liquid Body ... 111

Flame 7
Infested ... 124

Flame 8
A Dragon's Traits   138

Flame 9
The Black Panther   150

Flame 10
Headlines   168

Flame 11
Fall   181

Flame 12
Wings   200

Flame 13
The Defeat of Time   211

Flame 14
Artificial Intelligence   223

Flame 15
Goodbye   247

Flame 16
A White Christmas   254

Flame 17
Cleo's message   264

Flame 18
The First Hour   282

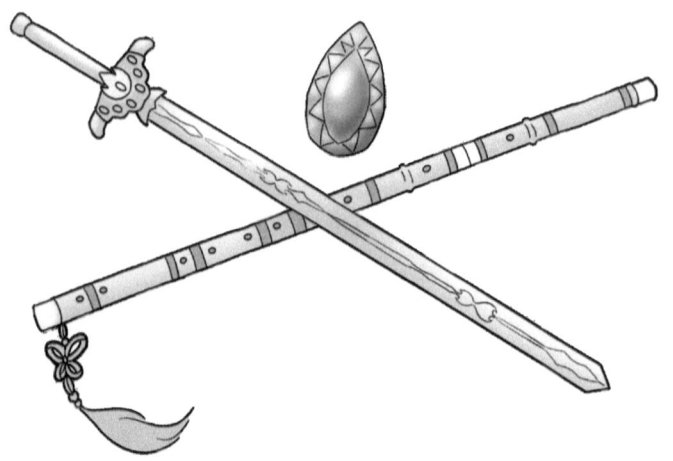

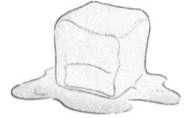

Prologue

A Frozen Midnight

2nd December 2015 Nottingham

Beyond the frozen lake of Nottingham's Lakeside Arts, reported the headlines of scientists and their midnight discovery of what they consider "a miraculous mystery". Biology professor, Doctor Lucy Lawson called for special equipment to dig out what she and her colleagues have detected through the thick layer of ice in the lake during the 3-degree weather.

"...it is eleven forty-five, we are out here at Lakeside Arts about to dig out what seems to be a person frozen in the ice of the frozen lake which is astounding, I have seen nothing like it," a reporter lady chanted loudly after a gust of cold wind blew past.

"... the weather has now dropped to 1 degree, a

temperature that doesn't explain how the lake is rock-solid..." she continued whilst the camera swiftly pans from her to the workers struggling to cut all the way through the thick ice.

Everyone switched on their mobile flashlights to fight off the gloomy darkness of the night and intensively waited for the large machinery standing on the concrete floors surrounded by grassy fields and trees. A children's playground was close by and pointed straight towards the University of Nottingham, a beautifully constructed university built on top of a slight hill. The tall clock tower next to the Portland building struck twelve as a shiny, black Audi car arrived at the scene. Connar Armsward, head of the robotics department in the depths of England and a world-renowned scientist with a big system of fascinating discoveries, black coat and denim jeans, with fair, black hair. He stepped out of the vehicle just in time to witness a clear block of ice sliding on the concrete after being transported from the water. Artificial light reflected across the surface and eventually, everyone was able to see what was trapped inside. Discussions of whispers grew in the background.

"Doctor Armsward, what do you think?" questioned Doctor Lawson.

Connar stepped closer, next to him, a child-like, humanoid A.I. assisted an optimum amount of light to see clearly a brown-skinned man with blue scars all over his shirtless body, white, dreadlocked hair tied up on the back of his head decorated with dark blue rings. He had the body of a wealthy wrestler wearing only a pair of trousers and thick black boots. He suddenly glanced at the lake and couldn't believe what he was seeing.

All the ice was melting away, all but the block they had ditched out, a chance for the report lady to speak to the camera again.

"What we have here is a black man-" started Lawson before she was interrupted.

"What we have here is a mutant, a brown-skinned mutant, there is no black man," Connar denied, he crossed his arms, he was confident in his judgement. You can tell Armsward has known Lucy for her prejudice and racism.

The word "mutant" taunted a lot of people but it didn't bother Connar, he suggested he takes this investigation to hand to give the mutant a safe home but Lucy bitterly disagreed with his offer, the wrinkles around her eyes folded on top of one another like a young shar-pei.

"I'll start tomorrow first thing in the morning, melt the ice and examine him," Connar suggested with no intentions of harming him.

"No, why would you want to melt him, he is a dangerous creature, we will take it in, it will be locked up and under no circumstances will we ever free it, a creature like this can cause us serious problems."

"Ma'am, it will cause problems once other mutants find out that you are keeping him hostage."

"And how do you suppose that? There hasn't been a mutant sighted for at least a year, the last one was detained, put down and quarantined in the Underground Prison of London for the freaks of nature," she referred to the Underground Prison of Mutants. "It will be kept under lockdown, we are not risking the safety of this city because you want to free it from the ice," she declared with a rude frown on her freckled face.

She slotted her ugly hands into the warm pockets of her long coat and walked away after a truck drove across the grass. The freezer-installed truck was sealed tight and transported the mutant to Lucy's lab and never seen again.

Connar and his A.I. Assistant Cyber 01 was left alone as he approached his car, the door shut automatically once Cyber took his seat next to him. Connar's mind illustrated a series of pictures and thought, he placed his hands on the steering wheel and gazed at the lake with an irritated expression.

"Did you get the pictures?" he asked Cyber.

"Yes sir, transferring photos to the system," he answered.

The instalment of his car unleashed a digital screen presenting all the photos of which Cyber secretly took before the mutant was taken away. He examined his features.

"Bring up the paintings," he requested.

"Transporting paintings," said the system.

A slide of paintings and photos from the late 1490s that he had collected popped up with a series of system sounds from the vehicle. The paintings and the photos were digitally compared on the screen, lines, dots and arrows pointed to similar features. Connar's eyes scanned from left to right and left again, back and forth.

"Go back," the patterns on his body were the same as the ones in the faded paintings, illustrating the mutant's time of greatness and duty, a souvenir of history from the Muman's war.

"Match found," the system picked out some very old and faint record, lastly, it zoomed in on the face of the mutant in the ice, his eyes were shut tight in a relaxed position. Connar watched and waited patiently for all the information to come to a halt whilst quietly drumming his fingers on the wheel.

"Identity found, Altas Silver."

Flame 1

Ninchanted Academy

224 B.C. Qin States
China, Planet Ervanna

Amongst the trees and bushes in the Forest of Past, blew the morning breeze sending the autumn leaves to peace in the calm skies. The warmth of autumn has passed, letting the winter chills take over the land. Birds flew across the blue sky above, a series of movements through the forest followed the noises that startled the wild. Those resting on branches flapped their wings tremendously to a more peaceful part of the forest but unfortunately, the disruption to nature rose. Far from the entrance, teenagers scampered across the crunchy leaves, rushing through the forest as if their activity was put on a timer. A group of boys painfully grasp their injuries and collapse to the ground whilst their peers try to fight off a fierce girl who they have decided to attack. Leaves swayed from the ground following the gust of wind created by Venas as she flips and turns across the soil. Her reflexes, better than ever, perfecting a smooth landing from the treetops after tying one of the boys to the branches with his own sleeves and strips from his hanfu and the rest of them tangled together with their sleeves in agony and bruised pain. She thumped on the ground with a crunch with a smile of satisfaction patting her hands together, brushed her clothes of dust and dirt. She wore a knee-length hanfu suitable for using her newly developed martial art skills. White underdress, unsymmetrically coloured, red and white, white hanfu boots, yellow belt and sleeves, on her head, the hair ornament gifted by Prince Emerald and long braided ponytail accompanied by red ribbons of which she took and flicked it behind her. Ever since she landed in this world, her eyes underwent a dramatic alteration. Before, whenever she sensed danger, the brown-hazel pigment in her eyes would swirl and turn red but soon disappear. After a short period of time, she has noticed that only her right eye has become permanently red. It was a strange mystery in her consideration.

Lastly, she ensured that the scroll she slotted in her belt was still there, thankfully, it was.

"Please, put me down," he yelped.

"Hmmm," she crossed her arms then stroked her chin, "how about no, good day," she grinned and rushed in a hurry.

"Ayyyyy, no, come back little miss!" he yelled and sighed, wriggling on the underside of the fat sturdy branch and soon heard some crunching noises below him. Who he saw put relief on his face.

"You can't even handle a little girl, ts ts ts... you call yourself a senior, talking about giving your master some face," said the boy.

"Lee, Hei gongzi, oh thank goodness you're here, please get me down," he begged, "she- she may look weak, b- but looks can be deceiving."

"She didn't even use her celestial, you big baby" Lee declared. Lee Hawk, as we call him, in the city, is known as Hei Li Bing, Hei gongzi is one of Prince Emerald's subordinates who works alongside Kayne Wen who is addressed as Wen gongzi. But today, he is more than just a royal employee, he has a different mission. Dressed in a grey hanfu, black belt and sleeves, his hair wrapped up in a bun with a grey ribbon flowing down his back. He crossed his arms.

"So... you can untie me now, I'm still waiting," he repeated.

Lee looked up at his peers tied to the branch and the ones sitting on the ground who also struggled to untie themselves without removing their clothes, he grinned.

"Enjoy the view, don't let the ants bite," he chuckled.

"Ants? No, you can't leave me here, help me please, we're classmates after al -" but Lee was long gone. Suddenly, his head twitches before his shoulders.

"So itchy," he declared, wiggling about like a tied up caterpillar.

"He was right about those ants," laughed the boys on the ground.

Lee travelled from branch to branch in search of Venas.

"If I remember correctly, Miss Xoular has tremendous speed," his head darted towards the direction where he heard the rustling of bushes and sprinted after the trail of sound, brushing twigs away and leaping over rogue roots. He chased the shadow closer to the assigned exit of the forest and suddenly stopped in his tracks. Silence grew around him, he searched anywhere but up and soon found himself being booted into the partly leafy bushes, face first. Venas pulled him onto the grass by the arm and planted her foot on his back without taking a closer look at who he was. Lee struggled for air with his face planted in the grass.

"It's me it's me it's me," he grunted when she locked his arm back, "it's me."

She recognised his familiar voice and gave him a chance.

"Hm?" she leant down to take a look at his face, "Hei Gongzi? W- what are you doing here, you know you can't sneak up on me, I can hear everything," she reminded him.

"Yes yes, now let go."

"Right," she loosened the pressure she put on him with her foot and before she knew it, he grabbed the scroll from her belt as soon as she freed him.

"Hey! Give it back."

"Not a chance," he grinned, raising the scroll towards the sky, her height was no match for Lee's.

She jumped up to grab it but sadly, she did not succeed. Lee was feeling a bit playful with his given task. He dropped the scroll into his other hand, she saw her chance to retrieve it until he punched it back into the air, and again and again like a session of kick-ups with a football. The scroll went up and down, left and right. Venas and her tiny legs only jump so high.

"Come on, you can do better than that," he teased.
"This isn't funny, I'm in the middle of something here," she yelped.

She stared at the scroll wrapped between the red ribbon that he held high in the air once again. Lee noticed the long pause and saw how focused she was. He nearly let his guard down when she picked up her fist and aimed it at his arm for him to dodge, her eyes met his eyes for a split second, another swing of her leg for him to duck, tipping over into a flip to land back into balance.

She's faster than I remember, he thought. The trees shook whilst being used as tools, stepping stones to perform their light-body kung fu with Lee creating the trail, trying his best to escape from Venas's lightning speed, hopping from one tree trunk to the other, the illusion of flying was taking over their martial arts combat until he landed on the ground to catch his breath. Venas didn't give up and chased him to do so until she had the scroll again. She leant down to grab it, he reached out and took her by the back of her clothing like a claw machine and pulled her up, one second after that, she spun behind him but he was quick to notice and flipped the other way to avoid her contact with the scroll. One punch blocked, avoided kicks and a serious gaze from her eyes to his.

His grin disappeared when Venas took a different approach and darted upwards, vanishing into the evergreen leaves. The rustling was everywhere. He could tell she was sprinting through the trees at top speed, trying to confuse him, blowing leaves and soil into his eyes to blind him. Even though he knew, it still worked and not long after, she swung upside down from a branch the closest to the ground, snatched her momently treasured gold and with the speed and force aimed from the treetops, aggressively spun in mid-air like a figure skater but more horizontally to make a safer landing before tapping a tree trunk nearby to boost her light-body skills for a swift escape into the far distance after giving him a light gaze. He was still dazed by her performance. He pressed his hands on his hips.

"She has tactics," he sighed.

What is the scroll for you may wonder? This is a 15-year-old girl who, a few months ago, landed herself in the Planet Ervanna that spins in an orbit inside the galaxy of Andromeda far away from her home on Earth in the Milky Way. The location of landing, Qin's Empire Palace in the Empire city of 224 B.C. better known as the Warring States of China. This hidden era is a place of danger and adventure, but mostly danger, land of martial arts and magic. How she landed here was a mystery that she had always questioned ever since the day she arrived. The bigger question was how she plans to return home. The art of portal magic is a challenge for mortals. In the meantime, in order to survive this crazy world, she took on the offer to become the first honoured disciple of Master Ocean to train under his supervision. She kept her word, she spoke of it to no one, respected the three rules of being his disciple. Respected her teachings and improved after many attempts and fails to rise up to this day in skill and tactics. The day of the exam. Today is the final day of the entry exam for Ninchanted Academy, School of Martial Arts and Magic. A bright day to congratulate the soon-to-be trainees of Ninchanted, an honoured educational site built in the Empire city of Qin States with a proud gold sign above the entrance gate that reads backwards:

(Qin States Ninchanted)

Venas finally reached the exit of the forest where the masters of the academy were standing waiting for their applicants. She was the first one to complete the task of bringing them the scroll which was merely a token of passing the exam. She fixed the stray hairs from her bangs and clipped them to the side using butterfly-shaped hair clips that she wore above each of her ears before being escorted to one of the school's courtyards by a worker. She was asked to wait here until the exam was over. The academy suffered great destruction during the battle with Tao Shi and his fellow monsters but luckily, it only took a few weeks to rebuild everything as people here are fast on their feet and like things done quickly. The educational site was built with many departments for medics, martial arts, celestial training, language class and many more areas that help with survival in this world. The ground covers a big deal of land and the courtyard Venas was standing in displayed pots of rich plants stumped on top of the pebble filling surface between the wooden footpaths that circled around it in the shape of a sturdy rectangle. Each edge leading to a different doorway from the entrance to the exit to the archways that led to the trainee dorms and education buildings. One of the very few things that survived the destruction was the highly valued cherry blossoms standing between each courtyard. Well, almost all of them.

The special trees bloomed all year round, the perfect scene to welcome a cute little friend onto the stage. From inside Venas's clothing, gleamed a soft light, her amulet released a stream of coloured energy twisting spirals in the air and puff. It was Petal, her beloved dragon charamol. Petal was used to resting in her Oracle, she would always stay in there when Venas was on Earth to avoid being discovered but here, she forgets that she can roam freely. She flapped her wings with joy as she flew out and landed onto a branch to stretch her tiny little limbs and lastly shake her body like a wet puppy from head to tail.

"Hi Petal," Venas greeted her with a paw shake.

Then noticing how quiet the courtyard was with just her, Petal and the academy guards by the doorway, she wondered what her friends were doing, they were still in the forest striving to keep hold of their scrolls to reach the finish line.

Returning to the tree with a boy still tangled upon it, by-passed a young teenager wearing a tea-brown hanfu, white boots and trousers. He crunched his way slowly when he saw the mess of bodies. Erra looked up at the boy who seemed to be half asleep as it had been nearly an hour since Venas put him there.

"Hm?" he heard an incoming human and broke out in relief, "oh finally, fellow gongzi, please help me down, I've been up here for an hour," he begged.

Erra was thinking about helping him and his friends but noticed they didn't possess a scroll from the masters at the entrance and he didn't know who they were.

"I think not, how do I know you don't try to steal my scroll when I free you down," he stroked his chin. "Answer me this, which way's the exit?"

"Over there," he gestured with his head of which was the only body part that he could move freely.

"Oh thank you," Erra followed the gesture and made for the exit.

"Huh, no wait, don't go..." he relaxed his muscles when Erra disappeared amongst the trees, "why am I so hopeless?"

After countlessly encountering tricky obstacles such as a variety of traps and ditches made from applicants to fall in, live obstacles like Lee Hawk and his peers who were in their last year of training at Ninchanted volunteered their assistance to challenge their junior classmates. Unlike Venas, many applicants failed to bypass the seniors but at the same time, many others succeed including Erra Stone and Markcas Black. Eventually, the exam came to an end. A total number of 345 juniors entered the forest and 200 managed to pass at a high ranking, 70 with a lower ranking and the rest vow to do better in their retake... for next year

The morning mist was quickly replaced by a ray of sunlight shining from the highest point in the sky. The juniors were split between courtyards before entering the process of unfolding what their set rankings were to continue their application. A long scoreboard noted everyone's names in order of their grades. Everyone hovered over the board to a series of writing, scanning vigorously for their names. Venas became lose amongst the people, she wasn't as eager as everyone else to know her rank, in her mindset, she was bound to find a way to return home but she tried anyway to squeeze past her fellow peers and searched through the middle of the board for the name "Xu Jing Xing," written in seal script Chinese. Petal struggled to stay put on her shoulder and nearly slipped down her back when a peer bumped into her. Venas lifted her back up securely. Petal looked wherever Venas was looking. Her name was nowhere near the left where the lowest ranks were, nowhere in the middle. To her surprise, she was at the very right of the board.

"Look someone received a rank 2, 430 stars," said a peer who was so hopeful that her name would be at the front, "Xu Jing Xing? This name sounds familiar."

Venas heard her name and rushed towards the highest ranked names.

"Luo Wen, your name should be there, you worked hard after all," said her friend bitterly.

"You're right, it should be me... oh, I know now, she's the hero who took down the monster Tao Shi, younger brother of the King of Neverlight... hmph, they probably gave her the highest rank in the year because of it, look, she's the only second-ranked trainee in the year."

"I'd like to see this so-called hero."

Luo Wen wasn't very happy at this point. She was a girl with a need for gossip and looking down on people who she disliked with the most obvious of hints, she received a 3rd rank with 350 stars out of 500 calculated from their performance alongside their written exams the day before. The crowded chatter didn't stop Venas from hearing every word the girls were saying, this prevented her from being seen by their judgemental eyes. Petal dropped her wings in empathy for Venas and wrinkled her little forehead ready to have a go at teaching them a lesson.

"It's ok," she stroked Petal's chin to comfort her and walked away from the crowd.

In her mind, she was thinking about two people, Erra and Markcas.

"Where in Ervanna could they be," she muttered.

The number of people made it hard to find them, Petal

would be able to fly up and spot them but before she could do that, an academy guard gestured to her to line up for the introduction assembly, following the open path that eventually led to the main outdoors training ground. By the entrance, stood Master Shi, one of the masters of both medicine and martial arts. She put her hands together and bowed, Master Shi, bowed back and handed her the academy uniform with a red belt to symbolize rank 2. Master Shi is the owner of the famous magic shop in Empire City and has had his eye on her and her potential since the beginning of the exam and was delighted to congratulate her. His magic shop was the same one of which Venas, MArkcas and Erra had entire for answers during the ruling of Tao Shi.

"Thank you," she bowed again and went to change.

"Hey Black, your name's there, see," Erra pointed near the left of the board to guide Markcas to his rank. Markcas rotated his attention to his point and sighed.
"That's good enough for me," he took his long braid and flicked it behind him. He wore his blue attire with strips of fabric flowing down to his ankles on top of his underdress, his blue eyes and lengthy black hair that grew out in the last two months enough to tie back.

"Fourth rank, you must've fell during the written exam, let's go get our attire," said Erra who was graded with a third rank.
"Hey, where's Venas?" Markcas looked around.
"I don't know, haven't seen her since dawn."

"I heard some gossip, she's ranked second," he and Erra scrolled to the right of the board "see, the highest in the year." Erra's name was a few slots away.

"Can't believe one can improve in such a short amount of time, impressive, come on, let's go," Erra praised.

"Yeah, she's pretty amazing," Markcas muttered.

They followed the rest of their peers to the training ground where everyone assembled a few minutes later in their new attire, white hanfus with strips of red fabric and the faded belt colour of their rank. Red for second, black for third, a sort of purple for fourth, brown for fifth and white for sixth. First is represented with gold.

All the boys and girls lined up in flawless rows like army soldiers and chatted amongst themselves whilst waiting for all the Masters to take their places on a small stage in front of them. On each side of the stage, corner and edges of the training ground, academy guards patrolled in silence. The flooring of the ground was a smooth stony texture and fenced at the back between two staircases that led down to the school building. Venas stood near the middle at the front far away from Markcas at the very centre and a bit closer to Erra as the order was according to their grades. Petal snuggled comfortably on her shoulder, her soft paws gripped onto her clothing quietly keeping Venas company. The same for Spike who crawled into the chest opening of Markcas's hanfu to take a little nap.

"Good afternoon, children," announced Master Shi,

who flicked his long, white hair behind him, neatening his blue and grey hanfu under those big floppy sleeves hanging from his shoulders, "freshmen, I would say, congratulations for passing your exams, those of you who have registered for the academy dorms will soon be escorted but first of all, you must understand that training at this academy is not fun and games, we have high standards for each and every one of you," the old man bellowed, he introduced the rest of the teachers who are in charge of the first years. Professor Gong, a rather young looking master of medicine in his 40s with a small moustache, a half-up hairdo resting on his rich navy overcoat capped over his blue and green hanfu. Mistress An, master of kung fu in her late 20s, her hairdo was a simple ponytail parted with braids, she has the posture of a noble soldier in a purple embroidered hanfu. Professor Qiu, master of celestial magic also in his 20s, his hanfu seemed tailored to a more immortal look that suited the subject, shades of blue silk that reached the floor. Professor Ning, master of language and poetry reaching his 50s, Mistress Jiang, master of medicine, Vice Principal Tang, master of a mixture of celestial magic, martial arts and medicine in his late 60's and Headmaster Hua, master of all reaching his 70s. Pupils will just refer to them as "teacher", "headmaster", since addressing a senior by their name is impolite. Addressing family members is deemed the same along that line. Each master waved to the students on the call of their names with a warm and welcoming smile before Master Shi continued to the rather boring part of the introduction.

"With great disciple comes disciplinary measures," he reached his left hand out for Mistress An to relay him a sea-blue hardback book that opens up like an accordion, "hopefully you all have noticed the wall of rules by the entrance, the same rules in this book, our "Qian Tiao Xiao Gui" that every student must follow," Qian Tiao Xia Gui is the translation of school rules of a thousand, one thousand rules for Master Shi to chant to the students for the next hour.

You can imagine the reactions of the students who were about to stand the whole way through a reading of a thousand rules, Master Shi began.

You will adhere to:

- No talking whilst your masters are talking
- No private/personal conflict in spars
- No using your teaching to bully others
- No activities of shadow arts and dark magic
- No interactions with those that are involved with shadow arts and dark magic
- No action of selfishness and greed
- No ownership of forbidden substances
- No misuse of sword arts unless on act of self-defence
- No misuse of celestial magic
- No misuse of martial arts
- Respect your peers
- Respect your teachers
- Respect your teachings and learning outcomes
- Respect academy property
- Respect the dorm curfews set at 10 o'clock
- No leaving academy grounds after curfew
- No drinking within and outside of the academy

- No journeys and entries within brothel hotels
- No acts of inappropriate behaviour
- No skipping training...

And the list continues.

40 minutes later, legs become dreary and mouths continue to yawn. Petal was fast asleep in her Oracle, Spike, who never woke up in the first place, Markcas rested his head in his palm supported by his other hand and Erra ended up cloud watching but eventually, it was over. Probably the longest hour the students have ever experienced. Venas was reminded of this experience when her previous school in northwest London took the class on a day trip to the Shakespeare's Globe where they stood for a whole hour to watch the play, Romeo and Juliet whilst most of the other schools were granted seats. Her legs became exhausted and heavy.

The students were finally dismissed to return home or to their dorms provided, with a note of starting their train first thing tomorrow at seven a.m.

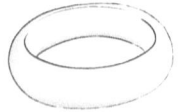

Flame 2

Jade of Health

After the assembly, Venas just remembered that Master Ocean requested an errand as soon as she could. To purchase some remedies and decorations from the city markets. What the decorations are for? Venas did not ask any follow-up questions. What her master tells her to do, she does. So in a rush, she gently transports Petal back into her Oracle and manipulates her light-body skills to run and created an illusion that she floated into the roofs to avoid the crowd below to the other side right before Markcas took a glance up into the sky and missed her by a second. Venas grabbed the things Master asked for and kindly gave the shopkeepers a few taels of silver lumps.

"Thank you," she greeted with a generous smile and took off amongst the crowd.

It was a fine day for the civilians to shop and explore the Empire City, the streets were festive and busy full of fresh steam that came from the food stalls and restaurants sizzling with delight. Venas couldn't resist and stopped in her tracks to hover over a stall of savoury pancakes and popping hot steam buns. Red beans, black beans, pandan, strawberry, custard and char siu pork, her favourite.

"Greetings, Miss Xoular, what may I get you today," said the stall owner who sees Venas come here very often for her uniquely delicious recipes.

"Three roasted pork, three pandan and two pancakes please," she spoke loudly to fight the street's liveliness.

"Here you go, thank you," the lady passed her a brown paper bag with the steaming good and offered a bean bun as a treat.

"Thank you," Venas gave her eight taels and scurried back to the Empire Palace with the bags of goods magically stored inside a small pouch hanging from her belt. After she enters the main buildings, presenting the Sword of Jade Dragon as a token of identification, she makes her way back to the Crown court past Prince Emerald's pavilion stand. Kayne stood outside on guard and pretended not to notice her.

Venas enters the underground library and approaches Master with a warm smile. Master was kneeling at his desk, he looked up at his disciple.

"Greetings Master," she held her hands together and bowed politely.

Maser smiled back and put down his brush.

"Someone's in a good mood," said Cleo, leapt from the bookshelves and landed next to her. "Bought everything?" Venas handed her the items.

"Look, I even bought you some buns," she shared.

"Buns?" Cleo excitedly raised his head, then his other hand for the tasty food, "thank you- thank you."

Master received the items and took them away.

"Master, I noticed everything you asked me to buy is red for the wedding?" She followed him.

"Why ask if you know?" Master replied.

"But the Palace guards and servants have it all booked."

"These are considered a gift."

"A gift?"

"A gift of wealth, a gift of health and a happy and long life," said Master.

Venas was sent to a very fancy store in the centre of the city that sold quite expensive things, things that only rich citizens could afford.

So they're not just decorations, she thought. Master removed a small cylinder case from the shelves and opened it to reveal a polished, white bracelet made purely of jade, also a gift to the bride.

"White jade, a sign of good health and luck, it can pacify the mind, nourish the body, calm one's soul and blood, it must be cherished, if broken, all that its promises will wither away with it," he quoted, "you will give this to Infanta Ocean."

"Why me?"

"You may do as I say."

"Yes Master," she kindly took the case from Master's hands.

The bride, Aiisha Ocean, Infanta of the Qin states arranged to marry the Crown prince of Zhao states.

"Zhao State's Crown Prince, Lan Zi Yi arrived yesterday, I haven't seen him around," she referred to Lucas Blue, the Prince she met during the Queen's angelversary two months ago.

"He's resting in his guest room, I've met his parents, they are to leave after the marriage ceremony to Zhao States tonight," said Master.

"Tonight? But the distance from Qin's Empire city to Zhao's Imperial city is a three-day trip."

"Not if you ride by carriage, the idea of a girl getting married at a different location than the one she is getting married into."

"Even with celestial magic, one's abilities have limits," Venas justified.

"Does Venas have anyone on her mind?" Master questioned.

"Me? Who would I possibly have in mind?" she denied.

"I say it would be Markcas Black, he's a fine gongzi he is," Cleo teased.

"Him? ... No no no, we're just buddies, two people

who have the same problem and are trying to work it out, somehow," she reminded Cleo and Master Ocean that she is never giving up on finding a way back home.

"I say you should give him a chance," Cleo suggested.

"Shush, eat your buns," she replied.

Cleo lowered his furry head, shrugged his shoulders and took a nibble from his bun.

"Master, aside from the wedding, I was thinking about Portal arts," Venas continued.

"Oh?"

"That's not new, when do you ever not think about portal arts?" Cleo commented. Venas looked down and gave him the eyebrows.

"If dark crystals are so powerful that they can create portals from Ervanna to Earth and back, then are there any alternatives that I could use to go back to Earth?"

"You know you can always go for the dark crystal option," Cleo joked whilst munching.

"Absolutely not," Venas declared.

"The Arts of Nature's Oracle," Master chanted.

"What about it?"

"A one of a kind read, the only copy belongs to Prince Emerald, you can give that a good read," Master suggested.

"I guess I'll ask his highness after the ceremony."

It was time for the ceremony to begin. Venas stood in the throne chamber amongst the rest of the Ocean family and their guests, waiting for the two main characters of the day.

She gripped the case Master handed behind her back maintaining a noble posture of the historical era. She was standing behind Master Ocean who knelt at one of the tables by the side of the chamber's footpath. All the members of the Ocean family took their knees, Prince Emerald, his uncles and aunties, grandparents and the youngers whilst the servants stood behind them including Lee Hawk and Kayne Wen who never looked colder. Venas stood across from them and looked at Kayne and thought, why does he look like he's attending a funeral?

The chamber was decorated with red paper flowers hanging on the walls and pillars, red streamers, silk curtains that gave the scene a calm and heavenly feel with the perfect amount of light blazing through the windows. The shadows create common patterns on the floor from the design of the windows. King Ocean took his seat on his throne and took a sip of tea placed on the table in front of him but the eunuchs, they both backed away in tiny steps once they saw the bride and the groom outside. Aiisha's long, red gown followed her along the large mountain of stairs on the way to the top and was still touching the stairs when she reached the door. The couple wore the lucky colour of red hanfus with draping sleeves and skirts embroidered with rich yellow patterns from shoulder to toe. Prince Lucas had a big, red paper flower pinned to his right shoulder and to his left, Aiisha was smiling under her thick red veil also embedded with rich threads along the edges, it laid on top of her heavy headpiece with several dangling pieces and golden carving that no one can see. No one could see her face at all, after all, it is bad luck, Aiisha too, could not see anything, she gripped the tail of a paper flower whilst Lucas held the other tail. Her other hand was held by a Palace maid to guide her but she wasn't the only one assisting the infanta. Several maids wearing the same maid attire as Rose White, Aiisha's former personal Palace maid who sacrificed her life for Aiisha during Tao shi's attack, they trailed behind the couple lifting the excess pieces of their clothing as they walked down the aisle. When they reached two kneeling cushions of the colour... red, in the front of the chamber, the maids crotched down to neaten their clothing and walked to the side in an orderly fashion whilst two stayed by their side.

The traditional ceremony consisted of giving the Immortal Gods a kowtow, a bow to the ground, the highest form of reverence. A maid assisted Aiisha when she and the Prince knelt on the soft cushions below.

"Bow," chanted Xander, the noble General Zhang who was the one marrying the couple off.

Aiisha and Lucas bowed resting their forehead on the top of their hands on the floor.

"Rise," they rise, "bow."

They bow again slowly.

"Rise."

They rose slowly and stood back up. Aiisha required the maid to help her up.

"Turn to your partner."

It was at this point when Venas could hear a continuous thumping sound that came from inside the chamber and grew suspicious, she looked around but no one seemed to be reacting to the noise. The thumping noise sounded like... heartbeats.

"Groom, bow to your bride."

Prince Lucas returned to the floor to bow. Venas could hear the thumping beat faster and faster.

I can hear someone's... heartbeats, Venas thought. The level of her hearing has been enhancing ever since she stepped foot in this world. The particular heartbeats she could hear belonged to Aiisha, of course, she was nervous.

"Rise," General Zhang waited for him to stand up again to say, "Ceremony completed."

The joy on everyone's faces couldn't be happier.

Transported to another room away from the crowd, the two drank their wedding wine before the maids raised two trays in front of them with a pair of scissors and small yellow sachets decorated with embroidery and tassels. Two other maids took the scissors to carefully cut a small piece of hair from both of them to place in the sachet. Lucas and Aiisha exchanged the sachet with one another. All the maids then take the trays and leave the room in two single files. Venas was outside with Petal perched on her shoulder, waiting for permission to enter, as she did, she took out the case and handed it to her politely with both hands.

"Venas greets Consorts," she bowed, "before you go, I'd like to gift you this, a token of good health, luck and a long life of happiness," she said nervously.

Aiisha accepted the gift with a bright smile that no one could see.

"Thank you," she said.

"H- have a safe journey," she then glanced over to Prince Lucas. Lucas looked back and excepted something from her.

"And you didn't get me anything?" he teased.

Venas then reached into the sachet hanging from her belt and a mist of steam flew out with another case. Master had given her two to gift, this one was a bigger size.

"One for you too, your Highness."

"I was only joking but it looks like you came prepared, thank you," he kindly took the gift.

"You- you better be good to the Princess, better than the concubines," she warned him but her threatening was rather the cute and harmless type.

"Okay, no concubines, take it that you're the hero of Qins, I'll give you this face," he chuckled

She chuckled back, so did Aiisha.

"Take care," said goodbye to the newlyweds, wishing them a safe journey to the Imperial Palace.

Venas remembered that she intended to seek Prince Emerald so her next destination was the common pavilion house in the Crown Court where she met eye to eye with Kayne Wen, he guarded the room like a statue.

"Afternoon ice-cube," she saluted.

"Quit the nicknames," he replied emotionlessly.

"You don't like it? How about stone face?" she stroked her chin, "rock head - Mr Cold, cube face does nicely," she finished.

"I prefer not, Wen gongzi would be fine."

"Hmm, anyways, can I -"

"No," he interrupted.

"But I didn't finish," she frowned.

"Okay, ask away."

"Can I see the Crown Prince?"

"No," he answered again.

"Please?" she pressed her hands together and begged.

"Xiao Loon, is that Miss Xoular?" called Emerald from behind the pavilion curtains of many layers of silk.

Venas couldn't hold it in and cupped her hands over her mouth with a cheeky smile.

"Xiao Loon?" she laughed at the nickname Emerald gave him as they both walked in.

"Your Highness has never used that term of address before," said Kayne to Emerald.

"I heard Miss Xoular trying to give you a nickname, Xiao Loon sounds good," Emerald grinned whilst knelt at his table drinking tea and reading scrolls. Xiao refers to "little" and Loon refers to "dragon" which is in Kayne's Chinese name Wen Kai Loon.

"Your Highness, Wen gongzi is more like a Da Loon," she clarified. Da refers to big rather than "xiao".

"Your right," Emerald agreed and rested his hand on Thunder who sat next to him. Thunder raised his head and panted with joy when he sniffed Venas before she even stepped in.

"Please, no more," Kayne turned to Venas and pointed his covered sword at her, "what do you want?"

Venas pushed the sword away as Thunder charged towards

her in excitement like the dog he is, he circled multiple times around her hitting his tail off the side of Kayne's leg as he did so before settling down for Venas to pet her.

"Hi Thunder," Venas returned the joyful greeting although she still didn't find it enjoyable when being licked on but it is how dogs express themselves.

"How about a game of wei qi?" she requested.

"Glad to," said Emerald.

Ever since Venas commenced training with Master Ocean, Emerald has been taking advantage of having an extra person to play wei qi with him whilst others are busy but of course, even though he wins almost all the time. Luckily, Venas developed a liking for the game. A traditional board game of which has been played for the past three to four thousand years using a high-level intellectual value. One player plays the white counter and one plays black and the objective is to end the game conquering the most territory on the board. Venas finds the game rather addicting but what didn't help was that she kept losing to his royal highness. This time, she was especially focused on where she went wrong, predicting Emerald's possible spaces of attack and where he could capture her pieces. Within fifteen minutes, Emerald's black counters have already captured over twenty of her white counters. The black counters took up sixty per cent of the board.

"Useless," Kayne commented.

"Who you calling useless," she looks up at him from his seat, "I know I always lose, it's fun… but frustrating at the same time," she described.

Kayne eyed over the table watching her take a counter

from the counter basket next to the board. Petal lept from Venas's shoulder to the table and also over the game too late to see Lee Hawk marching under the canopy, holding a decorative tray of desserts that resemble the shape of colourful mooncakes. Flur was perched on his shoulder and fluttered down to meet Petal. Flur is Emerald's Charamol, an elegant green peacock with a comparable size to Petal. He helped Lee choose some desserts for high Highness from the selected gifted by Lucas Blue.

"Your cakes, your Highness," he carefully placed it on the table.

Lee noticed Venas staring at her.

"Anything the matter, Miss Xoular?" he knew what she was going to say.

"You were trying to stop me from passing that exam this morning," she crossed her arms.

"Oh, still mad about that, are you? Did the professors not mention any live obstacles?"

"Live obstacles?"

"Yes, you have traps, the inanimate obstacle then there's me, one of the final years who volunteered as live obstacles to give you more of a challenge, my apologies, the idea of not telling you beforehand to mimic a sneak attack when least expected."

"Oh... I get it, I feel bad now," she mentioned.

"Bad for?"

"For the senior that I tied to the tree."

Lee hoisted his head in realization.

"Oh," he laughed in remembrance, "don't worry, he's fine now."

"Sounds like an interesting exam," Emerald squeezed into their conversation.

"It... was alright," Venas answered before Emerald placed his counter on the board, capturing three of her counters, "there," he said gently whilst taking the win. Venas pouted.

"As usual," commented Kayne.

"I discovered something today, during the wedding," she skipped his comment.

"Oh, what is it?" Emerald replied.

"I can hear peoples' heartbeats... from afar," she said excitedly.

"How can that be possible," said Kayne.

"No really," I heard the Infanta's beats during the wedding, they were beating fast," she confirmed, "I heard thumping but no one else could hear it then I realised, it was heartbeats."

"Fascinating, if you observe this ability further, you can maybe establish the personal difference of everyone's heartbeats, for example, you can tell if Markcas Black is around you by listening to his beats," Emerald suggested with a teasing smile.

"Markcas? Why bring him up all of a sudden?"

"I'm just teasing, have a cake," Emerald knew that she and Markcas would have something between them, if it wasn't sooner, it'd be later.

"Have you told Master Ocean?" he questions about her discovery.

"No, not yet. Another thing... the..." she tried to remember the name of the book she sought, "...The Arts of

Nature's Oracle," she clicked then continued to munch on the delicious treats.

"The book?"

"Yes, Master says you have this book, can I... maybe... maybe I can read it?"

"The Arts of Nature's Oracle..." Emerald began to think, "I remember donating a batch of books and scrolls to the academy, The Arts of Nature's Oracle was one of them I believe."

"You mean it's..."

"In the academy's pavilion library, unfortunately," Emerald confirmed.

Venas was a little disappointed that she had to wait until tomorrow to get her hands on the book, but no matter. And until tomorrow she waited.

Six a.m. arrived at the surface waiting to meet the fresh rays of the winter sun rising on the horizon. Markcas was fast asleep in the boy's dorms. The beds in his shared room were really just one long, wooden bed that reached from one wall to the other. Each section the boys slept in were separated by thin curtains. Everyone in the dorms was up and about preparing for their first day of training whilst Markcas dozed through the continuous sound of daily activity dreaming his superstar dreams dressed in his plain, white qipao. He'd hug his pillow but the pillows in this era aren't as huggable as our modern pillows so he hugged his duvets, luckily, they're nice and soft.

"Morning Lu Wei," one of Markcas's roommates who greeted Erra as he wandered into the room, he and Markcas were assigned to different dorms. He knew that Markcas wouldn't wake up in time.

"Morning," he greeted back and glanced at Markcas, "Venas wakes up at dawn every day so it's not an Earth people's thing," Erra always wondered why he wakes up so late every day, "he mentioned that he's British, whatever that is, it must be that." Rocky, Erra's labradorite rhino Charamol jumped from Erra's shoulder to the bed as he, unlike Petal, Spike and Flur, could not fly, rhinos don't fly. Rocky charged at Markcas and bopped him in the head but the impact was low. He looked up at Erra and he returned with a nod. The little Charamol did what he always did to wake Markcas up when he oversleeps or is about to oversleep. 3, 2, 1…

His eyes flashed open straight away and left his comfy sleeping position.

"I'm up, I'm up," he held in the pain.

"I can see that," said Erra, he regarded all the other boys who are now gazing this way from Markcas's squeal of pain and laughed.

"How many times do I have to tell you, stop Rocky biting my ear, it hurts like hell?!?" Markcas blurted.

"How many times have I told you to stop sleeping in?" he sat on the bed and crossed his legs.

"Sleeping in, the sun's barely out," Markcas knelt on the bed with his duvet over his shoulders.

"This is China and we are disciplined people, waking up nice and early is the best way to start the day and puts you in the right mindset," Erra explained.

"The right mindset to snooze during the day," Markcas muttered. He scratched his head.

"What was that?"

"Nothing," he was now wide awake thanks to Rocky. He looked down at the little creature but who could stay mad at his cute little eyes whilst he scratched his tiny head like a puppy.

"I'll go get you some medicine for your ear, be dressed by the time I get back," Erra left the dorm and returned to his dorm to retrieve some essentials, taking Rocky with him. Markcas pressed down on his ear and yawned.

"Why do I have to put up with all this?" he left his bed and grabbed his clothes sitting by the shelves next to the doors. Everything in the room was made of rich wood, the doors, windows, floorboards, the beds and the stool he sat on to pop on his socks and boots.

"Spike, where are you?" A glimmer of his amulet sitting on the shelves, shimmered out his little dragon friend, he flew over to his owner and landed on his lap, "tomorrow, you're staying out to make sure Rocky doesn't bite me in the ear okay?" Spike glanced a peek at his left ear and saw the fresh bite marks, he nodded to obey. "Good boy, let's go eat."

Flame 3
===

The First Day

Before the first lesson began, Students of Ninchanted Academy roam freely, meeting new people and seeing old friends from other states, chatting and catching up with each other. It was a very intense morning of winter chills, lots of students wore their winter cloaks to stay warm from the frosty bites. Markcas and Erra too wore their cloaks, Markcas's was of a mute blue and Erra's was a mute pastel brown, both with a furry hood. Markcas stood by the corner of the building they were about to have class in and hoisted his head towards the sky.

"What's wrong," Erra asked.

"Nothing, just tired, I wanna go back to bed," he whined.

Since yesterday, Erra has noticed the number of girls that have been gazing at them, usually in a flirty way. He thought it can't be him they're looking at, no one would ever notice him, a one-eyed teenager, rather it was Markcas they were attracted to. He looked at his friend and did notice he was quite a good-looking boy, his short hair was different to everyone else's, he gave off an attractive vibe that the people here have never seen before.

"Hey Markcas, by any chance did you alter your hair with your celestial?"

"My hair? Yeah, I changed the colour to fit in more, though adding a braid would look cool too," he answered.

"Colour?"

"I have naturally fair hair, British people are usually blonde or fair."

"Oh," Erra nodded, trying to imagine Markcas with fair hair.

Whilst he was thinking about Markcas's hair, Markcas on the other hand suddenly started thinking about a person. A girl in particular and where she was since he never saw her yesterday at the end of the exam or the assembly. This is when we speak of the devil or in this case, thinking of the devil. Right from around the tight corner, within a flash of the eye, a figure suddenly darted hastily into Markcas with a painful impact as she bounced to the hard stony surface below. Markcas was pushed back and pressed his hand on his torso of which Venas nearly drilled into. He soon noticed it was Venas.

"Venas?" he pulled her up.

"Sorry, I wasn't looking, you're not hurt, are you?" She shared her concerns.

"How've you been," Markcas asked.

Erra could see how excited Markcas was to see her and crossed his arms under his cloak.

"Not bad, morning Lu Wei," she waved past Markcas to Erra, he waved back with a friendly smile.

"Morning Xoular, how was the wedding?"

"Wedding?" said Markcas.

"The wedding between Qin and Zhao, it was alright," she replied then muttered, "but it's not exactly historically accurate according to Earth's Chinese history."

"What was that?" Erra heard.

"Nothing."

"Oh, that wedding," Markcas remembered from the news board in the city that was announced three weeks in advance. Sadly, the marriage between Qin and Zhou wasn't enough to declare peace between the states.

Venas suddenly heard the same thumping sound she heard during the wedding, clearly enough this one came from Markcas, his heartbeat was slowing down until Venas confidently put her ear up against his chest, close enough but not touching.

"W- what're you doing?" he looked troubled to have Venas this close to him. Erra however liked where this was going, he grinned.

"You're nervous," she guessed and stood up straight again.

"Nervous? How can you tell?"

"I can hear your heartbeats and it beating pretty fast right now," Markcas and Erra looked confused. Swiftly, Markcas tried to cover the noise of his beats with some movements.

"You look like you're freezing," he grinned, "you're not wearing your winter cloak, you can have a good listen to my heartbeats from under here and stay warm," he hoisted his arms and wrapped his cloak around her, "how's that?"

"Markcas, no, let me out," the playful Markcas has awakened from his snooze, he started to tease her.

"Lu Wei, help!" she yelled, her voice was muffled under his cloak.

"I rather not, you look like you're having fun," but Erra's grin disappeared and Markcas stopped moving when a random girl approached them from behind with something in her hands. She gazed at Markcas with a shy smile. Markcas waited for her to say something but she remained silent. Venas didn't move because she was able to hear the beats of another person.

"Uhhhhhh, can I help you?" Markcas broke the silence.

"Umm, I... my name's An Lin, I want to give you this," she said faintly and passed him the sachet she was holding but was fairly disappointed when Venas brushed Markcas's cloak aside to give herself some air, she looked at the shy girl. She was taller and looked frail. Without saying anything Markcas slowly and confusingly took the sachet.

"Uh…" he mumbled.

Suddenly the girl looked excited and smiled again although Venas and Erra didn't have the same look. Erra unfolded his arms and was going to do something but she thanked Markcas and ran away, she ran into the building they were going to have their lesson in.

"Must be one of our classmates," Markcas said and turned to Venas and Erra who gave him some kind of stare. "What? Did I do something wrong?"

"You took the sachet Markcas, you're not meant to take the sachet?" Erra blurted.

"What's wrong with the sachet?"

"It's a form of confession, that girl just showed her love for you and by taking the sachet, you accepted her confession," Erra looked a little bit frustrated. Venas didn't know what to do, she didn't mind that much, not as much as Erra.

"Lu Wei, don't be mad, he didn't know," she said.

Erra took her wrist and escorted her to the classroom.

"Come on, let's go," he said to Venas.

Markcas trailed after them and was thinking about giving the sachet back to the girl. He felt stupid.

"Good Morning Pupils," Master Shi chanted.

The students stood next to their kneeling tables and all bowed in sync to greet their teacher who rose from his desk to provide for the reading of today's language lesson. During the lesson, students are not to talk to each other or interact.

They must focus on the work like it was an exam. They must remain silent until asked to do so following the thousand strips of academy rules. Poems were a big part of high-level education so he was ready to chant them for the next hour. A simple first lesson for the first hour to lead on to the next lesson, more of a martial arts training session which is the main subject taught in the Academy to prepare students for real-life crisis and danger that they may face in this world. It was the key focus of teaching. Master Shi wished to observe the students abilities closely, this session was a sparring session. The class consisted of 40 students and each was called up, two at a time to take each other on. For a master to teach one they must understand the techniques of their fighting style, what kung fu style everyone uses and their level of ability. The session took place outdoors on one side of the training ground where the assembly took place o. Everyone sat round in a wide oval leaving plenty of space in the middle for the sparring to commence on a raised wooden platform like a big square stage decorated with traditional Chinese ornaments dangling over sturdy wooden poles on each corner. Master Shi took out a wooden scroll of the register and called out two names on shuffle.

"Luo Wen and Tang Yang Ling," the scroll soon disappeared under Master's long, draped sleeves.

Luo Wen pulled a dirty smirk and rose to her feet to face Yang Ling who took on the look of an elegant and honest girl who seemed a little nervous. Luo Wen on the other hand was confident that she could beat her as she was graded third rank whilst Yang Ling was one grade lower. The majority of the class was placed at third rank. The girls bowed to each other.

"You may begin."

A breath of intensifying silence struck the floor. Master waited patiently. Venas tried to control her hearing abilities to block out the loud thumping noises which was something that she needed to focus on for the time being. She and Master Shi watched closely their starting positions before Luo Wen left her stance and stormed towards Yang Ling who almost got hit by her heavy fist. Yang Ling blocked another incoming punch with the back of her wrist and repeated it many times leading from fists to kicks. Although their uniforms were long, dangly and looked hard to fight in, they felt surprisingly flexible to move around in. Luo Wen seemed fearless when put next to Yang Ling who lost quickly after a boot to the hard surface from the opponent's last kick but once the next name was called, she soon dropped down a level against a boy named Lee Xiao Li. XiaoLi Hawk was Lee Hawks' younger brother. No wonder Venas saw the familiar look in his facial features that resembled his older brother. If they were brothers then he must be a powerful one in kung fu following up to his brother's expectations. He beat Luo Wen with no mercy. Xiao was waiting all day to show her some colour after hearing her unnecessary gossip about the hero of Qins, her rude comments continued from yesterday spread like coconut oil. Master Shi skipped the satisfied look on XiaoLi's face and called the next subject.

"Next, Let me see," Master searched the list, "Lu Kai."

both third rank boys fought it out. Lu Kai gave off a calm and relaxed look, he and XiaoLi resisted each other's contact for a good ten-minute spar, a refreshing warm-up for the morning but XiaoLi took the win again as he did for the next seven spars, it was at that point, Master decided to give the other students a chance and dismissed XiaoLi proudly calling two other students to spar and two others after them. Erra and Markcas were up against each other at one point but to no surprise, Erra took the win as he did with every opponent he faced, he never lost. Venas too, defeated a number of her peers using different styles of kung fu to how she saw fit and surprised everyone with an unexpected number of kung fu styles. She defeated Luo Wen who wasn't very happy with her failure. Venas was soon assigned a spar against XiaoLi not long after.

She quickly approached the centre to meet with XiaoLi and decided what techniques to use against him, after his long seven rounds of defeat with the other students, she was able to establish his fighting style but she needed to be careful of Master Shi to not establish her usual fighting style, a style taught by Master Ocean and she was told to not expose her identity as Master Ocean's first disciple. XiaoLi was internally enthusiastic about this round with the hero of Qins. The two exchanged a bow. Venas remained still until XiaoLi budged from his stance.

He likes to attack from his right, which is his left to lock his dominant hand from gaining anticipation to strike, she thought carefully, dodged his swift punch by twisting her torso to the side, grabbed his wrist before he retracted it and launched her grip overhead facing his back to trip him over.

So fast, he thought. He attempted to flip his legs backwards for a backflip but Venas caught his ankle and swiped it to the ground landing him on his tummy with a loud thud on the wooden planks. After a page of silence, everyone applauded when they realized what just happened. Everyone but Luo Wen.

"That was fast," Lu Kai commented.

"That was a quick defeat, I didn't expect it to end so soon," XiaoLi admitted.

"I didn't expect it myself," she helped him up and smiled.

Master was impressed with her speed and everyone's efforts during the session.

"Very good, that will be it for this session," he said.

"Wait," the students were prepared to stand up and bow to Master Shi to his dismissal before Luo Wen interrupted.

"I'd like a rematch!" she declared.

"A rematch? With who?" Master replied.

XiaoLi looked concerned with her attitude and predicted that she's going after Venas. Indeed, he was right.

"Xoular," she said after giving her another stare, "I won't accept my defeat."

Master didn't wish for this rematch, it wasn't the point of the session. The primary objective was for Master to understand the students' styles and abilities.

"What makes you think you can have a rematch?" XiaoLi argued.

"Because- because I just want a rematch," she repeated.

"People who refuse to accept defeat in a small event like this need to fix up their mindset," Erra stated as he sat on the floor with his legs crossed and stared at Luo Wen who followed his voice to where he was sitting. She glared at him.

"That's right, I refuse to accept being beaten by some overrated hero who never knew anything about Kung fu and was still able to take down a monster, don't you think it's a bit odd?" she questioned rhetorically, " it's been two months, how could one possibly improve this much in two months?"

"What would you know, you were probably hiding away in fear when she was out risking her life," Erra blurted from across.

"Who said you have to know martial arts to defeat someone, there's plenty of other ways to fight," XiaoLi clarified. He and Venas remained stationary in the centre of the oval.

Luo Wen became irritated that nothing she says is convincing them to agree with her. She glared at Venas who made eye contact with anyone but her. She felt a little bit attacked by Luo Wen's attitude.

"She's done nothing wrong for you to pick on her."

"You! One-eyed boy, you are obviously the strongest out of the boys, you beat everyone," she said.

"Your point is?" Erra replied though he didn't like how she addressed him, he felt a little bit offended.

"If I can't get a rematch then you fight her, see if she really deserves to be in rank two," Luo Wen challenged, "I bet she only received a rank two because she defeated a monster."

"So that's what this is about, you're jealous you didn't get a higher rank," XiaoLi noticed.

"I worked hard," she squealed.

"So did everyone else."

"Taking your personal problem out on other people," Erra commented, "by the way, the name's Lu Wei."

Luo Wen clenched her fist of internal anger and turned to Master Shi.

"Professor, what do you think?"

Master Shi thought about it for a while, he did not pair Erra and Venas together for a fight during the session, he was curious to see who would actually win although he did not take any attraction to Luo Wen's impolite manner, he would have to do something about that later. She's already broken several rules from the Wall of a Thousand Rules.

"Very well, Erra, please make your way."

Venas and Erra exchanged troubled glances, they didn't want to battle with each other at all. On the other hand, Luo Wen looked satisfied. Erra replaced Xiao Li in the centre and bowed to Venas. Markcas noticed how troubled they looked but could only sit and watch. The entire class debated in their own minds who would take the win. It would be a tight battle.

Are you going to start or am I? Erra questioned as if Venas could hear his thoughts. Her body trembled, she prepared a stance and gazed at him until she decided what to do.

I've never fought him before, she thought. It has always been Erra and Markcas who spar with each other during practice, she would always watch and suggest tips and tricks for them to improve. There are many forms of kung fu Venas has learnt from Master Ocean, her personal favourites are light-body kung fu, the praying mantis, snake, leopard and the tiger style. Animal style, of course, mimics the animals' movements into a form of kung fu, tiger and leopards being more powerful in her list of abilities for martial arts but crane style consisted of many useful fists formations. For the past two months, she trained hard to perfect the tiger style along with her light-body skills, these two being the main focus of her course. Master would give her a sack of sand and request for her to throw up in the air and catch it again and again for a long period of time to strengthen her wrists and the grips of her hands that imitate the claws of a tiger when she catches it. Since then her punches became stronger and her dou qi skills have been more stabilised.

Venas took this as an opportunity, Erra is strong enough to keep up with her speed right?

Tiger style it is, she told herself as soon as Erra's front foot slid on the floor from the push of his back foot. She blocked his fist firmly with the back of her left hand after he dodged her right-hand attack, weaving it under his armpits before the blink of an eye to relocate his arm from her left to her right where she ends up standing behind him but he was quick to notice and darted to the ground, whipping his leg around like that of a compass. Venas predicted many possible movements with the flash of an eye and was ready to flip backwards to avoid tripping over quickly to return to his side. They blocked but neither of them landed a punch, their hands weaved and retracted congruously and incongruously after some time when Venas finally landed a jab under his rib cage with a snuck-in crane style phoenix eye fist complemented with a firm flat-palm hit on the chest pushing him backwards. He clutched his torso from the force that was almost enough to knock him over. A breath of tension spread between them and everyone around them when they were thinking to themselves what to use on each other and instantly resumed to hand in hand combat that dazzled everyone making their heads spin with their overwhelming performance. Master was respectively pleased to see such amazing skills on the first day. In the middle of their fight, a woman saw Master Shi and his class whilst walking past the training ground and approached to greet him during her break. She was Mistress An who showed her interest in the combat of Venas and Erra. The two Masters commenced in some small talk whilst observing the fight.

"You know this young lady's style of techniques looks very familiar," Mistress An mumbled to Master Shi.

Venas heard her comment and released the fist formation she was going to use and tried to keep up with Erra from the minor distraction.

They're figuring it out, I mustn't expose my techniques, she demanded to herself. She wanted to slow down but Erra expected her to be quick. He heaved an arc above her and landed a vicious thrust from his palms to her shoulder with a strong spark of power.

Venas flew backwards, within a split-second, she tried to stop herself from falling but his push was too heavy, catching a breath of pain in the spine when made a thump on the hard surface followed by a bang in the head. The pain travelled back to her shoulders not long after. The strength of Erra's attack sent her far from the destined raised platform. A small tornado of gasps replaced the air.

"She lost," whispered a classmate.

"That looked painful," said another.

XiaoLi was so positive that she would win, he and Marrkcas sprung up from the ground in shock whilst everyone else remained seated whispering amongst themselves through the prompt of Luo Wen's comments.

"Venas!" Erra jumped off the stage and dashed over to help her.

"Oh my goodness," Mistress An gasped, "we need to inform a pharmacist."

Master Shi nodded in agreement and called one of the students.

"Lee Xiao Li, go get the pharmacist," he ordered.

"Yes professor," he bowed and dashed away whilst Master trotted to Venas.

"Heavens girl, how are you feeling," Master felt guilty, this was not what this session was for, "Lu Wei, hold her up would you," he requested.

Erra dug his hand under her head and held her in his arms for more comfort, whilst Master ensured everything was ok. The feeling of being tossed across the training ground was no different than having a bad accident in a car crash and flying out of the car. Her back could feel no touch, it felt numb from the impact.

"I'm so sorry, I didn't mean to - I thought you'd be able to dodge judging by how quick you are -" Erra wasn't sure how to express how sorry he was.

"It's okay," the pace of her speech was concerning, she grasped her head as a ringing sound grew louder in her ears.

"You suddenly let your guard down," Master noticed, "you must always be on guard, no matter what happens to distract you."

She understood and was ready to say "yes Master" but he dismissed her from doing so to save her breath.

"What did I say? If you can beat Tao Shi, you can beat anyone," Luo Wen started, "she's a fraud, she doesn't deserve second rank."

"That's enough," Markcas barked.

"You're not going to hit me are you," she said confidently.

"I wouldn't mind punching you in the face, you need to watch your mouth," the slight rage in Markcas's eyes thundered into hers. Luo Wen shivered in frustration but to her fortune, half of the class agreed with her. The commotion took to a halt when Master Shi walked back to the students.

"Class dismissed, you may have your break before your next lesson."

"Thank you, Professor," everyone bowed and chanted in sync before trotting to the common rooms.

"Not you, Miss Luo, you may come with me," Master made his way to the teacher's office expecting her to follow him. Luo Wen's friends couldn't help her and left her to Master Shi while they followed their classmates. Markcas approached Erra who carried Venas gently to the academy's medical room where XiaoLi informed one of the doctors to come prepared for Venas's injuries. She looked like she was ready to take a nap. Erra dismissed Markcas from going with them.

"You go take a break with the others," he stared at them, "I can take care of her."

Markcas took the hint that Erra was still uptight with him for accepting An Lin's confession. He made his way to the common to set it straight with An Lin. Well, that is, once he finds her. He entered the building into the common room now crowded with students taking on all kinds of activities on their short break after two hours of training but his goal was to find the girl. The common room was built with oak planks slotted smoothly on the floors, painted and polished.

One long table and benches sat in the middle of the room displaying games and hobby interests along with books and scrolls. Noise hovered over the tables into an arch that led to the second section of the first floor rummaging with students that he's never met before. He didn't know anyone here and the people in his class were nowhere to be seen. Adjacent to the common room building were more study rooms, the oversized academy pavilion library and the medical centre before hitting the set of stairs down to the outdoors and indoors bathrooms where students from the dorms go to have a refreshing wash after a long day of training. The academy was lively on the first day, everyone was so outgoing and polite to each other, it was only Luo Wen that didn't get along with people by spitting mean comments at them for no apparent reason. Young strangers smiled at each other, they were kind and always open to making new friends. The older years were open to giving advice and directions as the academy was reasonably big and compact, it was a maze for those who didn't know where to go. Some trainees were on break and some were having lessons.

We make our way back into the medical centre still able to hear the commotion of conversations and joyfulness from outside.

"Why did you hit her so hard? It was only a simple spar." XiaoLi questioned Erra as they waited outside the doctor's office.

"I got too caught up in the moment," Erra muttered

and thought: she's not going to get a concussion, is she? He put his fingers to his lips anxiously.

"I knew something wasn't right when Mistress An arrived," XiaoLi noted.

"What do you mean?"

"Mistress mentioned something about her fighting style reminding her of an old master she used to know," he mentioned what he overheard during the session leading Erra into a deep process of thoughts.

"An old master?"

It wasn't long before the doctor emerged from the office.

"Doctor, she's ok right?" Erra prompted.

"She should be fine in the morning, just let her get plenty of rest, luckily, no concussion to worry about, here's a medical prescription, the pharmacy is right next door, next time, take it easy," the doctor informed and handed Erra the prescription.

"Thank you," he rushed in after saying goodbye, "Venas," he stumbled, "thank goodness you're ok."

"I'm fine, it's no big deal," Venas sat up and rubbed the side of her head. She gazed at him and noticed he had guilt plastered all over him, " don't start apologising, it's fine... where's Markcas?" she questioned.

"He… he's taking a break in the common room, probably looking for An Lin," he paused… "are you sure you're alright, no headaches, how's the pain?" He unconsciously touched her on the shoulder for some form of comfort and concern and noticed the silver butterfly-shaped hair clips she wore were on the bed, "These are the one's Markcas gave you right?"

"What... oh, yes, they are, you're not still mad at him?"

"Mmm... I'm not mad, not exactly."

"Don't be, there's no reason to be mad," she said kindly.

XiaoLi wasn't quite sure about what they were talking about.

"You can make it to our next lesson, right? We still have an hour until medical training," he inquired.

"You should be fine by then," Erra hoped.

"I'll be fine," she nodded, "thank you... both of you."

"So what's this I hear, Venas getting beaten by a punk?" strolled in a familiar voice.

"Hei gongzi?" said Venas.

"Who you calling a punk, who the hell are you?" Erra questioned.

"Hei LiBing, Xiaoli's older brother," he introduced himself to Erra.

Lee brought along some of his friends and wanted to introduce them to Venas since they were the ones that lost miserably to her during the entrance exam. There were four of them including the one she tied to the trees with no mercy.

"Oh, right you were the one that I... tied to the tree," she said of guilt now that she knew it was only part of the course, "I'm terribly sorry."

"I got plenty of ant bites you know," he mentioned as insects in China are a lot meaner than in the West. Venas hated mosquito bites and she only got them in China on her first day there when she was little, it was her foreign blood that attracted them.

"Bites? The ants here bite?" she asked.

"Quite a lot," he answered and gave her an intro, "I'm ChaoLing, same year as LiBing, I wanted to come along to meet you properly, it's very nice to meet you and sorry about the exam, it was only our job," he apologised and bowed to his greeting.

And the other three seniors that she tied alongside ChaoLing by on the ground below him greeted them with a bow, cupping their hands together, the usual.

"Gwang LiMing," he greeted.
"Tang Zhen."
"Xue ZhongWen," said the last one. They then all looked at Erra who noticed and realised.
"Oh right, Lu Wei," he bowed.

They were all tall standing at five feet seven except for ChaoLing who was five feet five. They all shared smiles of friendliness and built up a good conversation before they all set off for lessons.

Venas ate her prescriptions and suddenly felt well again, she felt restored from the elixir pill that the doctor gave her. She saw Markcas and sat next to him on their kneeling tables ready for lessons. Erra trailed along and sat next to her feeling a bit better now that she was okay. Her recuperation abilities were quite quick, it must be all that happiness as it is helpful to be happy 24/7 than it is to be gloomy and miserable, it causes wrinkles and also has a negative impact on ones ageing appearance making them look less attractive but Venas was the opposite of that, she was lively and always smiling. Occasional crying doesn't hurt, like the day she woke up from her coma after the battle with Tao Shi. Master Ocean was there to comfort her after all.

"Feeling better?" Markcas asked.

"Yep, I'm good," she nodded before Master Shi strolled in to give them a lesson on medical topics, the very basics today. The practical lessons of actually making elixir pills started an hour later as miniature cauldrons popped onto their tables over a burning pot of fire with ingredients on the sides. Spike was perched next to Markcas, he was fast asleep. Petal approached him and stroked his head with her little nose and bonded with him whilst their owners were busy with the lesson.

Everyone took their teachings and applied them to making their first elixir pill, the use of this pill will be for a simple cold made of basic herbs, mainly thorowax roots in the water waiting for it to boil. Blue flames poked out of the cauldron of those who did well and followed each step. Soon, they were able to form their hands around the fire and concentrated their celestial magic on pushing thermal energy towards the centre where the fire burned tall above the cauldron. The pressure of heat will help transform the herbs into elixir pills ready for testing.

"Wait, do we put the ginger in too?" MArkcas asked, he was listening but he still wasn't quite sure.

"Yes, but you should've popped it in first," Venas

answered and continued to make her pill that was nearly finished. She could see effective results.

"Does it matter when I put it in? I'll just throw it in now," he released the pressure he was using on the potential pill he was forming to grab the slices of dried ginger and chucked it in.

"Wait, Markcas don't!!!" She released her formation, took her completed pill from the fire, and tried to stop Markcas from dropping the rogue ingredient, but she was one step behind him.

His class project exploded in his face before Venas managed to warn him in time as she was so focused on her own.

"Putting in an ingredient in the middle of the pill forming will cause a disruption in result it… reacts… like that," she said in an I-probably-should've-told-you-sooner tone.

"I see, well it seems to be too late for that," he replied.

His face was coated with a thin layer of black soot and some on his hair that was now pointing to the ceiling. He flicked his braid behind him as everyone started laughing internally and couldn't hold it in. the other girls thought it was cute that he was this clumsy and the boys thought he was a bit stupid but everyone laughed except Luo Wen who wasn't happy because Master Shi had given her a source of punishment of which she takes after school for the rest of the week. Markcas noticed his hair and didn't like the state it was in, the redness on his face from his embarrassment couldn't be seen under the soot. But he didn't mind after seeing Venas laugh too. Master Shi raised his head to witness his disaster.

"Looks like someone didn't follow the instructions," he said, "That's the end of the session now, please place your elixir pill in the container provided, label and leave them on my desk, you will receive your grades at the end of the day, class dismissed," he announced.

"Thank you, Professor," everyone bowed together and made for the exit.

After school, it was time for a fresh wash for Markcas and Erra whilst Venas rushed home to Master Ocean. Markcas followed Erra from his dorm and past all the other dorms to the boys' washroom. The room consisted of a long pool in the shape of a cross with white tiles at the bottom and a wooden border with stairs. On the side of the pool were water pumps, wooden buckets. All the boys bring in their own soap and hand towels hanging from their necks still wearing the white trousers that they wear under their academy uniform. Some boys kept them on, some wore their towels and strolled carefully into the washroom making sure they don't slip and find a spot to chill and relax.

"No barriers?" Markcas noticed.
"Barrier? It's not like we have anything to hide," Erra answered.
"A little privacy would be nice," he mentioned.
"Don't worry, you'll get used to it eventually."

Markcas was cautious, he wasn't as open to everyone as Erra was who had just his towel on him. Space got a little bit tight after some of Lee's friends walked in. Since Lee lived in the Palace like Venas, he doesn't use the public washroom.

"Hey, it's Lu Wei from the medical centre, how are you doing, had a good first day?" Chao Ling splashed in to join him when he recognised his familiar face. He swung his muscular arms around his bare shoulders.
"It was cool, Markcas had his medical project explode in his face- highlight of the day," he replied whilst Tang Zhen and Xue ZhongWen joined the spa-like pool.
"Really, is that why there's soot in your hair?" Chao Ling noticed.
"What, I thought I got it all out," he shook his relatively long bangs and snowed on the wooden flooring over the pool.
"Seems like you had fun, academy life is always great, I'm staying for a master's year," said Chao Ling.

"Masters, what about the wife?" Tang Zhena mentioned.

"What are you talking about, I don't have one, I want to be where LiBing is, his job is so cool," he admired.

"I'm going to get married after this year, no more academy for me, my parents want their grandchildren," said Zhong Wen.

"Our parents all want their grandchildren, at least you have a fiance," Chao Ling replied, "what about you guys?" He removed his arm from Erra's shoulder and sank into the water.

Markcas shook his head, "not for me," Erra had the same answer.

"Trust me, you're not missing out," Chao Ling jokes.

Before anything else was said, two joyful boys jumped into the pool making a loud splash.

"Hey guys," XiaoLi greeted.
"Hi," said Lu Kai.
"Hey," everyone greeted back at the same time.
"Did you hear? Luo Wen got set her punishment from breaking academy rules, she's cleaning everyone's dirty socks for a whole seven days," said XiaoLi.
"Legend, I'm guessing it was Professor Shi," Chao Ling mentioned.
"How'd you know?"
"Only Professor Shi sets penalties like that."

"How much is everyone?" MArkcas questioned.

"I think everyone who lives in the dorms," Lu Kai thought, he looked at Xiao Li to make sure.

"Yeah, that's almost two thousand trainees living in the dorms," he estimated.

"Wow, that's a lot of socks," Markcas commented.

After the boys finished showering, Markcas didn't know how to feel when everyone made an exit for the laundry house and started throwing their dirty white socks in a big wooden bucket, several wooden buckets. And the trail of buckets led to a girl. Luo Wen. But she deserved this much for not respecting the rules on the first day. Whilst everyone was relaxing waiting for the next day to approach, Luo Wen was busy pulling a disgusted face from the smell of the socks piling up. One sock is odourless on its own but nearly two thousand gives your nose quite the punch.

Flame 4

Midnight Wander

Two weeks drifted away uncontrollably since the first day of academy training started. Although Venas thought that she learned a lot more from Master Ocean in three days than two weeks at the academy. Master convinced her to attend to develop her social abilities with people other than the people she sees every day in the Palace. She has always wondered why she was chosen to be Master's disciple, why she is able to live in the Palace, roam in Palace and interact with the royal family when all she is is just an ordinary girl with an ordinary identity. The question had always struck her but there was more she wanted to be answered. These powers, becoming the Fire Mortal, a leap into the past, her possession of Petal and her Oracle, the questions that she's tried to ask but Master Ocean would always find a way to answer them without actually answering them. Master knows something, he definitely knows something and he doesn't seem to want her to know. Venas knows that Master knows but it seems that something is stopping him from telling her because she can see it in the way he responds, the expression in his eyes was proof of his denial. Other than these dying questions, Master can answer almost anything, anything about kung fu, the variety of styles, medicine, the arts of forming elixir pills with the help of dou qi, things about history, writing, celestial magic, his teachings never let Venas down. He is over three hundred years old after all, for mortals, that is a very, very long time.

Master was right about attending the academy which can expose her to the social society of young people like herself other than Erra and Markcas, she can make more friends, it was a sign that Master wished for her to stay in this world but it wasn't a secret that she wanted the opposite and in order to fulfil her wishes, she must train, learn more techniques and become strong enough and wiser to create a portal.

The first two weeks in the academy were enjoyable, Venas had almost forgotten about the event that took place on the first day but she was always reminded every time she sees Luo Wen in class and around the academy. One part of her feels violated by her comments, another part of her chooses to ignore her but one thing that was quite hard to ignore all week was Markcas... being an attraction for love confessions. It wasn't easy to miss. Erra was relieved when

Markcas returned the sachet An Lin gifted her but it didn't last long when he too noticed the number of maidens that come looking for Markcas. One more thing that he's noticed was the maidens usually babble a lot of negative comments about Venas, why was this you may ask?

"They're jealous you get to be with Markcas all the time," Erra confronted her.
"I spend a lot of time with you guys, you're my friends, who else would I hang out with?"
"You seem to be getting along well with XiaoLi and Lu Kai," he added.
"I guess so."

The two casually chatted during an outdoors fitness session with Mistress An at the training ground, he was perfecting sit-ups whilst Venas was pressing down on his legs as he came up and back down with every word he passed onto her.

"How many have I done?" he continued to sit up and down.
"104," she updated, "105, 106, 107… 108, 109, 110… you can stop now, you've already hit the target number," she notified.
"I want to do more."

Everyone did their sit-ups in a long row, Markcas was eight spaces away from them, he wanted to be closer to Venas but instead, he could barely see her and he was paired with XiaoLi who was doing the sit-ups like a bodybuilder. He huffed like crazy.

"You like her," he casually commented between his synchronised breathing.
"What?"
"It's pretty obvious," he said.
"Is it?" Markcas tried to deny it.
"Although, you being surrounded by girls half the time doesn't seem to be giving her a good impression."
"It's not my fault that they have legs to approach me," he joked.
"Well you gotta choose one to marry," XiaoLi continued.
"Marry?"
"Yes, marry, we're basically near the age."

For you but not for me, Markcas thought otherwise, people here marry early in life, but he didn't think that XiaoLi knew where he and Venas were from. But if Earth humans don't know anything about Ervanna then Ervanna humans don't know about Earth right, well, false. The system of planets in Andromeda is hidden by its own magic to prevent the Earth humans from discovering them therefore Ervanna and her brothers and sister don't appear on the radar of their intergalactic research.

"Be more open to her," he added, "or else she'll just see you as her little brother," he teased.

"Open?"

Mistress An dismissed today's training to remind everyone who signed up for the field trip taking place tomorrow, a chance for the students to pick up skills and practice living in the wild. It is a common event to encounter when you live in an era like this.

"Yes, can't wait," Erra turned to Venas, "usual place for dinner?" Venas, Erra, Markcas, XiaoLi and Lu Kai would often eat at Erra's family restaurant after the end of academy training.

"I'm starving," she nodded as she transitioned to packing the floor mats back to the storage room by the indoor training hall before scanning amongst her fellow classmates for the rest of her friends after bowing goodbye to their teacher.

Lu Kai and XiaoLi both intended to eat at home today with their families therefore it was just the three of them left, Venas and Erra stepped outside the academy doors that reached up like a tower to wait for Markcas who was about to meet them, he couldn't help but be held back by a few more girls from other class groups.

"Gongzi," they all called at their own pace. It troubled him when they scurried around him trying to get his attention in a rather flirty way.

"Woah woah, can't you see I'm trying to-" he started when one girl excitedly cut his speech.

"Gongzi, you're so handsome," one said as she attempted

to wrap her arms around his arm but he lifted it up to avoid that.

"What's your name," another said even though she already knew his name.

He had almost made it through but they just kept following him and touching his arms not giving him the time of day. He eyed Erra on the other side for help but Erra returned with a gesture that told him:

"you're on your own buddy."

"I reckon, there's twenty girls over there," Erra estimated, "the poor boy."

Venas exchanged sudden eye contact with Markcas telling him to accompany them when he's done.

"I'm about to be sick," she commented on the girls' cringy behaviour, like something from a t.v show.

"Wait, don't go, guys!" he yelled when he saw his friends leave.

Girls, please leave me alone, he thought the words that he really wanted to say out loud without being rude. Markcas tried to get away from them when he saw her friends storm off the other way.

"Why are you in such a rush, stay," said another girl, how flirtish she was.

Past the populated city streets of Qin's Empire, dinner time roams the air leading hungry tummies to crowd the restaurants, bars and market stalls. Hot, fresh steam travelled from Erra's hands as he brought to the outdoors table his bowl of crispy beef noodles specially made by his beloved mother. Venas sat at a table after Erra bought her a bowl first, she sat by the restaurant doors under a sturdy canopy. Erra was about to sit down when he forgot his chopsticks and rushed back in.

As usual, Venas would always add some Chinese vinegar into her noodles so she reached over the table and picked the vinegar from the condiments tray and started pouring. Like her amazing ability to hear things that other people can't hear, she also possessed the immunity to sour foods. Erra came back and tucked into his food until he noticed Venas was still pouring the vinegar whilst her eyes were dazed, her head in her left hand and elbow on the table. He clutched her wrist and gently removed the wooden bottle of vinegar from her hand.

"Hey..." she realised after returning from her daze.

"Don't you think you've had enough vinegar today?" he read her. Referring to vinegar as the Chinese homophone to jealousy.

"Huh, I'm not jealous, I just want some more flavour, that's all," she answered to his I-know-what-you're-thinking stare.

"Is that so," he said and gazed at her trying to vacuum the truth out of her with silence.

She tried to avoid talking by slowly filling her mouth with food, her left hand holding her chopsticks uncomfortably whilst Erra forgot that he was still holding onto her wrist but it wasn't long before someone came along and pulled their hands apart. Venas was so distracted, she didn't notice the footsteps of Markcas.

"Looks like you're not the only one that's jealous," Erra grinned, "I'll go get you some food," he scurried off to fetch him his dinner. Markcas sat down next to her.

"What were you talking about?" he questioned with a shy feeling.

She curled her lips in thoughts about how to go about his question.

"Uhhhh… bunnies," she said.

"Bunnies?"

"Bunnies," she nodded, " the cute white ones with the red eyes," she added.

"The ones they sell in the city market?" he pointed in the direction behind them as there was a pet stall by the corner occupied by fluffy little furballs, "why? Do you want one?"

"Do I want one? Why- why would I want one, pets-pets are a bother," she stuttered and began slurping on her noodles again before Erra returned again with a fresh bowl of noodles. He then saw Venas moving her hand closer to the bottle of vinegar again and snatched it away from her.

"I told you, that's enough, you'd be drinking vinegar at this rate… it's not a good look on you," he teased but Markcas wasn't able to understand what he meant after Venas stuck her tongue out at him and said:

"I'm not, if anyone's jealous, it should be you."

"Oh? Why's that?"

"Senior, Mei's in second year at the Academy right,

she's also been getting a lot of attention from the boys and they're older guys too, don't tell me you haven't noticed," she grinned at him giving him the eye. He did not heed Star for a while now since they would never be at the same place or run into each other, the academy is a very broad area of ground.

"No, I haven't noticed, I've been too busy with the course," he admitted, "she just sees me as a little brother so there's nothing going on between us," he said sadly, "it's not a big deal, we grew up together, after all… here, my mum made these pickled moolis, they're so good," he bought along a plate of pickled goodness to the table and tucked into dinner. "Soaked in sugar- added flavouring, yum," he enjoyed.

The city market commenced with a gradual decrease of civilians after dinner hours, leaving more space for the trio to wander more freely without budging and squeezing amongst a large crowd. Remember the bunnies? The bunny stall was still open and it was a chance for them to feast their precious eyes on some adorable furballs that were too cute to miss. There were bunnies, little birds in their cute little cages, goldfish and pocket-sized tortoises. Venas tried not to touch them as they feasted on their juicy carrots and leaves in a wooden cot scattered with hay. She crouched down to get a closer look at the one sleeping softly in the corner.

"They're so cute."
"You are quite cute," Markcas muttered with a delicate smile.
"What was that?" Venas was too distracted by the

bunnies, she missed what Markcas just said even though he was standing right next to her.

"N- nothing," he gazed at the sky to ease his blushing.

Erra crossed his arms and set off an internal chuckle. He heard exactly what he said. He figured Markcas wasn't talking about the bunnies and felt like at this rate, they were going nowhere.

"Why you giving me that look?" Markcas turned to Erra who paused in silence before patting him on the shoulder. He was about to whisper something into his ear but Venas would hear either way. He wiggled his two-finger across his palm, one character at a time to tell Markcas without actually telling him. Markcas wrinkled his eyebrows and stared at Erra's palm and gradually realised that he was writing inkless characters of Chinese with his fingers.

"You know I can't read all that," he confessed, "I can barely read Chinese when it's down in ink."

"Markcas, you're hopeless," Erra blurted and wiggled his eyes, pointing them towards the cot of bunnies and he instantly understood.

"Oh...," he squeezed his lips together and shook his head.

"Why not?"

Markcas thought about it and turned around to notice that Venas had wandered away to look at other attractions. Now was his chance.

A while later, Markcas approached Venas past the mild crowd with a soft smile. She looked at him, he looked at her.

"What?" she said.

He looked down and held it up to his face with his big hands. The bunny's red eyes complemented his almost luminous blue eyes as the evening grew darker.

"You bought the bunny?" she gasped.

"What'd you think? I didn't steal it," he said excitedly as he held the bunny ever so gently between his long slim fingers and warm palm, to him, she was just a handful.

"But the academy doesn't allow pets, where you gonna put… her, our Charamols don't really count though?"

"She's for you, you don't live in the dorms," he stepped in a bit closer and carefully passed her the little furball who eagerly twitched her tiny nose and sought for a comfy pair of hands to sleep in. She shut her beady red eyes once she was in the hands of Venas after Markcas felt the sudden heartwarming touch of her hands. Erra took this opportunity to take a picture, how you may ask, cameras did not exist in this era, well, he has been discovering Markcas's apple iPhone that he's always found intriguing. It's a metal box that lights up with paintings inside, is what he described it when he first set his eyes on it. Paintings and manual ink prints were the only forms of pictures in this world such as lino stamps for books and leaflet copies.

He remembered how to take a picture and that was the only thing he could do. Everything was in English, something he will never need in his life and never understood.

"Did you just…" Markcas flinched. Then he shuffled through his pockets, "When did you?"

"Skills," he grinned and tossed the phone back to him. With panic, Markcas tumbled it in the air in hopes that it doesn't drop to the hard ground.

"I'm… gonna go home, it's getting late, we need to wake up earlier for the trip," reminded Venas.

"It's not like we don't get up early every other day," Markcas complained.

"If you don't want another bite in the ear, you better get up in time," she said whilst staring at Erra who looked away with no guilt, "thanks for the bunny," she beamed a charmful smile and hiked towards the Empire Palace.

"I'm getting tired too, let's head bac…. k, Markcas?" he waved his hand over Markcas's face, Markcas who felt his heart melting when he saw her smile like the way she did.

"Oh, what?"

"Come on," said Erra.

Markcas followed him back to the academy dorms, he turned his phone back on to admire the photo with him and her in the middle of the dim, night-time scenery. He smiled softly.

On the way to the Palace entrance, Venas gave her new bunny friend an affectionate touch, stroking her soft white coat of fur as she slept and unconsciously started talking to her.

"What should I name you?" she bent over the side to admire her cute little whispers, "a Chinese name... or an English name? What am I even supposed to do with you, I've never had a pet before, it takes a lot of time and effort to raise pets, maybe...," she thought for a while, "oh, I know," a lightbulb struck above her head when she thought of a solution.

"What, you want me to take care of..." Emerald started whilst he was kneeling at his table under the Crown Court's pavilion house.

"It's a she, you like animals right, please, I have my hunting trip tomorrow, first thing in the morning, I won't be back in a while," she pleaded, "Look how cute she is," she carefully raised her arms to give him a closer look at the creature.

Kyane backed away, he knows Emerald's conscious thinking, he will say yes and Kayne himself does not like pets.

"When she wakes up, you'll see her adorable red eyes."

Emerald looked up at Kayne, he knew he didn't like pets but Venas's request was too cute to reject.

He switched his gaze upon the sleeping bunny once more and sighed. The part that Kayne did not like the most in this situation was what was coming closer with time when Prince Emerald gave him a gesture with his two fingers to come collect the bunny from Venas. She noticed his glance towards his subordinate who tried to avoid eye contact with the cute creature.

"We'll take care of her," Emerald whipped out his paper hand fan elegantly and accepted her adorable offer.

"Really!?!" She pounced.

"But your Highness…" Emerald stared at Kayne to stop him from saying what he was about to say and dismissed his speech by ordering him to take the bunny into good care.

Venas carefully transfers her to him and bows to his royal Highness to say thank you and goodnight. He fanned the cold air around him and knew Kayne felt uneasy holding the bunny but he was gentle or at least tried to be gentle not to wake her up. He glanced back at Emerald, still seated on his cushion sipping on his tea and pulled a rather cautious expression with a twist of concern, thinking back to the day Venas first set foot on the planet, when their Oracles started glowing simultaneously when they met or rather when he found her lying on the grass, unconscious and cold. The unspoken thought continued to ring in his mind, and the more he thought about it, the more his concerns grew. But why was he thinking so carefully about it?

Nevertheless, he never thought to ask her himself but when he sent his thoughts to Master Ocean, he answered as if he knew the reason why but it seems that he was trying to hide the real reasoning behind the curation. He knew that Venas wasn't as simple as a stranger with powers. He couldn't help but notice how much her power has grown these past two months, all the better to utilize them in the rogue world on her wild expedition into an unfamiliar forest.

Far from the Empire City, a journey upon an ambush of grass and pebbles trotted the trail of galloping horses and pegasi pushing the fallen leaves from the soil below to dance in the wind through the trees. The crisp breeze swept past the heat of the travellers leaving a mist of breath behind them on the way to Taiyuan Mountains near the border of Qin States. Several students rode horseback and plenty rode their friendly pegasi beasts through the celestial forest of Taiyuan, the capital and largest city of Shanxi province in modern China where it became the capital or provisional capital of many dynasties including the Pre-Qin dynasty of which is the era Venas and Markcas have landed in. Although history in Ervanna differs from that of Earth in terms of the people and relationships between each other. The ride to Taiyuan put a strain on Venas's legs as she continued to grasp hold onto her saddleless Snowflake throughout the entire journey for the invention of saddles did not come to place during this era. Snowflake is Venas's pegasus, one of the pegasi sent from Planet Astriom, Celestial Planet of Immortals by Master Ocean's recognition of being a human immortal. After bonding with this magnificent creature, Venas discovered that Snowflake, along with having the ability to hide her horn, can also hide her wings, therefore at this moment, Snowflake looked like any other white horse.

The effort of staying on her "horse" was challenging when she first learned to ride but even now, it was still quite a task. Especially on a dragging trip extending over six hours with two small breathers in the middle. The commands of galloping riders sped across the dead leaves soon to be covered by

December's winter snow as sudden snowflakes drifted from the cloudy sky.

"Ja!" The command world for telling horses to gallop faster filled the air until snowfall became heavy, heavy enough to cause a hazard so for the sake of their safety, students and their two professors heaved their horses and relaxed a little bit. Snowfall in China every winter wasn't an unusual occasion, it snows heavily every year because when China decides to snow, it snows like crazy, the case is the same of course for the other climates. Neither the less, the snow began to plaster the forest until no grass could be seen, until no flowers to be untopped and no trees to be left undressed under a jacket of frost.

"How much longer do we have?" Markcas soullessly questioned as he stretched his muscles whilst trotting at walking speed on Nebula, his trusty pegasus that looked like an actual pegasus during the ride. Venas cast an observation upon the sky, judging by the position of the sun shining mildly through the light clouds and the initial time it takes to get to Taiyuan mountains:

"One more hour," she answered as accurately as she could, leaving Markcas to slump forwards with a great yawn. The current time was two o'clock and he was, as the British describe it, knackered.

"You're doing great, it's only one hour, we'll be there in no time," Erra butted in.

"Only one hour," he whined.

"We're used to taking cars and trains," Venas added.

"How long would it take by car?" Markcas wondered.

"Ummm… rough four to five hours," she estimated.

"What… is a car?" Erra questioned.

"It's… like carriages but without the horses and more…" she tried to think of a description that Erra would understand.

"Relaxing," Markcas finished.

"Not for the driver though," she corrected.

Markcas agreed.

"They can go faster than horses," he said.

"Faster than horses, how can anything be faster than horses?" Questioned Erra.

"A lot of things are faster than horses, planes, trains, motorbikes," Markcas listed, but he didn't expect Erra to understand what he was talking about and continued focusing on the trail ahead of them as the snowfall gradually disappeared leaving thick coats on the landscape.

Hoofprints trailed behind the group. There were twenty-five students from all years and tier two leading professors. Star Mei, Lee Hawks, Lu Kai, Xiaoli were also here and the leading professors were Professor An and Professor Shi. The first years ride in front of the group followed by the second year followed by the third years. Venas glanced back to the end of the line and found Lee Hawk in her field of view and slowly backed up to approach him for a friendly conversation. Markcas released a raging yawn and took upon notice that Venas had left his side to join the seniors. He peeked over his shoulders whilst keeping himself balanced on Nebula with Erra next to him seeing right through his thoughts.

"Hei Gongzi," she addressed him.

"Miss Xoular, what wind blew you here?"

"I was thinking, how much do you know about celestial magic, does the academy teach anything about portal magic?"

"You seem to find all sorts of different ways to ask the same question," he teased.

"The day I stop asking is the day I get a satisfying answer," she declared.

"They don't," he answered.

"They don't?"

"Not even the professors can master the technique, let alone teaching it through formal training, it's too advanced for mortals to accomplish" he explained.

"That means…" The idea of Kasey blew into her mind, he came to Earth and was the reason that Markcas was able to come here to Ervanna. Markcas mentioned to her how easy it was for Kasey to conjure up a portal on silent command. "He's not mortal, he's one of the demon monsters," she mumbled.

"Who?"

Venas came back to reality.

"Oh, nothing," she said right before a great, soundless yawn and covered her mouth.

"What's the matter, didn't get any sleep last night?"

"Actually, it's quite the story," she opened her eyes after giving them a massage.

"Does it have something to do with sneaking out of the palace at midnight last night?"

"How- how did you know?"

"I'm a palace guard, the subordinate of Qin's heir, you think I'd let a little girl sneak past me unnoticed, are you underestimating me Miss Xoular?"

"I did think I was doing a good job, yeah no, I was going to the academy," she began to pitch to Lee what occurred last night during her midnight wander. "The library was my target. I went there for a clear search of all the books and scrolls but before I got to the rest of the search, Markcas suddenly showed up."

"You mean you didn't hear him?"

"I was too distracted," she admitted.

Venas mumbled to herself reading the titles of the books she flipped through on the polished bookshelves in the library with an area count of a mansion but no bigger than Master's underground library. Stumbled upon the entrance of the library occupying one hand with hot flames that she used to see through the dark winter night and found Markcas, who was still in his academy uniform like Venas was, standing in front when she let her guard down. After all, in that one night, she scrambled through five hundred books and five hundred scrolls but nothing helped her interests. They gazed at each other astoundingly, he thought he saw someone lurking into the building from the courtyard therefore followed the figure into the time-limited access of the academy library and ended up meeting face to fire upon her lit flames making him jump.

"Venas what are you doing here, you gave me a heart attack!" he whispered wildly.

"Sorry, I thought you were the academy patrol."

"What are you doing here, it's one am in the morning?"

"What are you doing here?" She asked the same question.

"I…"

Venas vacuumed the fire back into her body and crossed her arms in the darkness waiting for an answer. She leaned in closer to see him more clearly past the glow of the moon glimmering through the windows and the door behind then that was slightly open. Markcas felt the thump of his chest and shivers under the pressure of being alone with Venas this late at night. Suddenly, ears twitched and warned her of a source of movement approaching them from the courtyard. Soon, Markcas also took to his awareness of the creaky footsteps outside. He swiftly grabbed her wrist and dragged her to a hiding spot within the library to avoid contact with the patrolman. They squatted down on the floor. A middle-aged man with his hair in a bun and his dark coloured uniform. He held a metal fire-lit lamp in his hand and held it up to the direction where he heard some motion but nothing was to be seen.

"Strange, I thought I heard something… it was probably the wind," he muttered and walked back to his position.

"That was tight," Markcas whispered.

He turned around to face Venas and took her by surprise when the two of them ended up almost touching noses. He was too close. An internal gasp filled his mind before he froze in the moment taking a loud gulp from his mouth.

It was clear where the thumping came from in fact it came from both of them. The sensation ran through their bodies, distracting them from the crickets of silence. Venas's ears sensed a rampage of thumps that helped spread shivers down his spine. Her eyes flickered between his deep blue eyes amongst the darkness with only a strip of light seeping through the windows of the library and past the bookshelves. Her balance was almost lost when her shivers travelled to her legs. They felt a connection, some kind of spark but only a few seconds later.

ARRRRGHHHH!!!

The moment was lost. Cancelled by a morid scream that trembled from the direction of which the patrolman was heading. They glanced sharply at the exit, glanced back at each other and left their post to see what had caused the commotion outside. Their footsteps rummaged over the crispy leaves and polished floorboards on the rim of the courtyard. From one courtyard into the next under the stone archway between them, Venas and Markcas discovered the body of the patrolman resting on the ground. Venas gasped.

"Stay back," Markcas commanded with cautions, he squatted to visually inspect the body, adjusting his vision through the darkness. He paused for a moment and informed her, "he's dead."

She stepped back grasping her mouth with her two hands. The man's face was deformed and seemed as if it had been melted with acid to the skull, his clothes were torn and his skin was covered with patches of black. These features were not clear to inspect during the dark hours; it was enough to attract a sense of horror and anxiety that surged through their pulses.

"Who the hell did this?" Markcas muttered.

"More like what did this, I didn't hear anything else other than him," she confronted.

He rose from the ground, building up a sense of awareness of his surroundings and the same goes for Venas. Her sensitive ears quickly detected rustling from the far distance amongst a long tension of silence. The rustling of long clothing, crackling of old bones and the friction of dry skin...There! A horrifying shadow emerged from the corner of the courtyard revealing only a limited volume of its appearance that camouflage into the darkness. It was arduous to identify what the figure was before it disappeared again.

"Markcas, there!" Before Markcas found the time to react, Venas had already ascended from her post to catch the cryptic character amongst gloomy frost misting in the air behind them.

Circling the campus of the academy, the figure stormed past every pillar, every courtyard with stagger speed that challenged Venas viciously as he tore the air apart thinking that he was succeeding his tremendous escape away from the live mortal not excepting Markcas to swing in from ahead after a whole lap around the academy.

It doesn't have a pulse, I can't hear its heartbeats, she thought. A bulk of lightning ice ripped out from his hands and engaged with the creature, he partially missed but was able to dislocate his arm that froze and flew across the yard. After the shadow uncoiled from his long ragged clothing from the shock, it was clear what the creature was, his blood-red eyeballs, cracked and bruised skin, his lips chapped like the dry clay and peeling glue. He turned around to guide away from Markcas's brutal attack in time for Venas to stun him by lighting a circle of fire to forbid his escape any further. The flames burned luminously and blew her into shock.

"A living corpse," she justified.
"What's a living corpse doing here, I thought they've all gone," Markcas bellowed.

The corpse growled and snarled with his nasty and irregular breathing patterns from the cold air. He stumbled in the circle of fire, parts of his body shredded to ashes from the cold and hot attacks but he was able to distinguish the fire immediately with a fling of his dark, bloodstained clothing and nearly escaped under Venas blew an ear sharpening tune on her celestial flute after throwing a soundproof spell at Markcas on the other side of the living corpse. The harsh tune pierced the corpse's dry ears causing him to wheeze his breaths and snarled horrifyingly, he was almost able to attack her before withering to the ground under the moon's bright midnight rays. Finally, the tension of trembling in her hands faded but still throbbed after the body exhibited a loss of immortality. She dropped her flute and soon herself, inhaling and exhaling vigorously from witnessing the corpse petrifying facial features and his intentions to attack her. She didn't want to look at it anymore and avoided eye contact with his face.

"Hey, he's gone now, it's okay," said Markcas, who dashed over the corpse to join and comfort her, grasping her in his arms. He could see how terrifying she was and felt her shivering when he opened up to hug her. She stayed silent for a while to catch her breath.

"Where there's one…" she panted slightly, "there must be more, we should tell the professors," she didn't realize her tight grip on his arms but he tolerated the slight pain for her to calm down.

"So you're saying there's living corpses on the loose, more of them?" Lee summarised.

"They come from the influence of dark crystal, the aura from his eyes gave it away, the same aura from Tao Shi's skeletal spirits," he evaluated.

"But he's dead."

"That doesn't mean someone else can't make more dark crystals, we're not safe yet," she warned. She felt as if she was developing an irrational fear of the undead. Anything but facing eye to eye with a living corpse.

The trip to Taiyuan mountains was about to end but little did Venas know, an extra pair of ears overheard her pitch to Lee explaining what she saw last night but he was not a part of the academy group, a mysterious figure tailed carefully behind them from the beginning of the trip. A boy who possessed the element of dark crystal.

Flame 5

Home

By the time everyone had settled down in ancient houses in the mountains, it was already eight pm, the time to be getting ready to sleep. The group arrived at an old inn run by an elderly couple who have lived here for all their lives and the inn was their only form of income. The couple was happy to provide enough rooms for the group, five rooms for the students and two for the professors. They called on one of their employees to take them to their rooms.

"Right this way," he said joyfully.

The inn was plain and small but highly maintained to a

presentable standard, flowers and ivy surrounded the windows and the doorway that led outside to a backyard located in the middle of the building. It was a tiny courtyard following into the next sliding doors to the second half of the inn where the group was going to stay for the next week.

"Here we are, boys on this side, girls will be that way and two seniors, your rooms are over there, please call me if you need anything," he walked back to the counter as everyone opened up their rooms to see five wooden bamboo beds in each.

"The beds here never have mattresses," Markcas complained.
"You should be used to it by now, it's better for your back," Erra replied.

Markcas and Erra shared a room with three other boys, Xiaoli, Lu Kai and another classmate named Wen Tang. Venas on the girls' side shared a room with Star Mei and two other girls in her year that she never really talks to because of being too busy with her training under both the academy and Master Ocean. Straight away, she fell fast asleep due to the tiredness of the journey and the fact that she slept late the night before. Star was ready to have a conversation with her but didn't want to disturb her as she knew Venas had always been occupied with training in order to search for a way home. Star understood her reasoning for not putting an effort towards being open and making new friends, she missed home, she wanted to go back to her birth planet just as much as Markcas did. Both of them missed their homes and their family. Star sat by Venas's bedside and silently wished her goodnight upon her sleeping eyes before she headed for dreamland herself, ready for the next day.

The sun rose to the horizon at seven o'clock sharp followed by the chuckling noise produced by a rooster who lived on a farm distant from the inn. Venas was able to hear just a hint of the rooster's call like a pin dropping to the floor. She was up and ready before anyone else, at five am in her in-the-wild hanfu coloured with shades of blue that flowed down to her ankles rather than her usual red, white and gold colours to blend in more with her environment. She secretly visited the sacred temple near the top of the mountains, prayed to them, toured around the building where she saw monks roam here and there. Monks dressed in orange with one shoulder poking out of their clothing wearing sacred beads on their neck, bald heads and not a single hair to be found. Here, a monk's duty is to follow Buddha, share their sacred knowledge, fight off demons and protect the land from those who have criminal intentions. Monks must also not fall in love or marry, they must maintain a single marital status. Venas gazed at the temple buildings located on a steep part of the mountains, a very difficult climb from the land below. Once she took a glimpse over her shoulder, her eyes widened to the mesmerising view below. She could see everything. Small villages, the farm, the inn, Taiyuan forest that took over half the territory of land. The beauty of nature spread throughout the field. Somehow it made her think of home and how much she missed it as she watched wild mountain birds swarm past her. She thought about it so much that drops of water ran down her clothes and absorbed into the fabric once there was no water left to continue the trail down. She controlled her sniffles when she heard the footsteps of a few monks passing by behind her. Soon, when the sun rose, she returned to the mountain inn in time for breakfast, everyone was here at the inn's restaurant, everyone except Markcas. He must still be sleeping, she thought and strolled upstairs to his room to wake him up. She parted the doors aside and approached his bed, ready to attack him with an alarm in the morning call but she wasn't in the mood anymore. Instead, she tossed her amulet vertically into the air and stirred up some clouds before Petal popped into the air, fresh and ready. Venas caught the amulet and put it back on.

"Wake him up," she ordered Petal and returned to have breakfast.

Petal hovered in the air and nodded.

Once breakfast had been consumed, the wild expedition began. Educational tours around the mountains, temples, the forest all to get the students familiar with their surroundings, what to avoid and what to look for because a few days later, the professors set up a practical course splitting the students into two groups of the colours red and blue. The course was on a timer, a pot of water hung by its handles with a tiny hole at the bottom to let the liquid drip. The water and the amount of drops it can produce are worth thirty minutes. The game was simple, each student is given a wooden bow and safety arrows with a padded tip dipped in a vibrant-coloured powder of their team's colour and the objective is to retrieve an item of which the professors have hidden in the middle of the forest. Like the entry exam, it was a scroll, instead of paper, it was a wooden scroll, the only difference is this was no individual mission but a team effort. The game commenced when the sun had reached the highest point of the sky and the water started dripping. Venas, Markcas, and Lu Kai were assigned in group red, Erra and Xiaoli were in group blue.

Straight away, Venas took advantage of her ears to track down the blue team from the treetops where she rested with her arrow to the ready.

SWISSSH

She had a keen eye for aiming her arrows and since no one had noticed her, she was able to hit everyone she saw. Straight after shooting, she fed the forest with a storm of wind that came from her speed escaping the eyes of the opponent. Leaves and bushes fluttered and uncoiled after the wind she created as she flew past. The more red marks she makes on the opponent, the more points the team gets; soon, her ears failed her when a ghastly cry shoots into her eardrums after a long ten minutes of silence and listening to nature's ambience. Venas wasn't the only one that heard the ghostly terror, Markcas too jumped to his feet to the horror of the scream.

"There's no way," Venas muttered to herself as the scream awoke her memory from the night she encountered the living corpse.

She blasted herself from tree to tree towards the direction of the cry and hoped for the best that this wasn't what she thought it was. But she had hoped too soon when her track was disturbed by a black floating creature she quickly identified as an undead, her face almost skeletal, her long, ominous black rags and scruffy hair no different to the straw hair of a scarecrow. The terror grew in the reflection of her eyes as the live corpse glided vertically above her, she followed the shadow, shot her with a ring of flames burning the corpse to the grass below. Spits of flames bounced from the body to the soil and disintegrated under Venas's white boots, twisting her foot on the toes to stop sparks of fire from spreading through the forest. Since the daylight was still here, the corpse was not as frightening to set eyes upon but it was still a horrifying sight. All of her facial features were very distinct and ghoulish like. She took a deep breath and searched for the source of the scream. Markcas was already there when she emerged from the bushes, wiping them aside to find him observing the freshly dead body of one of their classmates. She threw both of her hands over her mouth, it was Wen Tang, the boy with whom Markcas shared his room. His features were the same as the patrolman on that night.

"He's dead," Markcas clarified.

"Yes, I can see that," Venas replied nervously, trying not to look too long at his horrifying features.

WHOOOOOSH!

"What was that," said Markcas.

"Another living corpse," Venas answered.

"Another one, what do you mean, another one?"

"I burnt the one that murdered him."

They stormed from their post to catch the loose corpse, maybe it can lead them to where they were coming from. They sprung from one side of the forest to the other and ignored the fact that they were still in the middle of a practical training session. Coming out alive was more important than searching for a wooden scroll but instead of escaping the forest, they decided to tail the reanimated bodies. Unlike Markcas, Venas hurtled after the aura of the murderous creature with the motion of a cheetah; there was a limit for her speed and since the living corpse was just as fast as she was, questionably faster, her energy gradually kicked off like a weak battery. Markcas however, reached for shortcuts, he covertly tailed the corpse with a useful ice trail spell therefore he was traceable no matter how fast he was. Markcas scrambled between the greens of the forest to catch even a slight glimpse of the corpse, from shortcuts to shortcut, he accomplished nature's stepping into a wild territory of ghostly corpses that made him freeze on the spot. He could've sworn his soul left his body when they all beamed their bloodshot eyes at him hurdling a swirl of anxious thought. Their vicious breathing tickled a shiver down his spine.

There's a family of them, he thought. He felt like a worm hiding from a flock of birds seeking tonight's dinner but before becoming a corpse himself, he pinched his palm to pull his sword out with a series of magical sparks hopping from his skin and slashed it blindly as a prompt reaction. The corpse squealed and squabbled trying to suck his soul from his body like their previous victims but Markcas did not allow that. These corpses are like no undead, they were strong, stronger than the ones that Tao Shi released. It ached when they take turns attacking him, knocking him close to the edge of the forest where a cliff stood high and tall over the ground below. Anyone who falls down has no possibility of survival. Unfortunately, after being able to deal with two corpses, the rest snarled courageously like a wild beast and thrust him to the side of the cliff. Pebbles and stones scattered across the surface, some flicked to the edge bounces off the cliff, bit by bit with nowhere to go but down, and down the steep cliff is where Markcas was heading right now. He had nothing to grab, nothing to save himself, just like the rocks, he was going down and down he went.

The final squeals travelled from one corner to the other, spreading to the ears of the other students, Lee was the first one to hear, he as a blue member loosened his grip on his arrow to warn the rest of his coursemates of the murderous calls. His warning concerned the rest of the academy where they will be responsible for the death of a student. Soon a pigeon flew to the academy and spread to the Palace of the unfortunate incident whilst Prince Emerald finalised the conclusion of a different thought that has been running through his mind since the day Venas arrived. He left his room and dismissed his servants from following him in the direction of the secret underground library to question his ideas to Master Ocean. He calmly stormed in with his hanfu gracefully gliding after him and asked Master one question and one question only. Master had already guessed what his Royal Highness was going to ask.

"Venas Xoular…" he said seriously, "Who is she really?"

Venas didn't even notice that the corpse she ended up chasing was a different one to the one she had met earlier, from the back, they all look incomparable and the reason how they're able to slip away from Venas so smoothly is the result of being dead therefore not having a thundering heartbeat whilst they're on the move.

When Venas least expected, another shadow raced past her, was it another corpse. She looked up.

"You," she mumbled promptly.

It was the shadow that followed her from the city to Taiyuan forest, tall but strong, his long brown hair followed him gracefully as he jumped down to the ground surface, his ruffling clothes, black and maroon red and matching boots. His dangerous black mask covered only his eyes. His slow-motion entry set off a source of consternation, a sensation of terror from his sudden appearance. He stared at her emotionlessly as he dropped from the sky to reintroduce himself but it seemed that Venas had never once forgotten who he was, how could she forget?

"Xiao Kai," she clarified.

"Long time no see," he replied. Kasey knew she wasn't happy to see him as she had already summed up a conclusion.

"These corpses belong to you," she said.

"What if I say they aren't mine?"

"Then I don't have any business with you," she said before eliminating the corpses before dashing away to continue her search but Kasey seized her by the arm. Forcefully, she tried to shake his grip off but one attempt wasn't enough, she tried again.

"Let go of me," she cried but he would not let go until she anticipated a stretch for the nearest tree trunk with her feet, facing head up to the sky, she drew a firm arc over his head and finally threw herself in the air to release a series of flames that nearly burnt his palm if he didn't unhand her, "what do you want with me!?!" She yelled frustratingly before striking her combat mode and made a beeline for under his torso where she enhanced the phoenix eye fist, aiming it straight under his rib cage. He kept in a breath of staggering pain and blocked her incoming aggression.

"I don't want to have anything to do with you, I see your dark crystal ring, whoever uses it or even has ownership of one is instantly my enemy," she tackled.

A silent yelp for pain rummages inside his head, he clenched where it hurt and dodged in time for her next aggressive defensive kick and the next until he finally was able to grab both of her wrists, popped them together and held them with his large hands behind her to keep her still and swiftly shoved a small black sphere into her mouth and pressed his hand over it to make sure she swallowed it.

"What did you just feed me!?!"

"Relax, a pill so temporarily shut down your martial arts," he confronted.

"What, if you're asking for the elixir pill you used to save me, I'm sorry, I don't have any."

"Since you know I have a piece of the dark crystal, then you know I can help you to go back home," he ignored her last comment.

"Help? I don't need your help," Venas sought any unoccupied direction and was ready to blank Kasey when he swung his hand up in the air as if he was shooting a ball behind him to mobilize a tornado of ghostly, deteriorated bodies. Once again, squealing and yearning pierced her concentration before she apprehended her presence was lured to the edge of the forest. Not knowing that Markcas was here a mere second ago, she scratched and cut her hand on the rough and stony terrain, taken by surprise, she felt the effects of the pill spread through her body as the corpses were able to sneak past to shock her into suspense, interrupting her ambitions to fight them courageously.

"You're scared of them," Kasey noticed her frightened behaviour.

"What am I scared of?" Venas groped where her heart was, feeling the sensation of losing her martial skills.

"These deadly corpses... are you going to be good now?"

"What?" she said impatiently, stuck to the ground as if she was bound by some kind of spell.

"You want to go home, you've been searching," he walked up closer to her as the living corpses made an open path, he removed the dark crystal ring from his index finger.

Venas stared at the ring that he placed out in front of her to consider his offer.

"Why would you wanna help me in the first place? The only reason you saved me was because of Akirou."

"So you don't want to go back... because Markcas is already on his way there," he glanced towards the cliff behind her and her eyes followed with a shock of terror.

"Markcas?" she halted for a moment of brainstorming, "you... you were the one that opened up the portal," her mind flashed her the image of nearly being strangled by a reptilian demon monster and falling into a deep black hole that appeared behind her. She remembers when Markcas gave her a tip that it was a masked boy that dragged him into this world, later identifying that it was Kasey, "you're the reason I'm here, you opened the portal that I fell through - WHY would you do that?!?"

"If I haven't, you would've been strangled to death."

"There are other ways!"

"Was there?" Kasey hunched over and glared at her whilst she was still glued to the ground.

His stares were the most frightening stares she had ever encountered from a human being. The eye holes in his mask were transparent enough for him to see through them from the inside but not enough for Venas to see his eyes from the outside. His mask is like a one-way mirror, she thought.

"You'll never be able to go back home by yourself, it's highly impractical that you'll master the arts of portals at this age… without the support of a superior power gem," he justified explicitly, holding his rings in front of his face trying to give her temptation, "For mortals with average or even above average, it requires tens of years to master the skill to even forge a portal that can transport an object fully in tack let alone a full fledge human being, even for mortals who devote all their time on portal magic, it still requires a decade."

"Why should I believe anything you say?"

"Because… I've tried. I've used rats for my test runs but they don't come back in one piece, you a power gem like the dark crystal, alone, it can do things far beyond a mortal's abilities."

"I know that- why are you telling me."

"Because you need to go home."

"I know I need to go home but why do you think I need to go home, it doesn't concern you in any way."

"To stop a crisis," he finalised.

A tantrum of silence broke through once Kasey spoke of the word "crisis". The ever-so-serious face he bared when he said it made Venas hold in a funny feeling that was bursting to come out. A laugh, in fact, a small chuckle.

"Me? Stop a crisis?" she blurted, "what crisis would

Earth have that needs me to stop it?" She continued to think that Kasey was only joking.

"This isn't a joking matter."

"I know I'm gullible but I'm not that gullible," she dismissed her grin.

She jumped back to her feet but Kasey stopped her from leaving.

"I'm being serious," he stared at her. She prompted an idea up her sleeve.

"I'll accept your offer… when you put all the corpses back to their graves, you shouldn't be tampering with the dead you know," she lied.

Kasey remained silent and considered dismissing these deadly creatures, he released the chant that he had put on them and returned them to their graves.

I can do it, Venas prepared to escape from his eyes, she didn't believe that he would peacefully take her to Earth, he led her here but that doesn't mean he was going to send her back otherwise what was the reason for him to lead her to Ervanna in the first place. Frankly, Kasey already knew that she wasn't being truthful, she was trying to trick him, to occupy his hands with the task of returning the dead. Rather than catching her spontaneously, he impersonated being clueless and excused one living corpse to chase after her within the next split second since he knew if he tails her, the chance of Venas being able to hear her would be high. The corpse snarled at her through the trees when she was caught off guard thinking she was so sure that she'd get away but the corpse pushed her back towards the cliff, back to Kasey who didn't have to wait long to see her worried little face again.

It's so fast, she trembled and swung her body over in mid-air to avoid its brutal attack. Its movements were sudden and forced her to use every single inch of her body to at least not let it have the chance to land a hit. Leaves and twigs entered the tornado that she and Kasey had created once he clashed between them to dismiss his puppet. The corpse was strong but Kasey was stronger and unlike the corpse, he actually knew what he wanted to do and that was to get Venas into his portals to send her away with what he thought was an unnecessary matter of explaining further his idea of "crisis".

The air around them cuts in two, whoosh and crunches from the leaves from jumping and harsh swings like they have a planned route. One avoided the edge of the rocks and one was determined to make a beeline that trailed straight down and it was clear who was going to lose.

"Give up," he demanded.
"No," she answered.
"Fine then, have it your way- do as you please," he said and finally pulled his last strings blocking her kicks and punches, violently launching her into the sky beyond the forest with an impulsive force that flashed from the elements of his dark crystal ring.

Venas wasn't able to process his intentions quick enough

to act and prevent being thrown into the air, not a second later stars and planets forged into her surroundings like ink spreading across a piece of wet paper.

"This is..." she opened her eyes dramatically, finding herself floating in the air like an astronaut, "the portal," the galaxy-like portal quickly swerved into a hurricane and shifted the area around her, dropping her onto the fresh morning grass of what she thought was the forest of Taiyuan. Venas took a wild minute to ease the pain in her knees and elbows after crashing into the hard soil and damp grass. Whilst she rubbed the pain away on her elbow, she finally gave the forest a good look, it looked like any other, green trees, grass, bushes... but the size of the trunks was a lot thinner, the patches of grass were thicker and the snow was gone.

"This is," she repeated.

The species of birds that flew past were different, the weather and the sky, it seemed as if the clouds had vanished, the clouds that when the last time she checked, they were sprinkling snow onto the forest. "This is a whole different forest," she finalised before taking notice of her sudden change of clothes, clothes that looked more modern. A pink, puffy jacket, blue t-shirt and black jeans with white trainers. She walked deep into the unknown environment thinking that the way she was heading was a possible exit; she dug deeper into the greens, bewildered by where in the world she was, what forest this was and how to get out but there was no magic that could help her with this. An unexpected encounter bumped her in the head not many minutes later...

but there was nothing there. Nothing was in front of her to bump into.

"What in the world, I knew he wasn't going to send me to Earth," she muttered in bewilderment, slowly reaching her hand forwards to feel for what she established was an invisible barrier, a forcefield, something one would find in Ervanna and not Earth because this looks like magic. It looks like magic to keep trespassers out of one's property. Venas looked at her clothes and questioned whether she was on Earth or Ervanna. "Now I'm just confused," after a while, she became impatient and struggled to navigate the grounds, everything looked the same and all the trees stood at the same height. "This is Earth, this is definitely Earth," she said to herself when she brushed leaves away from the trunk of one of the trees to sight her eyes upon some English writing engraved neatly into the tree that read, "I love you, C and K," inside a heart.

If this is Earth then my phone will work, I'll just use Google maps, she said inside her head. She rummaged through her jacket pockets but of course, it wasn't there. Magic can only help her if she remembers exactly where she left it. Under… no, it was in her bag and the bag was next to the table by the shelves in her room at the Empire Palace, the shelves were next to her bed, she rambled. It was there, she knew exactly where she put it and extracted it with a transportation spell that she learnt very briefly from Master Ocean. It was simple, she could also use magic to charge it, enough for her to search her location but before she finished typing, a harsh snap bent into her ears, her eyes and attention was diverted.

SNAP SNAP SNAP

Ropes were released from their knots and scattered the leaves laid on top of the net that they were attached to simultaneously activating metal traps on the ground below as if someone had tripped over a set of wires.

Traps? She popped her device away and rush away from the unestablished noises, she leapt into the air to grab hold of the nearest branch, making an arc for the higher points of the forest before heading towards the source of the noises but no one was there as the trail of traps continued to act on some sort of stimulation that was switching them on, the subject was up ahead and by the chaotic sounds of the greens, the subject was struggling to escape.

Too far away for me to detect whether it's a human or an animal, I need to go faster, she thought and blazed across the air past all the leaves and branches. It was a rather tall and skinny boy with fair hair undercut, wearing a murky green baseball jacket with matching trainers, a white vest, black jeans and he was dodging all the traps that he accidentally set off with his clumsy feet. Venas was only able to see his backside and not his face, not even when she swooped down to grab him after making a brave leap for a strong and bendy branch, gripping it tight between the back of her legs, allowing her to swing upside down and bring him up to the trees to save him the trouble of dodging those painful-looking traps. Trying to pull him up without the help of her celestial would have been quite the challenge which is why she did use it but was careful to prevent the Earth boy from noticing. They sat on the branch before expressing a relief of the escape from the ambush that finally came to an end. Both of them stopped for a second to catch their breath.

"Are you okay," she puffed then gulped.

"I'm fine," he panted, "Thank yo…" the boy belatedly turned around and they were both blown to shock when they found themselves staring at the face of a familiar person, it was because of their altered appearances that they did not recognise each other at first display.

"Markcas?" she blurted.

"You're here too, how'd you get here, do you know where we are because this doesn't look like the mountains?" he questioned.

"Kasey threw me into his portals, I was gonna check where I was before you started setting off all those traps," she confronted. Markcas scratched his head.

"My bad."

"Seriously, when are you gonna start being more aware of your surroundings."

"Sorry, everything here is just greens, greens and more greens, I tripped over and all I could do was run."

"Ever thought about going up," she made a point because all the traps were set on ground level.

"No, no I didn't," he admitted and scratched his head.

"Anyway, we need to find ou…" she suddenly paused in fear that the cracking noise she heard was coming from the root of the branch that they were resting on.

It was breaking and falling apart too quickly for any time to react and avoid the potential accident of collapsing to the ground and that is indeed where they ended up, on the ground after a loud thump and rustling leaves that followed them down with the rest of them where Venas settled on something warm and soft.

"That really hurt," she rubbed her arms on the part where it hit and dragged on the tree trunk before she hit the ground, afterwards, she finally noticed that it was Markcas she landed on. She soon became embarrassed as she was sitting on top of him.

"That did hurt a lot… if you weren't the one being used as a human cushion," he teased with a hint of pain, "that's gonna leave a mark," he sat up and rubbed his neck and then his back with one hand when the other was unintentionally resting on Venas's leg when she removed herself from on top of him and sat next to him.

"Sorry," she said shyly.

"Not at all," he secretly blushed.

A rush of silence broke in where both of them ran out of words to say to each other after the accident before Venas poked her hand into her pocket for her phone to continue her map search.

"We're in... the Epping forest, in London," she confirmed.

"London? Earth London or Ervanna London because forests all look the same, modern and historical."

"Markcas... if there's wifi for me to search online then that obviously means we're in the modern era, we're on Earth," she stopped and took notice of Markcas's fair, blonde hair where he lost the long braid that trailed down his back, she remembered when they first met, he had fair hair and that it wasn't always black.

The task from this point onwards was simple, navigate their way out of this crazy forest but as they left the exit of the wild greens, an unknown creature peered out from bushes and decided to carefully follow them back from the forest to the underground, the underground to St. Pancreas international overground when on the way up the lengthy escalators, Markcas found it easier to talk to Venas switching his position to the steps behind her because of their cute height difference.

They longingly waited for the next high-speed service to Ashford International and sat across from each other on the table seats as Venas eventually fell asleep with her head in her arms. Markcas leant over with his face pressed against one hand and one hovered over her hair, putting aside the loose strands as he too fell asleep waiting for the moment they reach their destination where they can finally go home.

Flame 6

Liquid Body

Strings of thoughts threaded through Venas's mind whilst she laid on her comfy bed, she thought of why she landed in the Epping forest and why Kasey didn't land her back at the school where he first took her away in the first place. It was a minor riddle that was in no rush of being solved. She also remembered faintly, Markcas running his finger along the side of her face, tucking strands of hair behind her ear. He felt how close he was whilst being half-asleep and wanted the movement to last a little bit longer being alone with him.

Now that she was home, she has felt a tiny spot of guilt

for leaving without notice but what else could she have done? Her mother was downstairs working in the take away like usual times; in her mind, her daughter had always been with her at home, she asked her mum some simple questions without telling her that she was actually gone for a whole two and half months on another planet. Kasey must have done something to make her think that I was here the whole time, she processed a solution. She even wanted to thank him for not having her mother worry but if it wasn't for him, none of the whole space travelling situations would have occurred. The same happened to Markcas at his house where his mother, father and his younger brother Oscar had not noticed his disappearance during the last two months. Firstly, he snuck into his bedroom through the windows and when he heard footsteps outside his door, he rushed into bed.

"Yo Markcas…" his brother called and stormed into the slightly opened doors, "why are you sleeping?"

"I'm tired," he faked a yawn.

"But you were just gaming literally just a few minutes ago."

"Was I? … Oh yh, well, I'm napping now, get out of my room," he dismissed.

"Oh …. Right then," Oscar shut the door behind him.

I was gaming? He thought and soon established that it must've been some kind of magic to make his family think that he was still at home all this time. Neither the less, it was about time he was allowed to sleep whenever he wanted to so he decided to snuggle up tightly in his bed all day until he was satisfied whilst still thinking about being with Venas on the train having their little moment.

Venas was scrolling through her iPad after making plans for Christmas and discussing them with her mother. She was visiting her Godmother, her mother's best friend who lives in the East Midlands area of England, more precisely, she lives in Nottinghamshire. It was a long way from here and it'll be where she's staying for Christmas, her first time travelling so far across England alone. She scrolled through social media feeds like the day was never going to end as the school had been cancelled for a few months of lessons due to the previous attack of Tao Shi of which the Earth humans still have no idea. All schools in fact have been shut down for the children's safety. Judging by the low speed of British workers, it'll take until later next year for them to refurbish all the damage, rather another three months plus the three months that have already gone by. Venas wasn't sure what to do to kill some time, it has been so long since she's done anything other than martial arts and magic. Her mother was working and there was no one else in the flat, or at least that's what she had thought. After the evening hour struck, she decided to have a soothing wash. When she finished, steam followed her out of the bathroom and into her room which was just across from the bathroom. She suddenly noticed the damp window sill and the water that was dripping onto the carpet but it wasn't raining. The sky became a bit dark, dark enough that when she opened up the curtain to close the window, she saw a reflection of herself in a set of comfy warm clothes and the reflection of another living being. In shock, her eyes widened to see a blue figure that stood mysteriously behind her. At the same time, he said:

"Took your time," he smirked and lifted his head to look at her as he leant against the wall.

She was horrified by the dim reflection of a white head wrapped around his forehead, his blue skin from the head to his waist under his unzipped green jacket, brown jeans and shoes. His hair was the same light green colour as his jacket and had blue tips. She gasps sharply and instantly surged for the door in shock; he expected Venas to run away at first instinct so he was ready to shut the door just as she opened it. For a second, he cornered her tightly to prevent her from escaping, she launched him away from her and attempted to twist the door handle again but he came back too quickly within a flash to grab her hand and lured her away from the doorknob with his blue hands. She decided to aim a few hits and kicks at him as he swiftly dodged every single strike like he knew what she was going to do. Finally, he took hold of her two hands and landed on the soft bed, using his other hand to grab the leg that she was going to use to boost him in the stomach but his strength was very firm.

"Woah Woah, calm down - calm down," he said whilst trying to keep her still, "I'm the good guy, easy on the kicks," he said.

"Tell that to the one that broke in!" she struggled to budge his strong grip, she could see he had a six-pack and his strength was beyond hers, "How'd you get in!" she ended up staring at him and his deep turquoise eyes.

"Easy, your window was open," he confessed.

"But it's not big enough for you to fit."

"Anything's big enough for me to go through," he said as he demonstrated a little sample of his body forging into water.

"You can turn into water, your skin isn't painted?"

"You think this is paint?"

"Well, it's not every day I see a blue…" then she noticed the odd shape of his ears.

"You're a…"

"I'm a…" he waited.

It clicked, she knew what he was and raffled to get out of his grip.

"You're a mutant!"

"No, calm down, well- yes I am- but I'm not going to hurt you, Cyris, Cyris Coral, nice to meet you."

"Like I can believe a burglar, unhand me," she struggled again, her wrist was turned red already, she was trying so hard, he used both of his hands to hold her still.

"No wait, I told you to calm down already."

"Don't you think this position is a bit awkward?!"

"What do you mean, I quite like talking like this, if I let go, you might use your magic against me and I don't want that."

"How'd you know…"

He coughed.

"I followed you from the Epping forest, you and that blondy you're quite skilled for a girl your size," he scanned her.

"Thanks for the compliment," she said sarcastically, since Cyris knew that she was no ordinary human, she lit a palm flame and burnt his contact away from her.

"Ow," he flinched and unhanded her from the burning shock.

"That hurt right, now get out," she ordered.

"What, I just got here."

"You say that as if I invited you here..." she walked over to the window, pulled the curtains to reveal the window, "get out the way you got in," she insisted.

"What if I don't? You're not gonna call the police, are you, cause those handcuffs will definitely stop me," he said sarcastically and sat on the tip of her bed, leant back and pressed his palms onto the mattress.

"Okay then what do you want with me, you could've raided someone else's house, why mine?" She released the curtains letting it swing from side to side before it settled down.

"Normal humans are scared of me, one sight and they act like it's the zombie apocalypse."

"So I'm not normal," she paused, "spill it" she demanded.

"After you tell me your name," he flirted but saw the serious aura that Venas was sending him, he went straight to the point, "I'm here for your help, you can magic which means you're no ordinary human, you and that boy escaped all the traps in the forest, somewhere that human tend not to enter from fear and the unknown."

"So you want me to help you with…. ?"

Cyris raffled his pockets for a piece of paper, a piece of the newspaper he kept from two weeks ago, it illustrated a picture of a block of ice and in that block of ice was:

"Atlas Silver, he's like the idol of all mutants- been missing for five hundred years and the humans found him in the frozen Lakeside Arts, Nottingham, a demon snake put him there, he froze the lake with some black orb of his," he explained and passed the paper to Venas as she read the headlines and the long paragraph places next to the picture.

"Demon snake, how'd you know it's a demon?"

"Because he's captured other mutants before but there was nothing I could do to retrieve them-"

"Why would he freeze them? Mutants all live together in London right, though I dunno where in London."

"Epping forest, we live there, that's why we set traps there if they get far enough, they reach an invisible field that prevents them from entering our territory, Atlas went missing after the Muman's war along with a lot more of us- but lately I've been sneaking into the city and discovered the demon snake freezing them and putting them in the rivers for humans to find but those were all in London, I only knew about Atlas's reappearance after the news came out."

"Snake demon? Why would he put only Atlas in the East Midlands and the rest of them in London?" Venas questioned like this was of her concerns now.

"Beats me, Atlas was the latest one to be found," Cyris finished.

"You're telling me this like I'm part of the solution," she shoved the paper back to him.

"That's because you are part of the solution, you're going to Nottingham for Christmas, you can take me with you, I only know the southern parts of England- because Atlas is the strongest out of all of us, if we find him, then we can rescue all the other mutants that went missing."

"We?" Venas disapproved, "what makes you think that I'm going there for Christmas?" she denied.

Cyris walked towards her for a notebook she placed on her desk behind her and showed her the plans that she noted down for Christmas.

"See here, you wrote down your Christmas plans and one of them is, going to Nottingham to visit Godmother," he read to her as she snatched the notebook from his hand and closed it shut but she was already caught.

"Fine, if you're asking me to take you to Nottingham then that I can do, I'm not doing anything else, the ticket costs a fortune so I'm not paying for that," she said.

"Are you not one bit curious about helping us mutants out, you can help me retrieve Atlas?"

"Don't you have other mutant friends to help you, why me?"

"Because you're a human and you know stuff that I don't, it's better to get around, plus I can just sneak onto the train, remember, I can turn into water," he reminded Venas of how he was able to sneak into her room in the first place, "and… they told me not to leave the forest because the human world is a dangerous place."

"It can't be any more dangerous than Ervanna," she muttered.

"What?"

"Nothing, so I'll just shove you into a bottle," she commented.

"Yeah, that's what I was thinking."

"I was joking, knowing me, I'd drink the wrong bottle," she thought for a while, "I'll keep you in a jar, but you know my secret and I know yours - I'm guessing you have the ability to disguise yourself as a human," she predicted, "so you better keep a low profile… now get out of my room before my mum comes back, I'm leaving in two days."

"So that's a yes?"

"Yes, now get out of my room," she demanded him to leave again.

"But I'm hungry," he mentioned as his tummy just so happened to grumble.

Venas wasn't too motivated to feed the blue burglar that broke into her room but she was feeling generous and grabbed some food from the kitchen. She grabbed a carton of soy milk, a packet of croissants and quickly put together some ham salad sandwiches.

"Here, I don't want to see you before my trip so go find some place else to live," she warned him.

"Sure thing cutie," he took the bag of food and washed out of the window only to be seen days later as Venas had told him.

In time for the journey to Ashford International train station where her mother kindly and lovingly dropped her off, she set off. She packed two small pieces of luggage, one on her back and a purple suitcase and wore her pink jacket, blue t-shirt, black jeans and grey trainers. She waved her mother goodbye before strolling into the station to catch the next train into the St. Pancreas station to make it early for the train to Nottingham, Long Eaton station, the second last stop on the way to Nottingham city. Luckily, she took the highspeed to make it in front of the large crowd that was waiting for all the trains that appeared on the giant monitor above them listing trains with different routines to Sheffield and Nottingham. Venas sat on her suitcase whilst she waited for her train to arrive at platform 14 listed on the screen and soon enough she was ready to feed the entrance machine. The machine ate her paper ticket and spat it back out as the door opened before speed walking to the far end of the endless train carriages past the first-class sections to the standard seating. A stampede of human beings rushed around her also looking for decent seating as the tannoy above announcing:

"This is the East Midlands Railway service to Nottingham Station calling at Ketting, Market Harborough, Leicester,

Loughborough, East Midlands Parkway, Long Eaton and Nottingham Station."

She was ready to put her suitcase in with the rest but then thought she could use some celestial powers to shrink it and pop it in her bag and that she did before searching for an unoccupied seat to sit at, preferably, the seats with the tables and by the window. The trains of the East Midlands services had rich red seats and had a long line of carriages although the platform of Long Eaton station was actually shorter than the train, therefore, she searched amongst carriages lettered A to E, the first five carriages of the train and sat down ready for the two-hour journey.

"I see you've stopped moving, can I come out now?" Cyris whispered, "it's getting a bit stuffy in here," he whined.

Venas wanted to pretend that she couldn't hear him but Cyris wouldn't stop requesting to leave the glass jar that he was in so Venas took it out of her bag but unfortunately, she recalled a ticket checking inspection that occurred twenty minutes into the journey.

"You better stay in there," she whispered amongst the crowd that strolled up and down the train's interior, roaming to put their luggage away and finding a seat.
"Wait, no, don't zip it out, your bag is as dark as hell," he whispered again but Venas popped the jar back in and plugged in her Bluetooth earphones and decided to sleep.

As she slept, a dark creature lurked the rear of the station, his reptile snake sniffed out the blood of non-human in his water form and the blood of a familiar soul, two victims to act as his prey today. He stood on the roof of the station where no one would see him, his long, blue robe dangled from his body with several snakes wiggling out from underneath, following the movement of the essence seeping out from the dark crystal ball he was holding in the creature's skinny, long hands. As Venas was asleep, she wasn't aware of the dark aura from the station as the train had left long ago. The creature's pet snakes began to speak.

"The girl isssss on that train Massssster Sssslevel," said one snake.

"Aren't we going to chase it," said another.

Before Slevel responded he stood in silence like he was conjuring a great plan.

"Be patient... the trip to Nottingham is only two hours," he replied.

"Looksss like we're making another trip to the Midlands," the forest snake hissed.

"And our goal?" question the second snake as a third snake, much larger than Slevel, emerged from beyond the roof and answered:

"To take the girl's oracle and find the Spectrum Dia," he wiggled his tongue like he just came up from a satisfying meal, "the blood of these British people is so untasteful," he spat out a few drops of blood, "it's disgusting, the things they eat need to be adjusted," he said as screams screeched down below to the sight of a dead human of which he just took a bit out of.

"We leave in an hour."

Flame 7

Infested

"This is the East Midlands railway service to Nottingham station, calling at Long Eaton and Nottingham station," announced the tannoy as the train's journey was close to the end.

The rummaging of footsteps and luggage flew through Venas's ear and out through the other whilst she was still fast asleep. Soon, a whistle from outside blew to signal the train to leave, waking her up from her slumber. She squinted her eyes from the brightness of the sky and read the sign that said:

She was almost there, just one stop left until she reached the station to her Godmother's house. The train was jam-packed with people, so many that the corridor was a bit full of people standing who, unfortunately, couldn't find a seat. Apart from the train, the station was also very busy. It is the holiday season and the shops amongst the platforms were embellished with festive decorations that soon were no longer in sight as the train started moving again. A little while later, people in the carriage that Venas sat in began to travel along with the shaking floors into the neighbouring carriages for free spaces. Apart from the passengers that circled the train, Cyris was just as active in his little jar, he swissed round and round out of boredom and longed to be released and be free from the darkness inside Venas's bag. Since he was water and he was squished inside, no one could hear him when he talked, his voice was muffled and only Venas could hear him but she chose to ignore and his jabbering was getting on her last nerves. Suddenly, the rear of the train fell into shock as a worker dashed from the back to the very front of the train into the driver's room to inform them of a strange black figure that was following them. Passengers were startled by the sudden thumping of the worker's rapid footsteps. Slevel was on his way.

"Sir! We have a slight concern- there's some sort of creature tailing the train on the railway," he informed.

"What? That's impossible, we're going at a hundred and twenty-five miles per hour, there's no way anything is capable of running that fast," said one of the drivers that was taking a break whilst the other driver was driving.

"It looks like a man," the worker said, "and he's not running."

Just as he said that he received a phone call from the other side of the train.

"It's a mutant," he said out of instinct, "he's heading closer to the train and he looks like he's about to attack us."

The nearby passengers overheard the warning and kicked off their reaction with a panic, promptly, people started to leave their seats and scurried down the front of the train. The train attendants quickly evacuated the back carriages as if it was helpful anyway. People screamed in terror not knowing what it was that they were fearing. Mothers picked up their children and abandoned their bags whilst the front of the train was still nice and peaceful... for now.

"What are we going to do?" said an attendant.

"I don't know, nothing like this has ever happened before," replied another confused and anxious.

They needed to ensure that there were no trains in the distance ahead of them before proceeding to the very poorly planned solution. Through all the commotion, one attendant at the front picked up the phone to dial emergency services and one pulled the tannoy's microphone, as calmly and as formally as he could, he warned everyone on board of the new travelling update:

"Hello, this is an emergency announcement, we have just pass Long Eaton station and are now making our way straight to Nottingham station, we are under attack by a mutant tailing the train and are going full speed to reach the destination- everyone, please make your way to the front of the train as safely as possible, I repeat, we are calling at Nottingham station, thank you," the attendant hastily popped the microphone back and didn't know what to do next, he heard mutters of complaints and concerns. He raged on a mode of panic

Everyone on board was just as confused as the people

at Long Eaton station who just witnessed their train that dangerously flashed past them before sighting Slevel and his venomous snakes trailing behind it. They started screaming from the fright of his ugly face. The train rumbled vigorously but the carriages were stable although the driver increased his driving speed, Slevel still seems to be getting closer.

"What, mutants don't go around attacking people, that can't be possible," Cyris commented.
"I don't know," Venas replied quietly.
"It must be the demon monster that's been trapping lost mutants."

Quickly, before her carriage became pitched with a crowd, she headed towards the toilets, towards the rear without taking her jar of water with her. People continually kept crashing into her with no concerns for apologising, instead, they all ignored her. She slid into the nearest toilet and cleverly used a bit of her celestial to change her clothes with an additional white mask that covered her from her nose to her neck. She stopped and heard the sound of a crash. The banging of metal and the hissing of snakes were ever so faint. They made their way to the tip and slithered past the first set of windows and poked their body's through by staining the glass with their venom and melting it away.

"They're coming closer," Venas said.

She disabled any cameras stuck to the train ceiling as the jar of water appeared in her hand. She emerged from the toilet stalls, opened the jar and chucked the water into the air whilst it emerged swiftly into Cyris who came out in his black-haired human form, when he saw that there was no one here but Venas who already dashed away, he morphed back into his blue skin and colourful hair. He fled after her before his feet even touched the grey flooring. He was just as fast as she was. Fast enough to spot a small snake creeping into the carriage and to throw it out the windows creating a fresh new hole in the glass.

"It's the snake monster," confirmed Cyris.

Venas wasn't very excited about this encounter but somehow she felt like she should be responsible for the peoples' protection because there's no way any normal human being would be able to handle these dangerous monsters. A monster that is capable of chasing and catching up to a train an hour after it leaves. Venas and Cyris zoomed across the slim corridors opening the doors by endlessly clicking the open button on the sidewall and rushed in from carriage to carriage just in time to meet more venomous serpents aiming for their delicious flesh and of course the so-called Oracle jewel that their Master is so obsessed with. Venas gripped her two fingers together and drew fire from her fingertips to burn them away, harshly swiping her hand to the side to get them out of the way, magically shutting the door ahead with her magic, chopping another snake in half.

"We're almost at the station," Cyris yelled.
"I see him," Venas warned.

Slevel grew a devilish smirk on his blue face, his body travelled at an angle as he was tall and his horns looked very sharp. Unfortunately, his speed was limited in the tight space but for Venas and Cyris, that was an advantage and they took it. When he met eye to eye with Slevel, he felt something strange but ignored it when a cannon of flames passed him from behind aiming at the serpent but he caught it and threw it aside like it was a squishy dodgeball.

"He stopped it," Venas gasped.
"I felt that," Cyris commented, he hopped into the seats to the tables and sprinted around Slevel boosting his strongest kicks at him whilst Venas released the sword of Jade Dragon from her Oracle and set the blade on fire from head to tail distracting Slevel for a mere second.
"The sword of Jade Dragon," he said in shock, "how do YOU have it?!?"
"Nothing you should be worried about," she said in a cool but serious way.

The fire burst into sparks and reflected brightly into her eyes before Slevel dodged every single shot she struck and just before reaching the platform at Nottingham Station, he virtually lifted her by the neck with the untouchable power of his dark crystal, squeezing the air out of her, Cyris leapt behind Venas, wrapped his arms around her and cut off the connection before all the doors of the trains parted widely for the passengers to escape the snakes that trailed behind them with a hungry task of their own. Some shouted, some screamed and some cried, the peaceful station became an action-packed horror scene pushing all the people away from the platform and luring the emergency service in, better known as the police patrol. Dozens of police cars surrounded the entire station, policemen and women pulled out their weapons to shoot the serpents, preventing them from injuring and killing any more people.

"Quick, this way!!!," bellowed a policeman, pointing the way to the exit as more screams shot into the air after the gun started to fire their aim.

"How are you doing, ma'am," said one snake to a policewoman which she had instantly killed and shouted:

"These things talk!!!"

"They're probably mutant snakes," yelled another.

"I was told there's a man who attacked the train," they moved further into the station to the next platform whilst there were people still running as fast as they could from the vicious hissing of the snakes. A rapid motion of wind wrapped the air ever so suddenly from a helicopter that hovered in mid-air above the station, three figures leapt out of the open doors onto the roof in their iron-steel super suits and their robotic helmet ready to respond in action to the emergency call they received from the department.

"Look, it's the heroes," screamed a random civilian.

"It's Astron and Neon," said another but she was quickly taken with the crowd that was almost cleared, many were too busy escaping the danger to even notice Armsward who went by the name of Astron whilst in his disguise. They left the work to Connar and his crew and lowered their screams and panicking rage.

"Connar, there's a pile of serpents by platforms four and three," notified Serena, the lady in her yellow and white robotic suit, the same as Connar's blue and white suit but with the helmet, he was unrecognizable.

"We'll go there first," he declared and jumped from roof to roof that were slightly opaque, down the stairs to the platforms, popping a device from his belt prepared for the mention of snakes over the phone.

The device released a dose of Black Cyanide onto the snakes, a chemical capable of killing snakes by entering their mouths and spreading like a bullet.

"Not bad for a five-hundred-year-old mutant," Slevel commented, giving Cyris the idea that they've met before.

"You say that as if you know me," said Cyris who was still holding Venas ever so tightly.

"You're five hundred years old?"

"Yeah, I am."

"Forget that, we need to run," Venas abandoned the topic and confronted the first part of her plan and flashed out of the carriage flashing past Armsward on the way out. She instantly recognised his robotics work from online media but stopped when their faces meet for a split second seeing her reflection on the screen of his helmet before she and Cyris tapped out of the station with Slevel trailed viciously after them, determined for his chance to capture them and obtain her Oracle.

"That was the villain, Connar, let's go," Serena snapped Armsward into joining the ambitious chase. Their third colleague, Zara, rushed back to the white helicopter that was still hovering in the air.

"The police have evaluated all the people but the villain is heading into the city chasing what seems to be a teenage girl in a white mask, black hair, blue jacket, a teenage boy black hair, green jacket, brown jeans - now making their way towards Queen's Walk," Zara announced through her bluetooth earpiece navigating Armsward and Serena on the ground using the wheels that surge out form their boots, whizzing into the shortcuts with the company of more serpents to terminate.

"We have incoming," Zara reported under the ear drumming noise of the propellers.

"I got your back, go!" Serena gestured to Armsward to move on, pulling out the chemicals to kill the deadly reptiles before they use their venom to murder any more people.

Armsward speeds past the corner shops and busy streets, following the direction that Zara was giving him from above in time to see Venas and Cyris in combat with Slevel on the grassy field of Queens Drive. He and his teammates who hovered from afar were astonished by their speed and actions.

"Ssssssss looks like this human doesn't want to live anymore, " said another snake. He and his scaly family shredded from Slevel's body and emerged from under his robe with the task of keeping Armsward busy.

"He's shedding snakes from his body," Cyris noticed.

"I've noticed," Venas sliced them into bites and noticed that Slevel was very interested in her sword so she slotted it back into storage and continued to throw her flames at him, later to be hit by the sudden swing of a large snake. She flew into the sky and landed harshly on the grass.

"The name's Phizzzzzzor," he snared slowly, "and I believe you're about to become lunch."

Phizzor's voice rang into her ears unlocking a memory. A memory that spoke familiarity.

"Slevel! You're that snake I saw before when you froze London, you're that same monster!" she exposed him.

"Very clever girl, too bad I didn't eat you then," he said.

"You knew I was there," Venas cut back the talk and tried not to become snake food leaping in and out of Phizzor's long body but he was fast for a snake his size and was able to catch up to her.

Phizzor swirled his body around her and gripped her tensely and instantly aimed for a big juicy bite for her shoulder but ended up pricking his venomous fangs into her left arm when she pulled it out to blaze his sully scales. Phizzor flinched and unwrapped himself whilst he let out a strong hiss and wiggled the pain around whilst simultaneously etched a mark down the right side of her face. She felt the painful sting before hearing an abrupt ringing series of sirens.

Sirens beamed brightly from the distance. Flashing lights and weapons as the police force step out of their vehicles tensing their fingers on the triggers of their guns, eyes on the moving target, Slevel and his minions.

Cyris zoomed across the field, picked Venas up from the ground and flashed behind the nearest hiding place behind the building, an alleyway full of trash bins, boxes and crates from the shops. He saw the staggering bit mark and the wound in her face whilst she held the slight blood in with her hand.

"My plan was to lure him away from the city but I didn't think he'd be that fast," said Venas.

"I don't think we can continue this anymore, we've already exposed ourselves."

"But Slevel's gonna kill them all if we don't do anything."

"You need to stay here, I'll turn into my mutant form, I'll let them catch me, that way, I can find Atlas."

"What- no, that's crazy," She objected as she heard gunfire shooting at Slevel and his endless shedding of snakes.

"Phizzor! You USELESS creature, You can't even take care of a human girl, if we can't get the girl's Oracle then we go straight to Spectrum Dia."

"She's under my venom, won't be long before she diessss," said Phizzor, Slevel soon vanishes into mid-air along with Phizzor, leaving them behind to keep the humans occupied.

Cyris didn't give it any second thought and ignored her comment leaving behind to keep here away from the chaos whilst he lured the humans further away from Venas's location until one policeman took his aim and shot him in the leg.

"The two teenagers are nowhere to be found, where did that blue mutant come from?" Zara questioned over her bluetooth communication device.

"Don't know, but he's a fast one," answered Connar who scanned the area searching for Venas and Cyris but luckily, for Venas, he did not find her.

She was worried about Cyris being so reckless even though she didn't agree to help him, she still wanted to be of assistance but then, a click of pain suddenly rushed from her arm to the rest of her body like the venom was aggressively attacking her from the insides, spreading into her bloodstream setting off a throbbing sensation surging through her chest, past her neck and into her head. She compressed the side of her head trying to ease the pain but it only became worse, so bad that Petal was able to sense it and puffed out from her amulet to see what the problem was. It was the venom of course and it was slowly killing her slower than other victims that fell under the venom as she was originally immune to poisons and venom but this was too much venom. Petal couldn't bear the torture and sniffed out the level of toxins in the venom and decided to enchantingly fly into her body to act as a source of protection. Venas felt a tickle of relief and saw illusions of one hand turning green and the other one turning a mute pink but as the pain was too much to endure, she collapsed on her side, the last thing she sees before fainting being a boy under a black mask before shutting her eyes into warm darkness.

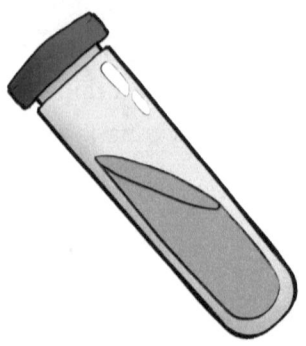

Flame 8

A Dragon's Traits

After the destructive incident, the city raged in panic and fear of Slevel returning. Family's fled to safer places provided by the fire brigades as police took action in preventing any more deaths caused by the snakes as their bites are extremely threatening. Catching up with the daily news, a reporter lady turns to the camera, citing the updates into her handheld microphone with the headlines travelling across the bottom of the screen.

> **NEWS**
>
> Body of a blue mutant discovered near Nottingham train station and captured during the attack of a dangerous snake man

A picture appeared on the screen of the same company of people who enclosed Atlas, storing the breathing body of Cyris Coral, showing signs of unconsciousness, strapped to the bottom of a coffin-like glass container. Workers pushed him into the back of a research van and started the engine, making their way to their biology research department where they intended to store him.

"What about the blue mutant with the horns?" questioned one policeman.

"We stay on patrol until he decides to show up again," answered another.

"But it's so powerful, it was able to catch up to a train at full speed."

"We have more men on the way, just be on guard."

Whilst the police officers have the whole city surrounded

from every corner to every block, yellow and black barriers line up the border of the city. Police cars parked ubiquitously, incoming police forces. Connar Armsward picked up a sample from the taunting trail of dead snakes. He locked it in a glass tube and tugged on a rope ladder to return back to the helicopter along with Serena who followed him up.

"Do you think they're taking the mutant to where they took the other one?" Serena questioned.

"Likely," Armsward replied, "we go back to the lab, I want to test the snake samples, see what these things really are, the police called that thing a mutant, there is no way that is a mutant because they don't attack people, it has to be something else, head back now."

"Yes sir," said the pilot.

The helicopter dangled past Market Square over the Christmas market where police roamed wildly, some wearing yellow jackets, holding weapons and their communicators. Connar's eyed from inside his helmet, the van that Cyris was in until it disappeared amongst the buildings. The helicopter flew in the opposite direction towards Nottingham University.

"What do you think? Where do you think the monster's from?" Serena questioned.

"I'm not very sure myself," Connar answered honestly.

The only place in Nottingham city that wasn't under surveillance was the underground. Deep down under the ground where trams passing by can be promptly mistaken for an earthquake, where the archways are dull and dark, holes and rocks, old, rusty dim lamps dangling from the ceiling connected along the walls into the electrical supplies under the property of the touring attraction store for the City of Caves. The lamp dangled over a well filled with mucky water next to a bridge built across a pit of water and lumps representing features of the historical era of Nottingham when animal dung was used here in this very spot to brew leather. There were radios hung across the ceiling, thin metal shelves, wooden benches, blunt weapons for decoration, old gas masks and posters showing the history of the caves. There was a tiny hole in the ceiling near the well where criminals in the past used to use the caves for illegal purposes and force young boys from the overground to drop a coin into the hole when they saw any police, giving them enough time to flee before they got caught. The metal bridge led to much smaller caves amongst bigger caves away from the limited tourist attraction area that only went around in a small circle. Past the barriers and blockages, the darkness found Venas sleeping on a rocky ledge with a blanket on top of her. After an hour of sleep, she gently opened her heavy eyelids to a blurry vision of the dark and warm setting of the cave that she was in. A faint image of flames burned in a pot and lit up the rim of the masked boy who sat across from her. She inspected him carefully and flung up from the rocky bed.

"It's you again! Where's Cyris?"

Kasey sat very still, waiting for something whilst he eyed

the fire ever so carefully. A flare of red light whirled around his hands forming something in the middle of the fire.

"You're awake," he said with a blunt expression.

He saw in the dim lights, Venas was shaken by his presence, "your blue friend's been taken away by the Earth humans, you should be more worried about yourself, it's a good idea to check your appearance once in a while," he hinted.

"What are you talking abo…" she set her eyes upon her hands. Each of them was different in colour, her skin and her hair…

"I thought I was hallucinating- what did you do to me- why is my hair white?!" She picked up the end of her ponytail and discovered that she no longer had precious black hair, but silky and silvery-white hair.

"I didn't do anything to you, this is your reaction to the venom, I've noticed your body has been immune to poisons that Tao Shi attacked you with, your body can only withstand so much venom that it nearly killed you until your charamol friend entered your system to sustain the portion that leaked into your DNA. If it wasn't for your DNA, you'd be dead right now," he explained, not making any eye contact with her to give her some time to process what he had just told her, "The venom is still in your system, which is why you look like that, it's altered your DNA and mutated your appearance," he finalised.

"Will… I be able to turn back?" She hugged the blanket.

"When you take the venom out… you will, you won't be going anywhere either, the city's been shut down- under surveillance until then, prepare for any changes," he notified her.

"Changes?"

The cave was silent again, the air was tickled by the sizzling flames from the mini bonfire. Streams of black and red fumes swirled around it. Venas watched as Kasey raised his hands with his fingers curled, forming a sphere of energy above the bundle of heat. He forced the elements together, compressing the medical ingredients in mid-air using thermal energy as his assistant. He looked as though he was cooking an elixir pill over the fire without using a pot of some sort. He sat on a rock and below him, Venas only just noticed all the bottles of medicine on the stony ground, clay and porcelain bottles capped with a cloth, short ones, tall ones filled with herbs and some with powder. She looked around amongst the darkness and found it hard to see exactly what this place is but her view was startled by Kasey who stepped in front of her giving her the elixir pill that he just made. She stared at it cluelessly.

"Hm?"

Kasey gave her the elixir pill that he had just mixed together.

"Eat it," he said bluntly.
"No," she rejected immediately.
"I said eat it."
"No," she repeated.

Eventually, he crammed it into her mouth before giving her a cup of water to wash it down with. She then drank and swallowed it without being told what it was for.

"I said no!" but it was already in her system.

"Well, you're too late."

"Where'd you get the water from," she tasted.

"From the old well in the caves," he replied emotionlessly.

Venas sprayed the water out into the distance.

"Relax, I got it from the stores, it's shameful that humans here sell water for money," he commented. Venas was relieved that it was clean water after all.

"So you just took it?"

"What else can I do? Pay for it?" He noted that he didn't have any money.

"Why are you even here and why did you send me to the Epping forest?"

"For fun," he lied and moved the fire closer. He grabbed a white bag with decorated pink and grey paint splats and chucked it at her, "I retrieved it from the train," then he went to the other side of the cover to fetch something, came back and handed her a mirror.

Venas gasped in astonishment, feeling her smooth but pinkish skin, shock flashed through her head when she took a close look at her eyes. The colour of her eyes was completely white like that of a moon child where a child is naturally born with all white hair and eyes with pale skin. Her ears were cutely pointy and she could see the scar around her right eye from Phizzor's sharp tail but the scar was unusually bright, almost like it was glowing. Her breathing became uneasy when her hand trembled over the scar, she was scared to touch. So the pill was her face, for the wound to heal.

"These are like Petal's features," she observed closely and embraced her heart with the touch of her hands when she remembered Petal rush in to help her, the thing that Charamols do best is to be their owner's guardian angels, to protect them and to comfort them, to make sure they are happy and safe but was she okay? Before thinking any further, she looked at her right eye, "You healed the wound," but he said nothing. Venas has always been very confused as to whether Kasey was a friend or an enemy, he may be raised by the enemy who is now dead but he may be like Akirou, she could almost consider him as a person she doesn't fight. But his appearance was still quite a frightening sight, especially in the darkness when the most visible part of him was the bottom half of his face.

"You're lucky the serpent didn't wound your eye, Slevel thinks you're dead right now so there's no rush trying to turn you back," he said.

"You say his name casually as if you know him."

"He's Slevel Moriyama, an old friend of the former King of the Neverlight Island," he informed.

"Tai Shi?"

"He's been on Earth for a while.." he paused.

"And…?

Kasey turned around and walked close to her, giving her the cold shivers and spoke slowly and calmly, the way he acted petrified her.

"He's after one of the Oracles from the Sword of Jade Dragon... the Spectrum Dia.. that and your Oracle," he finished.

"S- Spectrum Dia?" she stuttered and backed away from his approach with her blanket.

"You're scared of me," he detected.

"Scared, I wouldn't say scared... I'm terrified - why's Moriyama looking for the Spectrum Dia here, wouldn't it be on Ervanna?" internally, she was conscious of how close he was to her as he sat down. She tried hard to see through his mask, she imagined all sorts of different faces that would match facial structure. She's never even seen the face of the boy that saved her life and spirit but she doubted that he was ever going to show her or anyone else. She curled in the corner adorably in her mutated skin where she felt her hearing ability was back to normal, she could no longer hear Kasey's heart thumps.

"The Spectrum Dia is hidden in these caves," he informed.

"How could that be possible, how'd you know? If Moriyama has been searching for it all this time then wouldn't he have found it here long ago?"

"He doesn't know... but I know."

"Yes, we've established tha..." cold chills shiver through her body again when Kasey moved towards her with his stone expression, his hands close to her neck, she pressed her back tightly against the wall when his fingers touched her skin. Kasey ran his fingers across her collarbone and reached for the chain of her amulet, dragging it out from her t-shirt before she pushed him over, she saw that he was only trying to tell her:

"You're Oracle only glows when it meets a familiar Oracle - and it's glowing now which means the Spectrum Dia is in the caves," he dropped the amulet back to let it dangle off her neck.

"Oh, but I'm not familiar with it, I've never even seen it before."

Kasey didn't explain any further leaving her with a lot of empty spaces in her mind. A fraction of her thoughts included her growing enthusiasm to search for the Spectrum Dia, the diamond Oracle of Zhou States, now that she knew it was here somewhere. There must be a reason it was here in these caves but everywhere she went, there was no clue to where it could be but after a long stroll around the caves, it became clear that it must be inside the cave walls, wherever her Oracle glows strong is wherever it was.

"How am I supposed to get in there?" she questioned, she squatted down to think of a solution, could she be after to somehow break into the walls or use some sort of spell to extract the Oracle from the walls? Or could she ask Kasey for help? But then he would use his dark crystal and she didn't want anything more to do with that shard of darkness, it would be disrespectful to the lives that were used to make it even though it was the thing that brought her back to

Earth. She pressed her hand on the wall where the stone was glowing and shimmering like an enchanted cave. Then she discovered that her skin turned to scales and was stuck to the wall like chewing gum as she gently pulled it away from the rocky surface but it was super glued on. One final aggressive tugged and a long string of her skin and scales shot out from her hand, sticking itself to the first thing that stood in its way, Kasey. Her skin attached itself to his chest and pulled her in without hesitation. It winded her straight into him. Kasey moved back from the sudden impact. But it was expecting her to establish her new abilities. Venas panicked.

"Sorry!"
"I told you, prepare for any changes," he reminded her.
"I didn't know what you were talking about."

He seized her wrist to harshly remove her hand from his chest. He was still a bit scary to face and he looked as though he showed no interest in helping her but he was. It's like his facial expressions always express a sort of murderous feel. He never smiles. Doesn't joke around.

"What's the purpose of being here?" she asked.
"To hide."
"Hide?" does it have to be in the caves?"
"If you wish to get caught, then no, the city's covered with surveillance, do you really want to go out there?"
"The whole city?" she repeated.
"Because of this afternoon, humans are wrapping the

entire city, idiots like them think they have a chance of defeating a thousand-year-old snake demon," he criticised.

"I came here for the Christmas holiday and this is what I get… I'm going out there," she instantly decided.

"Be my guess, humans are weak anyway, their combined power won't even stand a chance against my one finger," said Kasey.

"They're weak but they have weapons- one gunshot in the head and you're dead," she noted.

"Do as you please," he was tired of talking and excused her.

"It's not like I was asking for your permission," she mumbled.

Kasey glanced at her and frightened her with his eye-stabbing stare.

Flame 9
===

The Black Panther

A few hours have passed as the sky begins to fade into a mist of gloom with no stars but a full half-moon hiding behind a pile of clouds. Moonlight beamed brightly through the ceiling windows of the biology research lab. The only sound that penetrated the silence was the sound of the door when the facility cleaner finishes up locking the cleaning cupboards to wrap up his day. He was aware of the rather difficult trip home with the city's surveillance set up. He switches the lights off and shuts the door behind him, the door to the biology lab of wild creatures, dead and alive. The lab stood under a thick glass ceiling with automatic windows on the side where the light led to a round glass tank surrounded by sophisticated gadgets, machines and android devices. The machines were all on to monitor a certain creature freshly caught from the city. The tank was occupied with a pink substance of highly developed perfluorocarbon liquid swirling in and out of the lungs of a blue-skinned boy, Cyris. He slept in the liquid, his body in one piece, his leg unharmed, his clothes were switched for a pair of plain white shorts and a series of thin tubes and wires were attached to his arms and legs as he drifted peacefully in the liquid. The wires were conjoined to a monitor where a screen shining bright and clearly displayed the humans' findings of his genes and background, his genes associated with the family of dolphins giving him a variety of sound defying mutant abilities but the scientists didn't know how powerful Cyris was, therefore, strengthened the security system of his capture. As soon as the room was cleared, he gently opened his eyes and rolled his eyeballs left and right keeping his body still. He looked for signs of sound waves, his abilities to see sound frequencies activated to detect whether the nearby rooms were empty or not. He detached the strings from his lungs and morphed into his water form swishing up and down searching for a way out of the capsule since it was extra secure.

There must be some way out, he thought. If he wasn't in the perfluorocarbon, he would've been able to let out a high enough sound frequency from the top of his throat to break the glass. Instead, he took the risk of streaming into the tiny tubes that were attached to his arms and travelled into the machines and leaked his way out of any gaps and holes. Just when he was ready to turn back into his solid body, a bang from outside the door startled him to shape into the wall as the security guard strolled in with his flashlight darted straight for the capsule that Cyris was contained in. he then worked out the other door after seeing that the blue mutant was still in the capsule little did he know, it was just a water clone.

The clone won't last very long, he said to himself, he slithered across the room, spiralled around the leg of a table to see the samples that the scientists took from his body whilst he was busy being unconscious after pretending that he got hurt from being shot in the leg, he was able to catch the bullet with his water form just as it shot into him to decrease the impact.

"This disgusts me," he criticised and soon saw the sample of blue blood that was extracted from his system.

The colour of a mutant's blood corresponds to the colour of their eyes and since Cyris has turquoise eyes, his blue was also turquoise whilst Venas's new mutant body would produce rather silvery coloured blood, she never knew why there was a messy pile of tissues next to Kasey with red and silvery stains on them, it was the blood from her face before the scar formed. Venas flashed at full speed around the city and just so happened to remember the logo of the biology lab that took Altas shown on the piece of newspaper that Cyris showed her and thought, that must be where they took him. It has to be. The biology research lab was a fifteen-minute drive away from the caves so she just about made it to the ceiling windows of the lab that Cyris had left not long ago. Her pocket started vibrating, she answered the phone to her Godmother asking why she wasn't home. To reduce the amount of worries, she lied and said she was staying at a hotel until the city is open again before she opened the window and disabled the CCTV system with a celestial click before she jumped down, landing softly on shiny floor tiles to face the empty capsule, the clone had already disappeared. She noticed the disconnected tubes and wires floating aimlessly in the pink liquid.

"He must've escaped himself," she muttered and pulled her mask up a little higher, lurking making her way out into the dark corridors with windows on each side showing the tubes of creatures trapped in their glass cabinets like lab rats. Wild animals like tigers, rats, snow foxes, beavers, hares and cute little mice. "Such a random collection of wildlife, she" she commented and placed her hand on the glass by the snow fox that didn't look one bit happy to be stuck in such a tightly confined cabinet.

It was natural that she wished for her to be freed. The last cabinet was rather big and spacy like the one with the tiger and it contained a helpless black panther in his sleep and the one across from it was a large tank with a dolphin. Helplessly, she made for the exit and followed the corridors down the corner and came across red rods of light circulating the entire hallway. The lasers beamed brightly like no lasers she's ever seen, shooting from one side of the room to the others leaving no space at all to wiggle through, it wasn't as obvious as following steps from a spy movie. Then she glanced up at the tall ceiling, the only way was to travel through the air. And the only way to do that was to use her newly discovered ability as her celestial powers aren't as strong as it was when she was in her human form.

"I pray for the moment I can get out of this body," she said and jogged on the spot for a little warm-up before she anticipated to shoot a strong thread of her scales onto the ceiling in hopes that she swings across the entire obstacle. She tried, again and again, to run up, ready to jump and swing when her scales touch the ceiling but always ended up reversing her thoughts with a lack of confidence and hesitation.

"This ain't gonna work," she doubted herself after running back and forth ten times. One more go, she shoots one final thread at the ceiling, sticking like a mousetrap, she jumps and speeds across the wall instead of swinging across and as her hair was so close to the lasers, she suddenly spotted the laser deactivation switch amongst the channel of buttons located on the walls. With her other hand, she shoots a tiny thread from her palms and intensively hits the button before her hair was ready to set off the alarm system. She returns to her feet after hard tumbling across the floor to see a blurry blue figure landing swiftly in front of her. Before they could see each other's faces, Cyris ambushed Venas with a staggering speed of attacking motions thinking that Venas was a stranger in the dark. Neither did she notice it was Cyris, the hallways became wildly sombre with the lasers turned off. He lured her towards the wall allowing her to step on a vault to make an arc over his head. Enraged by her speed, he tried to grab her but ended up tugging on her hair, snapping her hand band, setting her hair loose. Venas tumbled on the ground again and entered the stand of a tiger as her silky white hair fell down to join her. Every hit she aimed at him missed when Cyris's power of seeing sound took a streak of success until Venas unexpectedly emitted a transporting spell reappearing behind him, knocking him over by the legs and locking his hands and feet to the floor with her shooting skin. A flare of flames lit in her hands illuminating their eyes when Venas finally established the identity of her opponent.

"Cyris?" She halts and forgets that she lit the fire to attack him. Then her attention was distracted by his lack of clothes with only a pair of baggy shorts, "what happened to your clothes?" she blocked her eyes.

"You know me?" he scanned her from head to toe and noticed that she was wearing the exact clothes of Venas, "you're… Venas!?!"

Cyris returned to the lab room for his clothes and popped his jeans and jacket back on.

"Looks like I'm at the right place," said Venas.
"You're not gonna explain?
"Explain what?"

Cyris gestured that she knew exactly what he was talking about.

"Because the last time I checked, you were human... I quite like it though," he complimented.

"Quit it, it was the venom," she still wasn't very happy with her appearance, "let's go before we get caught," she anticipated arm motion to shoot the ceiling with her scales when Cyris pulled her by the wrist.

"Wait, we need to find Atlas," he reminded her.

"We? I never agreed to do that, I agreed to take you to Nottingham."

"Are you not one bit interested in helping me, you know humans better than I do, that's a big advantage."

"For finding Atlas?"

"And getting the humans to like us, not treat us like scientist experiments, you see all this, they don't care about us, they think we're dangerous, they think the snake monster is a mutant and that doesn't help any better to clear our name. We find Atlas, he's strong and we can work together to save the city."

"Save the city? Slevel's not after the city or its people, he's after a jewel hidden under the city."

"What jewel?"

"One that can give him a lot of power," she summarised. She stared up at the opened window in the ceiling for a little while and sighed, " if the scientists found Altas in the ice then it's likely that they stored him in a freezer warehouse."

"A freezer?"

Venas observed the documents of findings on the table next to the capsule and scanned through the details that were found about Cyris within such a short amount of time, how old he was, his blood type, his characteristics, his abilities and his body functions.

Blue Mutant

Name ?	Surname ?	☑ M ☐ F
DOB —/09/1470	POB ?	
Height 5'7	Skin Blue	
Species Mutant	Decendant of Dolpin	

Ethnicity ?	Blood Type B+	Blood Colour Blue

Research Summary

Has x5 more cells in retina to allow him to see more than the average human eye.
Has 3 vocal cords (1 extra) ~~||||~~ |||
Warm blood
Dark blue markings all over body
Unusually shaped ears
Body in good shape
Has webbed fins on the back of each forearm

~~||||~~ |

Weight	66.37
Eye Colour	Turquoise
Hair Colour	Green + Blue

Date 19/12/2015

And piled up with the form of brief notes about Cyris was another mutant's detail, a black mutant with white hair and blue body markings. The paper had marker scribbles in the corner like someone's marker ran out and was trying to revive it. The amount of writing wasn't a lot which meant that the real documents were hidden somewhere else, probably stored away. It would be in this lab or somewhere else in the building like offices.

"There's another one here," she said.

"But it doesn't seem important if it's lying around like this."

"They're just notes."

"If only I can get my hands on the real ones and shred them into pieces," he rubbed his fist.

"Atlas is a descendant of a black panther?" she comprehended, "that explains why there's a panther in the corridors."

"What no, he's a polar bear, where the heck did a black panther come into the picture? " He corrected, "let me see that…" he read the paper. He scanned through it in disgust.

	Name Atlas	Surname Silver	☑ M ☐ F
	DOB - /- /595 A.D.	POB ?	
	Height 6'1	Skin Black	
	Species Mutant	Decendant of Black Panther	

Ethnicity African	Blood Type ?	Blood Colour ?

Research Summary	Weight ?
Found in the frozen lake of Lakeside Arts (Nottingham, Nottingham Uni.	Eye Colour ?
A participant during Mumans War 1514 representing mutants. Dissappeared after the war	Hair Colour White
Frozen in the ice for at least 500 years.	
Dark blue markings all over body. ✚✚ IIII	
One of the strongest mutants known to man. ✚✚ I	

Date 02/12/2015

"Well someone's feeling a bit racist this morning, Atlas

isn't black, he's brown and he's British, born in England-evolved from human ancestors like the rest of us, what are they playing at?" he raged.

"Careful you don't wanna be too loud, that's how society is... it says here you're a descendant of dolphins?"

"Yep, I can see sound and manipulate frequencies, stuff like sonic attacks," he said confidently, "and you?"

"A dragon I suppose," Venas assumed.

"A dragon? Good one," he laughed and then realised when Venas wasn't finding it very funny, "oh you're serious."

"Yes, I'm serious."

Cyris stopped when he saw a ripple of sound waves travelling along the floors seeping into the room from under the doors."

"Who's there !!!" bellowed a security guard when he saw the deactivated lasers in the hallway and rushed in the direction of where the channel of buttons was. Where he went, Cyrus and Venas went the opposite way to avoid meeting him. Across from the hallways, white floor tiles were a set of pipes from one side of the wall to the other creating a path into the other research departments without the trouble of doors.

"Up there," Venas whispered and pulled herself up with her sticky skin along with Cyris who followed her hastily.

Tapping fed through the site, lounging past the endless hallways of lasers and doors, the deactivation switch to these ones were not as visible as the last one.

"Hey!" a slim ray of light waves into their direction but missed a glimpse of them, the security guard knew he saw something, two humans running through the ceiling like monkeys swinging through trees. Soon, they discover a metal vault and left turn, the vault was locked and security was close behind.

"Quick, in here," Cyris unlatched an office door and they zoomed inside. He found a plastic cup to hide in as Venas unlocks her celestial powers to mobilize a very limited camouflaging spell whilst sticking herself to the ceiling with her front facing the floor. Another security guard walked in as the one chasing them stopped him to question whether he's seen humans running this way.

"Nope, no one's come by here, why would two kids be running about in the building, they won't be able to get in here in the first place?"

"I dunno!?! We should go catch them, this is a restricted area."

"And restricted areas come with high-security systems, there is no way two children can even complete without triggering one of the alarms."

"You're right, I must be seeing things, but some of the lasers were deactivated," he remembered.

"You must've forgotten to turn them on, I'm taking a quick break so I'll see you later," he announced and walked into his office, he sat down at his desk where the cup was.

Why did I have to choose this room, Cyris thought. The man was ready to take a ten-minute break, relaxing with his phone before he continued with his long night shift.

Come on, come on, leave, Cyris rushed.

I don't think I can hold it for much longer, Venas struggled to keep up her invisibility spell but it would be okay as long as the man didn't look up until following a long minute of texting, he sees in the corner of his eyes, the cup of water and slowly reached his hand out to drink it. The fear in Venas's eyes sparkled a strike of terror when he held the cup so close to his mouth and thought the only way to stop Cyris from being devoured was to expose themselves. Silence fell just as the cup touched his mouth before Venas aimed her sticky skin for a random bucket used to collect leakage from the ceiling and flipped it on top of his head.

SPLASH

The man, now, dripping wet from the waist up, tumbled onto the floor and just as he reached for the bucket, Venas shot another sample of skin around his waist, connecting it to a cabinet door.

"What the, what's happening?!?" The thread pulled him against the door as she conjoined his hands together. Cyris returns to his solid shape and they make an exit before getting spotted leaving the guard's cry for help.

"I feel bad," said Venas.

"Don't worry," Cyris enters liquid mode again and seeps through the microscopic gaps of the vault and forcefully turns the wheel on the other side, he could feel his body temperature drop. Venas pulled the vault from the outside, a tiny gap enough for her to squeeze through, the door was hefty and very difficult to handle.

"Come on, close it quick," Cyris whispers, he transformers back and tugs on the wheel with his mighty grip, shutting the door just in time before the guard cried for help attracting his colleague's attention. Venas slid down the back of the door in relief Cyris removed his hands from the wheel and joined her on the metal floor.

"That was too close," Venas huffed under her mask and finally understood why it was so cold in here.

She shook Cyris by the shoulder to get him to turn around and set his eyes upon her realisation. Not only was the floor manufactured with metal, but the walls and ceiling were too. Smoke of frost boiled around the enclosed room displaying an angular lump of ice standing ten feet all inside, was a brown-skinned body, his white dreadlocks held back with a blue cuff. Each dreadlock strand was decorated with shiny indigo rings that correlate to the imprints marked all over his body. His eight pack and other body muscles signified his hero title to the mutants, an icon for his kind before the Muman's war, during the war and after and yet, he's here, trapped and enclosed by heartless humans.

"Atlas Silver," Venas chanted.

"It's really him," Cyris bounced up and patted the icy cold surface, "he's just like how I remembered."

"You're gonna get frostbites if you don't take your hand

off the ice." Just as she says that an alarming burst of dismay feeds through the building like light followed by red beams and sirens.

"Someone set the alarm system on," said Cyris.

"Yes, I can see that," Venas replied. You tried busting her flames through the ice to set Atlas free but one blow of fire wasn't enough.

WHOOOOSH

She tried again and again.

"Come on come on," every try melted down a small segment of ice, with the alarm ringing into her ears, she felt a rush of anxiety and pressure, abandoned the idea of melting the ice completely and aimed for the sides to cut a rectangle out of the block. Atlas slid out and made a bang at the vault door where guards from the outside heard a faint and quickly approached the vault as fast as they could,

"I heard something - this way," one yelled.

"Okay, now what," Cyris panicked.

"I don't know, my magic's not powerful enough when I'm in this form," she confessed, "if it was, I'd teleport out of here by now."

"I can see them getting closer," he referred to the sound waves booming past the vault.

Water splashed onto the metal floors but not a single part of Atlas's body was touchable and the block was too heavy to even lift off the ground.

"It's too cold in here for me to do anything," her powers

weakened whilst she began to shiver in the cold, seeing her breath forming into clouds seeping out through her mask.

"Quick block your ears with these," Cyris chucked a pair of sound-cancelling earplugs to stick into her ears, to buy her a few extra seconds, he cupped his hands over his mouth and created a threatening ear-piercing vibration dart into the unprotected ears of the security guards and the policemen who just flooded in. Everyone covered their poor ears feeling their eardrums rupture into a million pieces.

"What's that horrible noise," one questioned, the sound wasn't loud but a frequency sharp enough to stab one's hearings, more powerful against an adult's fully developed ears but Cyris's can only scream such a volume for a short amount of time so he could only keep it up for a few seconds before his head starts to spin.

"Keep it up," Venas shouted.

But he couldn't keep it up, the veins in his neck were ready to jump out of his skin if he didn't stop.

"I'll open the vault," he stopped his screaming and reached for the door.

Venas unplugged her earpieces and wrapped Atlas who was still trapped under the ice with her sticky skin and slid back to the lab room with the ceiling windows still open and shot her way up. Cyris gave the now-smaller block of ice a big push up the window and leapt onto the machines to reach the window just as the guards surged from the corner to see that the capsule was empty and all the samples were gone. Venas had taken them.

"The mutants gone," one of the men bellowed across the hallway as he stepped into a warm puddle of water looking at the big hole left within the centre of the block of ice where Venas set her lasers to free Atlas, or at least, a liftable chunk. Whilst the humans in the lab were panicking and raging, Venas noticed dark spirals of energy surrounding the rooftops, a black figure emerged from the essence and grabbed her, Atlas and Cyris into the darkness and disappeared.

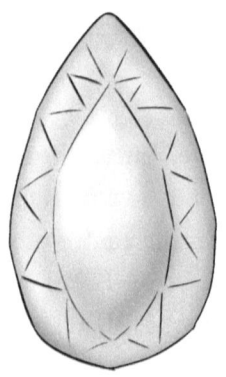

Flame 10

Headlines

Cyris tightly grasped his head to ease the throbbing pain after using his vocal sound powers for too long. He sat down on a rock seat in the dimly lit caves where Kasey was able to swoop in and save them with the power of dark crystal. They returned under the city but under which piece of property was unclear. Kasey released a microscopic spider with his aurora to creep onto Cyris and read his pulse to help determine what type of medicine to brew for his unusual headache. He perfected the same procedure when making a pill for Venas and handed it over to him. Cyris looked up.

"Can I trust him V?" he asked Venas.

"He's the one that healed my wound but I have my doubts sometimes," Venas wasn't really sure herself.

"Pass," he rejected the pill until another hurricane of throbs bounced into his head, he instantly swallowed it and let the pill do its magic, "who the hell are you?" Kasey remained silent. "I asked you a question."

"Ignore him, that's just how he is," Venas was in the cave next door with Atlas, still unconsciously laid down on a piece of rock representing a table. She was slowly melting the ice away with her palms, slowly to let his body adjust to the sudden warmth after being in the ice for so long. She had already melted the ice away from his face, chest and his boots, the highest points.

"I haven't used my ultrasound powers in a while, forgot that it can damage my head if I don't warm up," Cyris commented as he walked up to Venas feeling a bit more relieved after digesting Kasey's pill, he cupped one hand over her ear and whispered:

"Your friend there looks a bit depressed."

"He can probably hear you."

"What, no, we're pretty far away," he said while he glanced at Kasey's backside.

"Look at your shoulder," she said without taking her eyes from her task. Cyris peered on his shoulder and wiggled around.

"S-s- spider!" he hastily flicked the spider into the wall away from him and hid behind Venas to be wary of anymore.

"You're afraid of spiders?" she continued to defrost the rest of Atlas's face, "you live in a forest."

"I get spider bites and I'm not a big fan of it."

"He's still alive," she discovered a pulse and suddenly eyed a familiar aura circulating his body.

"What made you think he was dead?"

She followed the energetic sphere with her eyes, it of black fumes swimming through his body and was almost about to identify what it was and where it came from. It was a sample from the power of dark crystal but it wasn't from Kasey, it was from Slevel when he froze Atlas. The strange part was when the fumes slithered away and evaporated into the air. Venas didn't know what to do now that she freed Atlas from the ice, he was still in his deep sleep and throughout the long hours lying in the warm and cosy cave, he never showed any signs of waking up. Kasey sat up against the wall and remained still just like Atlas, his eyes weren't visible through his mask therefore it was hard to tell that he was actually sleeping whilst sitting upright and crossing his arms.

"Is he asleep?" Cyris observed from afar where he sat with Venas.

"I don't know," she answered, "he must be."

"I'm getting bored," he whined.

"At this point, it looks like we're gonna be here for a long while, I don't even know how to turn back into my human self," she thought, "I don't wanna be a mutant anymore."

"What's wrong with being a mutant? It's fun, we have all these fun powers."

"Nothing's wrong, I just want to go back to... the way I was," she fidgeted with her hands, looking at the new colours of her skin and the hidden scales on her arms that show a slight raise above the skin. Then she stroked her head and felt the white locks of her hair no longer tied up but flowing down. She mumbled, "get rid of the venom to turn back," she looked up at Cyris, "but how do you get rid of venom that's already inside your body?"

"Don't look at me," he shrugged.

"Why..."

"Why what?"

"Why did you choose me to help you, you saw me in Epping but I was with another guy, you could've asked him but instead you decided to follow me," she curiously reminded him.

"I tried, I did follow him and ask for his help since I thought he was a guy and he'd freak out less when he sees me... as a mutant," he rambled.

"What's that supposed to mean? What did he say," her eyes lit.

"I tried to pick the right time to approach him when he was in his house but his whole family was at home- he went into his room to play on his devices and that's when I knocked on his window- at first, he gave me the eyebrow, I climbed into the room and introduced myself as a human and he freaked out telling me to leave," he explained.

"Markcas dear, is there someone in your room, who're you talking to?" his mum called from downstairs.

"Nothing, I'm just gaming!" he yelled back, closing his bedroom door, "dude what the hell is wrong with you, get out of my room," he said to Cyris.

"But I wanna ask you for help."

"I'm not helping someone that just broke into my room, scram," Markcas demanded, grabbing the closest thing he could use to threaten Cyris to make him crawl back out the window and leave his house, it was his guitar.

"Alright… alright, I'll go… I'll go," he raised his hands up to eye level and slowly returned to the window of which he came from and took off.

Venas thought for a while.

"Breaking into someone's house isn't something you'd want to do, it's not very… it's just not something you do unless you're a bad guy and you're robbing the place," she tried to explain why Markcas kicked Cyris out of his house.

"Is it not? What am I supposed to do then?"

"See, we do this thing where it's more polite…" she leaned over her crossed legs, "it's called knocking."

"But I did knock."

"The door Cyris, you knock on the door, not his window."

"The door to his bedroom?"

"No, the door to his house," she finalised.

"Ohhhh, the front door but then someone else is gonna open it and I don't want them to see me."

"You were in human form anyways, it wouldn't matter, it's better than being remembered as a burglar."

"That does make sense," he stroked his beardless chin, "but I didn't even know his name, I know it's Markcas because his mum called him but that was after I broke into his room, I wouldn't have been able to address him at the door," he made a point, making Venas pause and speechless because he was right about that one, "point won, you were saying earlier that you wanna go back to being human again, if you don't you can always stay as a mutant and come to Epping, it'd be great."

"Absolutely not, I'm not staying like this forever."

"But you need a name either way."

"A name?"

"A name to go by when in mutant form, you can't go by Venas," he made another point.

"Oh, it doesn't hurt to give myself another name but I don't know."

"It doesn't have to be a proper name, it can be something like a superhero name, human in disguise name," he suggested.

"Superhero? I don't think we'll ever be heroes but it could have something to do with fire and flames, I'll have a think."

Cyris scanned the dim area of the caves and questioned why they ended in the caves that he never knew about and how she, Kasey and Markcas all have powers though they are human. It was a simple yet complicated explanation that Venas tried to express but Cyris understood it anyway, why wouldn't he, he was a mutant with powers, it was believable for him but for other humans, that would be a different story. They would suggest something is going on with your crazy mind. Venas mentioned the Spectrum Dia, a diamond Oracle gem that belonged on a sword of hers that came from the Jade Dragon who died under the hands of monster demons and that it became her sacred weapon but the only mystery is, why the Spectrum Dia is inside the walls of the caves, one possible answer was that someone put it in there, then it must've been a monster, one of the demons popped it in there and they must have a dark crystal, it couldn't have been Slevel otherwise he wouldn't be searching everywhere for it. There's another demon loose in the UK? And why did they hide the Oracle on Earth?

"That's something I'd like to think about tomorrow," she left the rocky seat and dusted herself off.

"Where the hell are you going?" he remained seated.

"I don't know about you mutants but I as a human, like to have eight hours of sleep every night so I going to sleep, don't follow me, humans like to sleep alone," she lied and returned to the cave with the blanket that Kasey had given her, used a little bit of her energy to magically make the rocks comfier to sleep on.

Cyris agreed with her statement of having eight hours of sleep every night but he intended to stay awake until Atlas woke up but it wasn't long before his head started bouncing up and down as he tried to stay awake. Soon, the image in his eyes of Atlas lying on the bed in front of him blurred into fuzzy, dark colours, he too, fell fast asleep. Everyone in the caves meets their dreams as a strange beeping sound trailed into the cave that Venas was sleeping in, a small device, or rather, an android that spun its tiny, little head vigorously after spying on Venas and Cyris and finding Atlas, the missing mutant from the lab before crawling out of the caves like a spider amongst the midnight air. It disappeared into the mist that soon faded into the sky that welcomed the next day whilst the morning sun rays shot into the wide windows of a robotics lab in a building not far from the city but a good distance away from the biology research lab. The lab consisted of white furniture and work desks compiled and almost hidden under a large amount of complicated equipment from small gadgets to half-built robots or rather soon to be A.I. androids. The walls were lined with glass cabinets and wooden shelves inside stacked with bottles and boxes of bits and pieces. The machines in the room were all switched on and powered up to perform their daily tasks alongside the first successful model of humanoid A.I. Cyber. Cyber's joints buzzed as he walked around the lab ensuring that all the machines were running smoothly and waited for his creator, Connar Armsward to return from his morning coffee not dressed in his iron armour like the day Slevel attacked the station but in black trousers and a nicely ironed blue shirt. He entered the lab and walked over to a table displaying a series of tubes and glass bottles and funnels flowing with liquids and steam next to a microscope with a glass palette nudged under the objective lens. Though he did not touch it, instead, he went over to grab the documents that he had placed alongside it from the night before after he discovered the properties of the venom and the snake bits that he collected. The severed flesh was placed in a small glass container of its own, unlike a full-sized snake that was later retrieved from the scene before the rest vanquished on their own. It was set down in another room more dedicated to biology research of unknown creatures. The results that Armsward took from the samples reminded him of the samples he took from past crime scenes in London where he found snakes like these. Armsward had never seen even a shadow of Slevel when he made a more subtle invasion of London, the same day Venas had spotted him on the way home from school because he had frozen everyone in time and only those who possess an Oracle are exempt to this enchantment.

Armsward's brain clicked, he rushed to his desk and the cabinet behind it, fighting with the powerful rays shining through the massive windows and neatly rampaged his folders for the one for "unknown cases of deaths", the one named "Reptile?" just for him to identify the case. There was a USB nudged between all the papers. He took it and popped it into his computer and once the files were reading and loading, he took a quick sip of water to refresh himself. He scanned through every case and the evidence found in each crime scene and all the DNA of Slevel's snakes detected matched the ones that were in the past cases. That was when he realised that this snake monster was the man he had been trying to track down all this time, throughout the past two years. He filed a reading into Cyber's database as Serena unlocked the highly secured metal door with her ID scanner to walk into his office. Cyber bounced up immediately once Armsward was done with importing information into his drive from the back of his head. He stormed over to Serena with excitement like a puppy.

"Morning Connar," she greeted, "Morning Cyber," she patted his metal head.

"Morning," he replied.

"Good morning Miss Varro, how was your sleep last night, mind rating it from one to ten," he spoke, his voice was still working progress therefore it sounded too much like a robot, Armsward wishes to make it more human-like.

"I would say a... seven," Serena answered.

"Seven, I will note that," said Cyber.

"Sorry, I feel like he annoys everyone he sees with questions like these," Armsward apologised, "I need to fix a few things."

"No, not at all, have any traces of the missing mutant yet," she questioned though only hearing about it only a few hours ago after she woke up. The news was plastered with information about it. From the attack of the snake man with the horns and his terrifying army of snakes to the case of the mutant discovered in Lakeside Arts going missing. Reporters went wild bulleting the biology research lab crew with plummeting questions, raging at the front door during a morning interview with the people involved with containing Atlas away, including Lucy Lawson and her colleagues. All the reporters shoved their microphones into her personal space and flashed their cameras uncontrollably.

"Where do you think the creature is now?"

"Do you think he used his powers to escape the ice?"

"The question of how the lake was frozen in the first place had never been clarified, what's your explanation to go about it?"

"Do you think we will be in danger because of its escape?"

"Wouldn't it have been a better idea to kill it before it does any damage to the city?"

Lawson's head was ready to explode after all these questions were thrown at her face like rotten tomatoes. Her colleagues attempted to calm the audience down, streaming on live television and trying to keep their reputation by not losing any face but they're already lost some face by losing an unknown mutant.

"Who knows where it could be, plotting to destroy the city like the snake man yesterday," said another reporter. Lawson answered as many questions as she could along with the questions about the snake man and the rough footage found of the two teenagers who interrupted the scene. No proper videos were taken as Venas had disabled as many cameras located in the area as she could but not all of them. The footage was blurry and it was impossible to fully identify who those teenagers were… and the questions continued to ambush mode.

It was obvious that the news was seen by the entire

world, Armsward, Serena and Cyber viewed the commotion on the big screen that hovered from the ceiling with a call of his voice. On the other side of England, Markcas strolled out of his bedroom, down the stairs to fetch a bit of something to eat after only just waking up from his slumber wearing grey joggers and a white T-shirt. His father was slouched on the couch in the living room spectating the news. And the words "snake monster" caught Markcas's attention, he was half asleep but not any more.

"What's this?" he asked.

"Oh, the mutant that they found two weeks ago went missing last night after the snake monster attack," his father answered, "you're heading into the kitchen? Turn off the cooker whilst you're there."

"Okay," Markcas switched the cooker off and opened his ears to listen to the news whilst quietly getting a few pieces of bread from the counter and butter from the fridge plastered with decorative magnets and stick notes.

He slotted the drawers open for a butter knife and dropped the bread into his fancy black toaster and ran back to the t.v. in time to see the rough capture of the unknown teenagers.

Even he wasn't able to identify Venas but he was able to identify the other one, Cyris, the boy who broke into his room. He was wearing the exact same clothes as when he met him.

That's the guy that broke into my room, what the hell is he doing there? Markcas questioned in his head. He went back into the kitchen and grabbed his buttered toast but when he returned the news had already carried on to a different topic of discussion. After he finished, he took a glass of orange juice and scurried back up the polished oak stairs into his room, nearly tripping over his acoustic guitar that just tipped over from the walls. He popped it back and searched the news on his laptop for further intel. His laptop was displayed amongst his unorganised desk between bits and pieces of stationery and gadgets, it was so messy, he couldn't find his phone amongst the untidiness. The topic of monster invasion and missing mutants interested him proactively as he sat and read, clicking from page to page.

CLICK... CLICK... CLICK... CLICK

He clicked through all the limited and poorly captured shots of the event, he still had no idea that the girl was Venas nor did he recognise Slevel as a Nevelean demon.

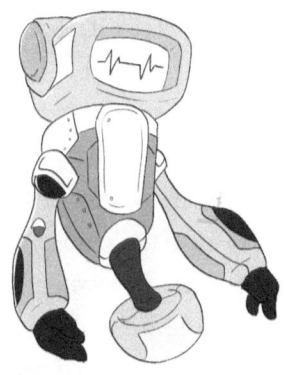

Flame 11

Fall

As the news made a hurricane through the internet, it concerned many but the most concerned people were the stars of the headlines themselves who were still in sleep mode under the city inside their cave of darkness. The caves let in no light to indicate that it was finally broad daylight. Water dripped one drop at a time breaking the silence of the slumbering caves and soon, a fluff of flames soared through the air with a swing of an arm and the other one. Soft orbs of fire spiralled across the cave and burst against the cave walls whilst Venas attempts to break it, that was where the Oracle was hiding. She tried and she tried, all morning, it went on and on and yet it woke up no one. No one but one.

A big, parasitic fly buzzed into view and tapped its small, lanky legs on the tip of Atlas's nose. He twitched his nose ever so slightly and felt the fly's weight fading as it flew away again before slowly lifting his eyelids to see the ceiling as a blurry piece of vision. Five hundred years he's slept, his body felt weak and soft, soft like a cushion. Atlas frantically blinked his eyes from the stiffness of his muscles and rose. The sight of the mysterious, gloomy caves was unfamiliar to him, there was no like, none but a dim source that flashed off and on every few seconds. For him, the ceiling was low, he could touch the top with his palms no problem as he adjusted to walking again, continuing to remember what had happened to him and how he ended up here. He didn't remember anything about entering a cave, the very last thing he recalled was a raging army of humans charging through the battlefields of a sandy and dusty area of London, a lively plane of land dedicated to the reign of mutants and humans, the Muman's war killing thousands and thousands of bodies. 1514, the end of when mutants had freedom to roam the streets, they were free like humans to go just about anywhere in London without question or discrimination. They were treated as equals before humans decided that they were Earth's threat, their powers were strong, humans thought it was too dangerous for the risk of a rogue mutant could destroy the entire country or that is what they considered to be the truth

The mutants, their numbers were low. They lacked weapons like the durable bows and arrows and crossbows as at the time, those were the main weapons developed in the Uk along with swords but it was a challenge to get so close to a mutant to even use them therefore arrows tipped with fire and poison were the key. He remembered defeat, the mutants lost the war and those who survived went into hiding, ever since then, live mutants, one by one go missing if found away from their hidden homes in the Epping Forest. The victory of humans raged tremendously, kicking mutants out, either out or sentenced to death, or at least, that is what they thought. Humans thought mutants were gone for good after slaughtering the children and women of their families. The cruel acts were unexposed to the Epping. But the last thing Atlas thought of was saving a family, a blue family, their skin tone was just like the colour of Cyris's muted blue, ears like the webbed feet of an amphibian, there was a baby, his mother and his father. He noticed Cyris sleeping in the corner of the uncomfortable rocks, all lumpy and hard. Through the dark, he could just about see the shape of his ears and the two-toned hair drifting over his headband. His centre of focus shifted like light and darted his eyes towards a warm gust of fire setting off sparks past the arches of the underground. A sudden surge of energy threaded through his body like a storm, his instincts reflected that of the war, his last memory lingered in him, he was aware for anything and nearly cost Venas her life if she hadn't noticed him flash from the cave openings ready to commit murder. He didn't recognise her scent nor has he ever seen her before, she had the scent of a human therefore considered as an enemy. And in his mindset, the enemy must die like all the other humans that threaten him and his kind. The hundreds and hundreds that charged at him were all dead within a second and it was then that no human would ever dare to even be in his presence but then how did they lose the war?

What in the world? Venas didn't realise that it was Atlas until she lit the whole section of the caves to witness his glowing white eyes and the raging veins popping out of place showing through the skin of his neck and arm muscles as he took the stance of a wild bear, his polar bear instincts. The hit that he gave her missed its initial target and externally damaged her left arm when she dodged him and barely made it through his next move, instead of her head, the wall behind her shattered into the air. Venas tumbled onto the ground in astonishment and fear after thinking that what happened to that side of the cave what meant for her, her heart tripped over a few beats huffing and puffing, she scrambled across the floor, finding it hard to stand back up from the shock of Atlas, she didn't think that he'd be this frightening even though he is the hero icon of all mutants, of course, he's capable of breaking down not just this one wall but a whole cave. A lightning strike abruptly zapped past her and hit the walls of the cave in front of her spreading its lightning blue colour like a high tech explosion before a series of hot stream smoked out from the surface. No one would want that anywhere near their body. There were more flashing around his hands ready to be released though they were not as strong as before he was trapped for five hundred years. He returned to his bear stance, all fours tensed up on the ground, his warrior rage said to Venas.

"Humans must die," his gravelly voice bellowed faintly into his ears, his eyes and body marks gleamed intensively, lighting everything around him and sent Venas into a sort of panic when she turned around from his fifth lighting strike at the wall to throw her off guard before ending her with his storm and thunder powers. All the neighbouring caves lit brighter than the sky at staggering force, drifting bolts like sparks that bounced onto the ground and disappearing along with the light only a few seconds later. Soon, dimness roamed and it was clear how Atlas didn't kill Venas who tripped over on the ground. She opened her eyes.

"Kasey!" If anything, one piece of dark crystal was just as strong as his current state as Kasey administered a dismissal of Atlas's assault. Kasey switched on a sort of mode, his mask always shows an angry slash scare mode. Right now, it was that but times three. His stance was calm and he saved Venas once again.

"Venas," Cyris charged in after Kasey.

Atlas regarded Cyris, he regarded his smell and dismissed his powerful glowing marks and his beaming eyes, relaxing his muscles when he saw a mutant helping a human. Then he looked at Kasey and detected his scent.

"You are no mutant nor are you human… what are you?" his ancient accent echoed into Kasey's ears as he kept the protective shield beaming out of his ring. It took a while for him to answer.

"I don't know what you're talking about," he said bluntly.

"What does he mean, not human?" asked Venas.

"He has a strong sense of smell that allows him to tell the difference between species through scent," Cyris summarised.

"But Kasey's human."

Before anything else was said, a throbbing pain stabbed into his head, his mind pulsed into eternity, collapsing onto the ground fairing quickly. He sounded from the pain.

"What's happening?" Venas questioned.

"He used too much power and energy after being in the ice for so long, his body can't take the sudden source of activity," he said calmly like it wasn't his problem to deal with but Venas begged him to help, "Why would I do that, he almost killed you," he said again with his emotionless voice.

"Because every life matters, his head's still stuck in the war zone, we need to give him time," she justified.

After Kasey helped him eased the pain, he went back to sleep.

"He looks like one of those Buddha statues," Cyris commented. Venas shrugged.

"I don't even understand why he's here," she said.

Kasey left Atlas on the ground, as he was still sleeping after giving him a pill to ease the pain, he was too heavy to carry back on the table therefore he stayed on the comfortable ground. Venas had a query about his body, about the marks.

"What are these, are they like birthmarks, there's so many of them?"

"That's an interesting question, those are scars- when mutants get wounded, they heal and form a different colour, they glow with our powers when we use them, like our eyes, see I have loads, they were mainly from escaping human attacks when I was a few hundred years old, we see them as a source of strength," he got up and removed his jacket to give her a closer look at his dark blue body marks, all over his arms and a few on his back and front, there were more under his trousers, Venas recalled roughly seeing them when they found each other in the lab but she wasn't paying attention.

"Like the ones on my face," she muttered as she felt the uneven surface of his eyebrow area.

"Think of it as a trademark, something special, it shows that you've experienced a battle, brave and courageous- I think nowadays, society isn't too harsh on us as they were back then- hunting us down one by one but now, we won't get hurt unless we leave Epping, the difference is, now they have stronger weapons, a more evolved defence mechanism equals humans living a better life," he flung his jacket back on and left it unzipped.

"Where is this place?" said a faint voice that came from Atlas who expectedly felt weak and tired, though he had been sleeping for so long.

"You're awake," said Cyris, "This is the caves, we're in Nottinghamshire."

"Nottingham? What," nothing crossed his mind that he is in an era five hundred years after the Muman's war. "The war!" he jumped up from his seat and propped his hands on each side of Cyris's shoulders, then it clicked, "the war, we're still at war, I have to go out there - how long was I sleeping - who's in the lead!?!" he initiated panic mode and started shaking Cyris around, he couldn't keep his balance.

"Atlas, calm down! The war's over!"

"What, how can the war be over, I was out there just an hour ago, we were all getting killed…"

"You've been sleeping for five hundred years, the war's over!" Cyris battled the harsh words into his ears, his shoulders hurt from Atlas's grip.

"Five hundred years? What do you mean OVER?"

"It's over," he tried to control Atlas's volume, "you went missing for five hundred years and we found you frozen in ice, it's 2015 now," he blabbed. Atlas paused.

"So you're telling me that… the wars over…"

"Yes."

"And we… are in the future," his brain processed slowly, "It can't be over, how can this make sense, it's not over, we haven't won yet, the humans - the humans… you," he pointed at Venas.

"Me?" she panicked.

"She's not human," Cyris blurted, "well she is human, she's just not like the rest of the humans- s- she's not afraid of us-,"

"Just because she's not afraid of us doesn't mean she doesn't hate us."

"You're not listening, calm down a bit, I'll explain

slowly. The Muman's war ended 1515, it lasted for a year, it's been exactly five hundred years since then, we're dealing with a snake demon right now. With assumptions, he was the one that took you from the war and froze you like other mutants that went missing just like you but that was after the war so you are the first one we've rescued from the mystery," Venas sat on the ground with her legs crossed and listened carefully to the story, "the humans nowadays don't kill us, they just put us in some kind of liquid and take samples from us and for many experiments," he remembered all the features of his capture.

"We want to know what happened to you, anything you can remember from before you were frozen," Venas mentioned.

"Yeah, anything," said Cyris.

Atlas started to think, the smallest of detail whizzed through his brain like a bullet. It slipped his mind but soon came back with a click. He imagined the scene and it felt like only just yesterday when he saw the shadow of a man with two large horns on his head and long navy blue hair. He possessed the advantage of something he couldn't recognise, it was the dark crystal, much smaller than it is now.

"The city was at night-time war, the humans pulled out their poison-tipped arrows and shot them out like swarms of bees, that one shot took down quite the number of us, ten thousand human soldiers and ten thousand of us but more humans kept joining until they doubled our size- the last thing I remember was snakes- I ran across a field- I was chasing the humans who tried to kill a blue child, the child had green hair, he cried and I heard him in time to grab him before they shot the arrows into him, I took him and hid him in a crate from the ruins- there was nobody there except for the six men that tried to hurt the kid, one by one I grabbed their weapons and snapped them - took them down with one blow of wind and dust- that's when he appeared..." Venas and Cyris exchanged nervous glances, "snakes attacked me when a man with giant horns on his head just popped out of nowhere like he was using black magic," he said with a nerve racking accent, "he didn't touch the kid though- I didn't know him and before I knew it- I was out and now I'm here," he finished. Venas paused and rolled her eyes slowly and stroked the side of her nose, thinking about what could've happened next but the blue kids sounded familiar.

"That kid- the blue kid with green hair," Cyris said excitedly all of a sudden, "you remember- it's me, I was the kid, that's why I came out here to look for you," he pointed to himself.

"That was you?" he said surprisingly.

"Yeah, I was forty-five years old," he replied, noting that Mutant's age differently from humans, him being 45 years old was the same as a 7-year-old human child, "my family told me not to go out into the human society but I... well I didn't listen..." he continued.

That either was the first time Slevel entered Earth or he was lurking about specifically targeting him and just him since he didn't aim for the child or maybe he just didn't see him," Venas brainstormed in her head whilst Atlas and

Cyris chatted away smoothly like two old friends accidentally bumping into each other at the mall.

"All the mutants in Epping avoid the big city, some go out but then they go missing so others go out in search for them but they usually come back alone or not at all - there's a prison, the Underground Prison of Mutants," Cyris mentioned.

"And that's where they are," Atlas assured, Cyris nodded, "well then guess where I'm heading," he bounced up but Cyris pulled him back down.

"What're you doing, it's in London," he reminded.

"You make that sound like it's far away," said Atlas.

"That's because it is, it's more than a hundred miles from here," Cyris estimated.

"It's highly secure too," Venas mentioned.

"Is that so... on the contrary, I refuse to believe that any human can accept us as mutants," he glared at Venas but then he paused dramatically, "what was that?" he asked.

"What was what," Cyris repeated.

"I smell it!"

"What do you smell," Cyris questioned nervously.

The caves were occupied with a long trail of silence and echoes, what was he talking about.

"The smell of the snakes," he said with an angry expression.

Venas lifted her head in awareness and tried to detect any

noise but she wasn't able to hear anything, Cyris struggled to see any visible sound waves before he heard a slight crack within the cave walls. Not the one Atlas had punched but a different section of the cave.

CRACKLE   CRACKLE

"Sssssssssssss, I smell... foooood," hissed Phizzor who emerged from a tight corner.

Venas felt disgusted by the serpent's crackling smirk, devilish and unpleasant. It got closer amongst the dark and did not slow down to give them a warning.

"Kasey, where's Ka..." she glanced back and he had disappeared.
"Where the hell did he go?" Cyris questioned.

"I sseeeeee the girl's not dead from my venom," he sniffed her familiar scent, "it lookssss like I helped in some kind of way," he smirked and aimed his first bite for her before Cyris adjusted his third vocal cords to beam a structuring screaming only the Phizoor can hear, he assumed these snakes monsters have a sense of hearing, unlike any other Earth snakes. Phizzor shook like a giant drill digging into concrete and his vision became blurry whilst he sensed the vibrations, hearing the high pitched frequencies. It was enough for them to rush and dodge into the other caves of the underground and slow down the process of being eaten.

"If Phizzor's here then Slevel's here too, he's gonna find the spectrum, I need to get it first!" Venas blurted whilst in mid-sprint.

"No, we're not going back, he's gonna catch up," Cyris stopped her from going back.

"Well, I'm not gonna let him take it!"

"Atlas what are you doing!" Cyris bellowed.

Atlas started to light up his whole body once he saw not just Phizzor but an avalanche of snakes piling into the caves, sparks and streams of light energised his muscles and blew a powerful gust of wind and lighting into their systems, electrocuting a whole den of snakes. Where rumbling hurricanes from above, a tram from overground rambling the tram tracks, shaking and filled with screams as flying skeleton heads with dark cloaks banged uncontrollably against the windows and ceilings. Thrasher spirits released from the dark crystal orb that Slevel hard hovering in front of him conquering a painful amount of land with emergency services on high notice and phone calls that rang continuously, ready to attack back but the skeletons grew in number before the first gunfire was shot. Bullets darted into the air like confetti. The trams weren't holding up very well as the first crack in the glass sounded at the rear and the skeletons bashed their murderous heads into the tram and spread. The driver anxiously ran through every button on the control panel and finally opened the doors for everyone to escape and run, some toppled over in cries and pain after being tugged on by the solid spirits. Sirens beamed and ambulances screamed. Soon joined by the fire department. A radio-toned voice sounded from a police woman's radio communicator.

"Get everyone away from the city, it's currently infested over here!"
"Got it," she replied.

The tram stopped after the train station on the tracks towards Hucknall.

Flying skulls emerged one by one into the atmosphere, chattering their teeth, flapping their rags and sinking their fangs into the shoulders of the policemen. Their venom came from formulas that Slevel had conjured up from his pet Phizzor who continued his manic chase underground whilst his master lurks the overground, filling the city with monsters, monsters and more. So much that it was impossible for the human emergency services to deal with.

"This is getting out of hand!" screamed one police officer.

The last to arrive at the scene was Armsward himself in his protective mechanical suit under the identity of Astron accompanied by Serena under the name Neon, Zara under the name Echo. There was one more, it was the man flying the helicopter that we never got the chance to see during the first city attack. His name is Cody News, wearing the same type of suit as the rest with a green theme under the name Bult. Following the helicopter were Connar's service creations, a bundle of new-looking blue and white androids with two arms and a robotic tail that followed them as they soared through the sky, shooting bullets from their arms to dispose of the skeletons. The androids colours set off a feeling that they come from the police station but they were Connar's precious babies.

"Cody, stop it over there," Neon ordered him to keep the helicopter hovering in mid-air over the open in Market Square.

The square was currently occupied with the annual Christmas market, with food stalls, games and an outdoor ice rink with a little entry hut next to it everything was plastered with bright and vibrant Christmas decorations and an oversized Christmas tree proudly stood behind them. A big festive sign above it read:

Winter Wonderland

NOTTINGHAM

"Copy that," as they jumped down and encountered the unfamiliar thrasher spirits that were unable to attack them in the helicopter due to the aggressive propellers. Each of them landed safely on the roofs of the market stalls and leapt down to ground level with ease. It was hard for the thrashers to bite through the team's suits which gave them a chance to eliminate them into bone dust effortlessly until more decided to join the party, trashing all the decorations and market stalls.

Dead humans rested on the concrete ground, falling one by one as gunshots continued to fire like crazy. Citizens fled the city like ants disturbed by bug spray. Quickly, people grabbed their children and blindly followed police orders to attempt to find a safe place. Skeletons snarled and growled their way into the underground, infesting the caves. Phizzor kept Venas, Cyris and Atlas busy with his monster army and spat his destructive venom at the walls, melting the hard barrier of stone. The rocks sizzled and spread with a black burnt texture. Intentionally, he just felt like destroying the caves for his own amusement, to make a collision, an avalanche and take care of the three running loose in the caves but to his surprise, he witnessed a glow from the far end of the thick mould of the stone inside.

"Now... what do we have here," he said to himself. He stared at the walls and knew exactly what he was looking at. At that very moment when Phizzor removed the Spectrum Dia from its settling place, a spark of light flew from the diamond to Venas's amulet, she felt the pressure of the amulet suddenly pressing into her chest. The same sensation to when she shattered the dark crystal to find two of the missing Jade Dragon Oracles.

"Hey, why'd you stop!?!" Cyris flung his body around luring the snakes to hell, eliminating them with a flash.

"It's the spectrum," she panicked and knew it was released from the caves.

Serpents slithered in harmony, darting their heads into the air as if there was something to bite before being slaughtered by Atlas's storm power washing the caves with a wave of thunder and wind, washing them away into a mountain of dead snakes. Atlas stomped on the ground with his heavy black boots and raged in fury. Cyris feared as he noticed another cracking sound coming from above. It was faint underneath the overground rampage but as soon as it was clear that the cracking was running towards them, Phizzor spat another mass amount of venom making the cracks bigger and bigger. A rush of anxiety strangled them as they helplessly watched it breaking the ceiling apart from one end to the other. Gravel and stone rained down and light shot into their eyes with a blinding shine of the afternoon sun. Venas's first instinct was to flee from the fallen stone that continued to snow. Taking down more of Phizzor's snake friends, she and the others rushed from cave to cave, in and out of the stone arches to avoid getting crushed into bone dust but space was limited. Atlas blew a hit at the cause of the event thinking that it would help.

"What're you doing, you're making it worse," yelled Venas, she glanced everywhere, all her surroundings and the only place to flee was up as more and more of the arches was blocked with boulders.

The ground above shook like an earthquake and the roads finally tore into it, demolishing the tram track into Market Square where the clock building stood. Venas took to mind that she has wings, Petal's wings. If they were any good, they'd show up now but before they did, the people above shook in terror and witnessed the rumbling, monstrous crack endlessly travelling towards the City Square.

"It's tearing the whole city apart!" Cyris reported as he was attacked with a ray of light.
"Wings, come on- come on," Venas left Cyris on the blank as she struggled to release her dragon wings.
"We can jump out of the crack," Atlas pointed.

He took Cyris by the arms and anticipated a powerful swing to launch him overground.

"No, what're you trying to do?!?" Before Atlas gave an answer, he launched Cyris into the air like a baseball and he rumbled in the mid-air trying to find balance and figuring out how to land unscratched. Just at that movement, destruction hit the square like a canon crushing the foundation of the square building, Nottingham's main attraction. Market Square is falling.

Flame 12

Wings

Connar sprung from the ground, dodging the impactful hits the thrasher spirits attacked him with. He slid down on the slight hill from Nottingham's Royal Centre on the untouched tram tracks back to the City Square followed by a dead trail of skeletons rolling on the ground. One of his service androids flew past him and obeyed orders through Connar's radio connections to set a new explosive device that he had invented not long ago. The android chucked the gadget swiftly into Connar's grip. He removed a tag with an orb dangling after it and switched the main device on, boosted the orb into a swarm of skeletons, hit the switch again and took the crowd down in time for him to zoom past to see Market Square rumbling in an earthquake of its own. Everything in the Christmas Winter Wonderland fell apart and partly sank into the ground sliding at an angle towards the centre where the ground continued to break into two.

"Uh, team…" he said in terror and shock, "I think we have a slight problem.

"You THINK?" Connar repeated

"I see it," Cody replied through his earpiece as he saw it from the helicopter.

"What is it?" Serena questioned as she could not see Old Market Square anymore.

"It's Market Square, I'm contacting the structure bots from their pods, keep going with the skeletons," Connar notified his collection of androids that are made to be involved with building foundations for his lab building. It has been a very long time since he's used them but he's always maintained their condition to the very best, they are his fine creations and robotics like Connar never leaves an android behind.

"Connar, it's starting to collapse," Cody paused as he saw something else worth noting, "I see a blue-skinned boy with green hair that just jumped out of the crack from the ground, he seemed to have come from the caves."

"It's the mutant that was captured yesterday," just as Connar also saw Cyris run away from the ground opening, the right side of the Market Square building began to sink into the caves.

"It's about to timber," cried Cyris, hoping that Venas and Atlas could still hear him through all the chattering commotion.

Venas heard him loud and clear and suddenly felt a sensation running down her spine. Light beamed from her Oracle following the strong tingling feel of her wings. Her eyes and scars started to glow. Atlas was astonished when he saw Venas pull her mask up as her clothes changed with the power of Oracle and soared out of the caves and zoomed in a tight arc towards Market Square. The building heavily made its way down with half of the foundation ruined. A pinkish-skin colour of sticky scales spat at the bottom of the attraction just when the rest of the ground around also began to disintegrate just like the broken tram tracks. The new ground opening spread into the fancy black architectural fountains that took the form of a water park. The fountain snapped at the bottom and water sprayed in all directions whilst the sticky scales that Venas shot out of her arms continued as she flew around the entire attraction wither chewing gum-like threads and finally took use of her Oracle for extra power to lift the building in time for any humans within to escape safely. Police officers were indeed inside with a few citizens that were less able to remove themselves from inside as the attack happened too quickly. Venas's Oracle glared red light like the crazy fire alarm at the fire station that received another call for backup service. All the fighters on the ground plus Cody could see a white-haired girl holding up the building with only her wings and her two hands attached to the strange threads. Under the noise of the propellers, Cody questioned with confusion:

"You guys seeing what I'm seeing?"

"I'm definitely seeing what you're seeing," Connar replied.

"What is that, I can't tell what it is?"

"I don't know but the bots are on their way," Connar activated the systems connected to the bots and they were zooming past all the rogue skeletons searching blindly for new victims. They end up getting knocked over by the zooming bots that won't stop until they reach their given destination.

Venas stretched her muscles and tugged harshly to hold it up. Her body could only take so much weight even with her celestial strength, she felt one of the scale threads ripping. Another one parted and soon more. The building lowered itself again until the structure bots flashed from one end of the square to the bottom of the building to replace Venas's drain out efforts, catching the building once she dropped it. She opened her eyes to notice a swarm of androids releasing their metal arm from their orb-shaped bodies and digging them into the bricks. The work of one hundred managed to hold the building upright for Venas to safely release her grip. The ground amongst the feral attack could barely be seen but it was still tearing the city into two and at the end of the trail emerged the main villain. Slevel and his pet Phizzor. Slevel bellowed a mighty cackle and raised his arms. One holding the dark crystal and one holding the Spectrum Dia.

"After Tao Shi foolishly lost two of the precious Oracle of Jade Dragon, I've been searching wide for these," he smirked madly, "and now, I finally have one."

"What," Venas mumbled.

As Atlas stomped out from the cracks she glanced over at Cyris and plugged in her ears. She and Atlas both gave him a nod. Cyris screeched a pitch that can't be heard with ordinary human ears and scratched Slevel's nails, sending him and Phizzor a painful headache. Venas took off again and blazed for the spectrum whilst Slevel was distracted but he saw. Without hesitation, he merged it with the dark crystal.

"NO!!!" She yelled, she was so close and was boosted away after she closed her wings, they disappeared as she rolled on the hard concrete into a messy rack of bikes, ruining the metal frames and dislocating the tyres from the bikes.

Slevel chuckled a bit more and walked up to her in his mental image of victory.

"The sword," he demanded.
"What sword?" she lied, her inside screeching in agony from the impact of the fall.

Slevel grabbed her by her purple cloak.

"The sword! Sword of Jade Dragon, you have three

Oracle gems that I WANT," his evil whisper circulated into a loud and frightening temper. She had the chance to look closely at his face. It was scaly and dry like a lizard that hasn't been in the water for decades. It was unpleasant for her eyes.

"Does it look like I have a sword on me?"

"You have the sword, you can either hand it to me like a good girl now or…"

"Or what, you'll never get it if you kill me," she exposed.

"So you DO have the sword."

"You just want the power to kill people, slaughter them for more power," she tried to grasp for air, Slevel had his scrawny hand around her neck, it seemed like deja vu.

"Threatening people is how one shows their power," he expressed his thoughts.

"Power? You'd be nothing…" one hard breath, "without- dark… crystal."

"Wrong, I am the one that made the dark crystal, therefore, I am powerful with or without it, unlike Tao Shi… dying in the hands of a mortal girl, you, you were that mortal," he knew, it was obvious to him that Venas was the famous Venas Xoular who saved Qin's Empire City from the Monster Tao Shi three months ago.

He knows that green rat? Venas thought in her head and finally decided to burn Slevel's hand into ashes waiting for his cry of agony from his withering hand.

"Why youuuuu RATCHET MORTAL!!!" He shot the dark crystal orb in the sky and aimed powerful solid energy at her that shifted into chunks of icicles. All the icicles stabbed the ground from missing Venas who fled like an eagle via the ground like a cheetah.

"GET HER," Slevel urged, "I want that sword and her Oracle."
"Yes massssssster," he darted his way into Venas but also missed as he didn't expect her to dodge so easily from his fangs.

Cyris and Atlas demolished a mountain of monsters very quickly. Venas was surprised to see Atlas stand in front of her to launch Phizzor into the deserted tram with one stomp. He looked at Venas who looked at him with stunned eyes. He seemed embarrassed after being rude to her earlier.

"You're quite cool you know that, I like a brave girl like you," he said at the beginning of a new friendship. Venas smiled.
"Thanks."
"The city is being obliterated and you're doing what!?!" Cyris said.

Slevel screeched, slanted his reptilian eyes and noticed Atlas. Under the gunshots and destructive noises, he spoke from afar, "Ah, it's you… it's been quite a long time since we've seen each other eye to eye… rather five hundred years," he said with a creepy smile.
"I remember," Atlas said coldly.

His eyes and all his scars glazed and glared through the daylight telling Venas and Cyris to stand back but Cyris had already fled into one of the police vehicles and grabbed himself some handle gadgets pulling Venas along with him whilst Atlas rages into beast mode but his attacks were barely putting a scratch on Slevel when he possesses the dark crystal. Both of them flew around and engaged in a powerful battle as Cyris and Venas watched from behind the opened car door.

"It's no use, that dark crystal is more powerful now that it has the Spectrum Dia in it," Venas stated.

"What do we do then?" Cyris asked.

"We destroy it, we have to destroy it to get the Spectrum back," she became determined.

"Here, human's lazy devices," he passed her a black object.

"A gun?"

"Yeah, we can use it to save our energy, I see humans use it and they don't need to move a muscle," he said.

"I ain't using no gun, put it back."

"Fine, I'll take two."

"You know there's not enough bullets in one to deal with all this."

"Where's the rest?"

"I don't know, keep that thing away from me!"

Suddenly, Phizzor found them hiding and fired a shot of his molten venom through the door window, Cyris and Venas dodged in opposite directions to avoid becoming roasted venom meat.

"Gimme that!" Venas demanded and at the same time, she opened the drawers in the car to find some backup bullets and trailed it behind her. One eye closed and Phizzor unexpectedly bled from the bullets that sunk into his hard scales. She kept going, one by one, continuously aiming upwards for the rest of the monsters in the sky as Cody drifted the helicopter out of the way when he saw Venas with a weapon and Cyris taking care of snake combat with Phizzor who was still well and alive.

"Come on die! How the hell are you still alive?!!" he shouted impatiently.

"Never," Phizzor hissed, "you need more than a few ssshotss to kill my old body," his eyes widened and he nearly strangled Cyris but released him quickly after he used the same technique on him when they were in the underground.

"Boss, the mutant's are helping us, the snake man has appeared at the end of Market Square and one of them's fighting him- it looks like he's got some kind of magical orb," Cody reported.

"The number of monsters has dialled down over here by NTU," Serena reported, referring to Nottingham Trent University.

"Same for me," said Zara who was busy near Corner house.

"Keep an eye on the snakes, I'm heading back to the Square," Connar updated.

Venas thought of taking care of the last few skeletons by levitating the bullets, slotting them out of their cases and simultaneously darted them like a series of invisible canons. One blast led to a flooding of bone dust down from disintegrating amongst a grass of fire that disappeared after she released her Aurora.

Just then, Atlas flew through the sky and landed on the fountain, drenched wet from head to toe. From the impact of the boost, he tumbled away and nearly fell into the cracks. One Zap of magic and he was frozen cold again.

"Atlas!" Venas called.

Slevel cackled again. His robes rippled in all directions from his latest movement of action, taking advantage of his freshly powered crystal to freeze the entire city into solid clear ice. The water froze and ice spread quickly across the landscape. Cyris attempted to back away but he too got caught. The frosty chills travelled around vehicles, busses, the tram, slowly creeping up the shops on the sides and along the tram tracks, it's contagious power captured everything it touched, the Christmas tree, all the market stall remains and the skating hut.

A large icicle rose from the ground and kept time still around the helicopter whilst it was still in the air, Serena, Zara, Cody... and Connar were trapped helplessly. The whole city was sparkling from the glow of the sun like an Ice Kingdom attraction.

"What in the nine heavens?" she muttered as she

feasted her eyes upon the dazzling view of Nottingham city glimmering under planes of ice.

Everything and everyone froze in time…

Everyone except Venas.

Flame 13

The Defeat of Time

Venas scanned everywhere for an uncaptured soul but everyone... absolutely everyone was caught in Slevel's spell. The power of Oracle protected her from the darkness of the frozen magic the dark crystal produced. The frozen city was filled with dark fumes, something that news reporters did not capture during their midnight discoveries on the 2nd of

December. The ice was fresh and thick but other than that, there was a layer of water spread on the top. Venas's first movement of action involved her butt falling onto the ice when she tried to run but the thin layer of water defeated her. She struggled.

"Much better," Slevel charged towards her but missed, sliding on the top of her force field magic.
"She's helpless," Phizzor intended to laugh at her sliding her feet back and forth trying to stay upright to find her centre of balance.

Whilst she struggled, she also kept her eyes on the crystal ball like a hawk.

"Get her," he said silently.
"Yessss master," he tried again but to his unfortunates, she found her balance and used the edges of her soles to perpendicularly push herself along the water surface and dodged Phizzor's first attack and the second.

She busted out a packet of flames and melted an area of ground to step on when she was about to lose control over her steps and managed to find her way back like a speed skater gliding across the arena. Phizzor closely gained after her, so close to biting her; to his surprise, she engaged in a sharp turn to the right as he bashed his scaly head into the lion statue of Old Market Square. This knocked him out cold just as Slevel took matters into his own hands to do the job right. Venas found his claw-like hand aiming a grab for her cloak. She was dodging fast. It was no surprise that he was going for the amulet she wore around her neck which was hidden under her shirt. He missed. His broken hand recuperated immediately and shredded a staggering number of peeling skin that morphed into snakes nearly as big as Phizzor. She fled and stumbled over the uneven icy coat that travelled over the cracks and fountain under the skating hut. Soon the topcoat of water froze under the pressure of mid-December weather, just the right condition to adapt to when Venas was trying her best to multi-task a crisis that made her think she wasn't going to make it. She took heavy breaths and felt her pulse running wild trying to catch up with herself. The rogue newborns stabbed their sturdy tails into the ice and shattered it into pieces as a result of Venas escaping her terror until Slevel rushed in, his long hair trailing after him as he dug his long claws into her hair missing her by a second and scratched some tears unto his clothing, marking her arms with stinging cuts. When she stumbled again, she found his claws sinking into the right side of her forehead, she was able to pull herself back to stop him from scratching her entire face. Because she ate Kasey's elixir pill, the wounds healed like the first one and glowed brightly into Slevel's eyes, blinding him to make any more cruel attacks. Her stance with all fours on the ground comprehended anger and rage, determination as a source of red energy flowed through her body and stormed around her.

I got it, Venas thought, she glanced over at the skate hut with her glowing white eyes. One after the other, potholes transmitted a trail as Venas first stumbled. She found the time to become a master at travelling across the slippery surface.

Slevel came to a halt once he saw something unfamiliar on her two feet. Skating shoes that allowed her to surge past and slice his pets with its sharp blades. Green blood splat onto the surface like paint, an artistic murder scene.

"What is this?" he bellowed hatefully with a slight expression of confusion.
"Give it up Slevel, you've already done enough."
"I'd kill you a long time ago if it wasn't for the sword of Jade Dragon," he sneered and threw his orb into the sky once again raising his hands in wildness.

Madly, he released more skeletons, abusing his power of holding the Spectrum Dia. Abusing his creations to handle just one girl. A storm rose within the city, catching cars and unhinging tram stops from the ground, nearly pulling Venas into the tornado of skeletons that swarmed around her like pigeons and their local feeder in a cartoon. Unfortunately, they weren't prepared to become bone soup from her explosion of flames so quickly. Slevel, equipped with dissatisfaction bellowed:

"Phizzor, get up you imbecile!" he demanded aggressively and ambushed a hurricane of icicles shooting from the ground in an attempt to stab her just once.

Venas flash towards Phizzor just as he gains consciousness and finds spectacles of ice shredding tinkling in his eyes as angled her skates for a sharp turn to spray him with a tsunami of ice. The helpless snake wiggled around in pain from the sharpness of the shards cutting his eyes.

"Why you ratchet mortal!!!" he cried as his master chased her with the dark crystal ensuring its safety in his hands.

When he grabbed it from the sky Venas blew another tsunami but with flames she produced with her bare hand with the motion of kung fu. The fire melted the ice immediately and it spread around her nearly burning Slevel into ashes. It warmed the whole city with its winter heat and gradually unfrozen everyone who was around the square but they were still stuck.

Venas disappeared amongst the flames and snatched the dark crystal from his dirty hands whilst he could not see or smell her whereabouts, stepped out as her ice-skated turned back into her regular shoes and smashed the orb into the concrete. People who were in the process of defrosting were just in time to witness Venas destroying Slevel's main source of energy and power, releasing millions of brightly-coloured Oracles into the sky. The feeling of deja vu sent Venas three months into the past when she destroyed Tao Shi's crystal orb and gained two of the sacred Oracles of Jade Dragon. After the mesmerizing field of vision displayed all around her started making their way into the air, Spectrum Dia sensed her presence, the owner of the sword of Jade Dragon. Now that it was free, it approached her effortlessly. Venas grabbed it as the rest spiralled into the clouds. Every single gem in the crystal had been trapped for hundreds and hundreds of years giving Slevel power that his body became dependent on it, now, they were free. They all stormed into the clouds, aesthetically pleasing eyes of every human being situated within the city. Venas pulled the sword from her Oracle and claimed the Spectrum Dia.

"NOOOOOO!!!" Slevel snarled, he struggled to escape the ring of fire without dark crystal and could only hear it shatter into pieces before the flames faded.

Once the dark crystal had gone, all the thrasher spirits, dead and alive, disintegrated into dust and disappeared with the cold breeze. Citizens, the services, Cyris, Atlas and Connar's team had never seen anything quite like it. The sky was literally overcast with jewels reflecting in every window and eyes. Cyris transformed into water and escaped the rest of the melting ice and freed Atlas on the way whilst everyone else was still half-frozen from the knees and down. Slowly, the ground healed like a timelapse video, the stalls, the ice rink, the Christmas tree, the roads and finally the building of Old Market Square. Slevel fell to the ground on the tram tracks in defeat and regret. Black fumes surged all over his body and caused him a stabbing amount of agony as he noticed his scaly skin wrinkling more than ever, his body flushed and burned on the inside whilst he trembled in confusion.

"What's happening, "Cyris questioned.

Dozens of serpents slithered out of him, his legs, his

arms, from under his traditional wear and instantly died. His clothes were the only things that stayed the same whilst he himself began to lose a high volume of skin. It started to shed then folded onto the ground as his arms began to deteriorate from his previous actions of abusing his snake shedding powers to infest the whole city, without dark crystal aiding him, his body could not take the sudden change of it not being there anymore. With no crystal to aid him, his pet Phizzor shrunk and shrunk and what was left of him was just his scales, rotten and withered with holes of blood.

"What's happening to me?" he bellowed.

"Without dark crystal, you're just a useless snake, you relied on its power for too long," Venas commented, "now that it's no longer here to support you, your body can't take it- admit it, you've been defeated."

Slevel snarled and hissed as a field of shadow energy spread through the city that blinded everyone before he noticed Venas getting bigger and bigger all of a sudden but unfortunately, he was the one getting smaller and smaller, his clothes became loose, all his hair strayed from its habitat and his horns shrunk too. His growling and curses came to an end once Venas grabbed him by his tiny neck and claimed her win.

"That's one point for me, zero points for you," she showed Atlas and Cyris Slevel in his snake body, weak and fragile.

Now he can easily be killed but Venas decided to spare him his life as the torture of being a helpless snake suited her satisfaction. The sensation of defeating Slevel felt a lot better than defeating Tao Shi. We weren't a bright fan of murdering living creatures unless it was absolutely necessary. Cyris and Atlas both suggested to end him for good but he was only a ten-inch-long snake. She put a seal on him, a strong seal that prevents anything, any magic like shadow spells to help turn him back to normal or maybe he began life like this. She wasn't sure if the seal was strong enough. A demon who was born a snake and practised morphing into a humanoid being like the famous Chinese legend of the White Snake but instead, Slevel was an evil snake, unlike the kind-hearted white snake. Venas was so caught up in the moment, the sudden sound of clapping slowly spread all around them started with Connar and his team who seemed more understanding towards mutants especially when Connar tried to take Atlas away to keep him safe instead of keeping him trapped in the ice like Lawson.

Venas held Slevel tight in her grasp by his neck area to ensure that he couldn't escape. At first, she panicked from so many humans settling their eyes upon her mutant form, Cyris and Altas but didn't think it mattered as much as half her face was covered and they were all standing so far away.

Market Square was restored to its former state after the Oracles left Earth, or at least, the foundation was. The beautiful sight of the shattered crystal still stormed in everyone's heads, they were stunned, amazed even though they were mutants. No one wanted to get closer. The clapping stopped.

"This... this is quite awkward," said Cyris, he glanced over at Atlas who wrinkled his face and feared the results of his potential actions.

"Humans," he sniffed the staggering scent of all the humans that surrounded them and prepared himself in a stance on his hands and feet.

Everyone quickly changed their prompt idea of thinking these mutants were harmless to them but it was hard to believe with Atlas bursting into anger towards them. The police armed themselves and held their guns up in the air aiming at the three of them. They were trembling and releasing clouds of anxiety into the air. They were scared of them even though they just helped save them. It made Atlas growl, even more, growling like a polar bear of fear that these humans were going to hurt him and his friends. He looked more fierce facing the humans than facing Slevel. The gun pointing only made the situation worse.

"Atlas no!!!" Venas demanded him to stay still but he was already on the move.

"ATLAS!!!" Cyris screeched.

"He's coming right at us!!!" called an officer.

Connar and his team couldn't believe that the officers were threatening their heroes with their guns ready to shoot. He quickly retrieved and joined Cody in the helicopter taking a giant leap and crawled in.

"Quick, start the engine!!!" Connar ordered.
"Yes sir!"

Just as the propellers fanned the ground below and blew everyone near it off course, gun fires shot into the air, bulletin towards Atlas. Venas flashed forwards joining him side by side to blast a source of power towards the bullets and repelled them back to prevent any of them from getting shot. Ten bullets fired at once and were all cancelled by her magic.

"It's not working!" one officer shouted before twenty more bullets blasted into the atmosphere one after the other and continued to shoot. The guns could be heard from the corner house and university where Zara and Serena were. Venas easily repelled them too as the rumbling of propellers that interrupted the connection slowly hovering above the tramlines where they were standing.

BANG!

Bullets aimed towards Cyris did not take on any effect. He was able to jump and morph into water moulding around each lightning-fast ammunition whilst Atlas remembers that guns were the human's form of defence instead of the old-fashioned arrows. Guns were a lot quicker than arrows, they were stronger and created a bigger impact when he saw them go through the snakes and thrashers but luckily Venas acted quickly to aggressively shield them from the bullets.

"Up here!!!" Connar called as the copter lowered to the ground enough for him to reach out his arm to gesture them on board.

Venas scanned his suit, his helmet and the inside of their helicopter. Out of all the humans, why would Connar and Cody help them and go against the others but there was no time to think anymore. She jumped and Atlas followed. Cyris splashed on board and remained in liquid form to save space.

"I'm sorry," he realised what he had done.
"It's okay," said Venas.

"Get ready and hold on tight!" Connar yelled.

"Everyone hold your fire!!!" demanded one police officer in shock and anger to see Astron assisting their escape.

They flew away with ease leaving everyone on a fuzzy confused as to why he was helping them.

Flame 14

Artificial Intelligence

Atlas sniffed around with his guard up and everything a new unfamiliar human walks past the lab room, he would growl at them like a cautious tiger but Venas specifically told him a million times to refrain from biting their heads off because he WILL do that. He will resort to violence with the instinct to protect his kind. If it wasn't for Venas, all the scientists and robotics engineers in Connar's lab would've all gone to heaven by now. Cyris chilled in a jar that Venas found until he wished to show himself to the humans close up in his mutated form for the first time in forever. Venas sealed it to make sure he doesn't get used in anyone's experiments or end up in anyone's tummy. She put an invisible field around Atlas to prevent him from doing anything stupid and walked up to Connar who sat peacefully at his desk in his shirt and trousers after revealing to them who he was under the helmet. Only Venas was caught up with all this information. She was a fan of reading about Astron and his team and now she could finally see who he is. Bearing in mind that she was still in her mutated figure. She pulled her mask higher to her nose and constructed a conversation with Connar who left them with nothing to do in his office but watch people walk past through the high tech windows by the doors. It had already been a while and Cyris thought that this place seemed quite safe. He swished out of the jar and wriggled over to the walls where played about with a panel that controlled the windows and found it entertaining. He's never seen automatic windows before and he can make them one-way mirrors and other things that kept him fascinated as he slowly morphed back into his solid form.

"I see your friend there is having fun," Connar commented.

"Spill it, are you helping us or are you doing the opposite? Is there a reason you just helped us out there?" Venas blurted without a greeting.

"It's very nice to meet you too, Miss…?" Connar stood up from his fancy office chair and gestured a handshake.

Venas stared at his hand and didn't know whether to shake his hand or not. Why is it that this man and his team of heroes decided to save her from the rest of the protection services? She released a string of her stick scales and avoided contact with Connar by tugging the thread up and down as it stuck to his hand. She winded it back in and continued. Connar observed his hand and tried to see what it was that she had just stuck to his hand. A pink soft but yet stiff piece of material that shot from her skin. It was fascinating to witness such a power.

"Nice to meet you," she said.

Hello, I am Cyber, it's very nice to meet you, how do you rate your visit," Cyber rolled over to Venas and greeted her with his metal hands.

"My visit?"

"Please ignore him, it's a working progress, he's asking everyone survey questions and I need to fix it at some point," Connar explained.

"That's pretty impressive."

"Thank you, it's very likely that we will be dealing with some more commotion in the far future but for now, let me introduce myself, my name is Connar Armsward, founder of Arms String Technology A.I... and your name is?" he said.

"I don't have a name," she lied.

"You don't have a name? How could someone not have a name," he questioned.

"I just don't have one," she tried to think of a name

quickly but nothing sounded right, "I want it to have something to do with fire or something."

"Wait a minute," Cyris slowly walked over, "you're Connar Armsward?"

"Yes," Connar answered.

"Then you're that man that secretly helps mutants," he burst into excitement and slammed the table with both hands.

"Well, it's not a secret anymore," Venas commented.

Connar grinned.

"It is still a secret, it's under the name of Astron, the team and I think there's potential in you guys, we think of you like you are our own... but you referred to me by my own name, how did you know it was me?"

"It rings a bell, both of your names, I know a mutant, we haven't really seen each other for a while now but he came to Epping after him and his family went missing, his name's Lucas, Lucas Lanheart, and he told me that a man Armsward saved him and gave his family a home- family of eight," he remembered.

"They're the only missing mutants that I've been able to rescue- I found them one after the other after finding Lucas... he returned to his home- how did I not know about this?"

"He came to tell us that not all humans want to kill us, he wanted some of us to go with him but everyone refused, they wouldn't believe a word he said, I could barely believe him."

"Interesting…" Connar grinned, "I don't expect anyone to believe it."

"The A.I. here is cool and all but how are you going to help us now, we're kinda in a tight spot here," Venas butted back in.

Connar walked over to the window and hovered his eyes over the city view. The window planes curved around half of the office and stood at eight feet. It was quite a tall building. They could see everything from up there. All the police cars dotted throughout the city. Firetrucks, ambulances, people that looked like ants.

"I've brought you here so you can hide," he looked at Atlas,"if I'm not mistaken, I believe Atlas is still in the war-zone from being in the ice for so long. Now that he's seen in public as a threat, you guys are going nowhere," he made a point, "I've looked it up, gathered evidence from the war and it seems that before the Muman's war, mutant's have done nothing wrong, they have no intentions of hurting humans, it is just a form of self-defence, if humans didn't offend them and think they were dangerous with their powers then there would be no war- we need to show them that you intend no harm."

"So we're just gonna stay here?" she replied, "and do nothing?"

"I dunno, this place does seem pretty cool," Cyris commented, "kinda want a tour."

"Not with Atlas around, if he sees any more humans, who know what he'll do," she said.

"I can take you for a look around," Connar agreed.

"Heck no, I don't think that's a good idea, Atlas... he won't be able to contain himself," she warned.

"You just need to clear your name," said Connar.

"So we ARE staying here forever... because we just helped contain a murderous snake demon and that wasn't even enough," she pointed to the glass jar containing Slevel in his tiny snake form, "his name's Slevel by the way."

"There's no way... if we could prove ourselves, we would've done it five hundred years ago, and what even are we trying to prove? The fact that we are also living beings with the same right and we don't cause any harm, there are humans that take on murderous crimes and all they get is a sentence and a warning- what are we? Atlas used to be the most generous mutant being in our society but now after what they've done to us, all he can think about is killing them... to protect us- it's not that easy to go out there and say, we want peace because humans fear, they fear us!" Cyris raged, "I also noticed that they can be a bit racist too, Altas, a black panther? This ain't no superhero plot."

"It's true," Atlas admitted, "I'm a descendent of a polar bear and I always get mistaken for a black animal, do you see my skin. It's brown, not black, BROWN."

"They thought we were all gone after they slaughtered all the women and children, they thought they did but before the war, our families sealed the Epping forest for us to hid in, the ones that didn't make it died but the ones that did hid away forever- traps get set off every day until they gave up- we lived with fear in our own homes because a lot of us go missing, they step out of the zone and never come back," he summarised, "we're scared of humans too you know."

"But now we're out here, they think there's a whole tribe out there. The reason why they attacked us earlier was because they think Slevel is a mutant himself," said Venas.

"Like hell, that ain't not mutant, he's the ugliest thing I've ever seen," Atlas commented.

"If he's not a mutant? What on earth is he then?" Connar questioned.

"He's just a demon," Venas said slowly without giving too much detail.

"Just a demon, are you sure he's just a demon, where does a demon even come from," Connar questioned curiously.

"He's just a snake that practised shadow skills to turn into a humanoid creature, but we made it worse for the other mutants when we decided to expose ourselves to Slevel, we might've beaten him but now what we're dealing with is an ambush of humans hunting us down, and they're gonna start with you," she said to Connar, "How does it work. They know this is your company and if society wanted to know who Astron is, they would've followed you here and questioned you."

"That's a good question…" but before he opened up to explain how hiding his identity works, Atlas sensed a source of bait.

"I smell snakes," Atlas sniffed.

Everyone turned to Atlas who was sitting on the guest seats on the side of his office.

"You smell snakes?" Cyris repeated, "but they're all gone now.

"It's faint but it's the same snake," he clarified with a hint of rage.

"You have snakes in your department?" Venas asked curiously.

"It's dead, we took it back to take some samples of its venom... you can smell that? But it's in the labs downstairs."

"I have an abnormal sense of smell," he said with no further detail.

"Can I... take a look?" Venas asked.

"You want a look at the snake?" Connar questioned.

"Yes... if you don't mind," she said politely.

"Right this way."

Cyris stayed behind with Atlas as he and Venas were not confident with him leaving the room until he learned to control his instincts and his violence, he looked like he handled small talk with Connar quite well. They were left in the office with Cyber and the other service androids to look out for them. Atlas took some time to get used to being in the presence of artificial intelligent species that have the scent of metal and bolts. He trusted them quicker than he trusted the humans because as long as they don't smell like humans, he knows he's safe. He played with them like they were kittens and puppies whilst Cyris stares out the window in curiosity. He's never been high up before, other than the helicopter that he came here on. He watched the people walked around the city with the ground surface looking as good as new like nothing had ever happened.

"So what's your special power? I can already tell that Atlas has courageous strength and impressive sense of smell," Connar questioned as they walked down the busy corridor.

"I...," she wasn't sure if she could say she has enhance hearing because ever since she became mutated, her hearing has dropped a level but she can still hear what others can't, "I have advanced hearing and fire abilities, Cyris plays with sound, he can see sound waves and create sounds that affect certain species and age ranges," she clarified.

"Oh, is that what the screaming was doing to the snakes? I didn't realise that."

"Yes, that's exactly what he was doing, he was trying to deafen it, it was a sound that only humans won't hear."

"Really? Then how did it not affect you guys?"

"He gave us earplugs made to block out his screams."

"That makes sense," she waved at the employees that greeted him as they headed down the stairs.

"You took a sample of venom to do what exactly?" Venas wondered as she walked into a well-lit biology lab with lines of tables occupied with research elements, including a tray covered with a scruffy white cloth.

The tray contained the dead snake coiled up within. It's stuck through her mask although the flesh hasn't rotted yet. She enchanted herself from smelling the repulsive scent.

Connar specialises more in mechanics therefore the building is mostly full of A.I. departments over the area of twenty floors and one floor dedicated to other topics related to biology and chemistry. Venas sighted the venom samples on the table. The building was occupied with just as many creations of robots and artificial intelligence with a given task of their day, it was fascinating to see them work whilst she opened up her ears to Connar's speech.

"When humans discover something new, we get curious, I study things I'm curious about to discover more features they have- example A, the venom here is highly toxic and kills you instantly, rats were part of the testing subject, they die almost immediately, yet we still haven't found where these snakes come from, I've never come across snakes as venomous as this one," he said, taking into account that Venas wasn't human.

"Is there enough venom here to make some anti-venom?" she questioned with concern.

"Unfortunately, there isn't," he said.

"Oh," she replied sadly but then common sense hit her, "what about Slevel?"

"What about Slevel?" he repeated.

"You can use his venom, he's still alive," she suggested.

"Yes, there is a possibility," Connar noticed, "but everyone who was bitten by them has already passed away so there is no hurry to make it."

"But it's still good to have it ready right?"

"Very well, I'll go get the snake."

"No need," Connar turned around to see Slevel already

on the table from Venas using her celestial to make it appear on the table but he didn't see it.

"How did you...?" he muttered, he was certain that the snake was in his office when he left and he didn't see Venas take it on her way out. It was there, right in front of him like it just magically appeared.

Without the power of dark crystal, Slevel was useless, his power had completely weakened to where he started off in life. His ability to shed his skin on demand was lost and now his fangs were being milked to create the potential anti-venom that Venas was so curious about. It was obvious she intended to use it to rid the venom from her system to turn back into a human. If it worked, that would be amazing. Before, in Ervanna, all she wanted was to go back to Earth. Now that she was back, she got her wish and this happens. Now all she wants is to go back to the way she was. It was one problem after the other. As simple as getting her hair colour back, her skin colour and as much as she loved her new eyes, she wanted them to turn back too. And hopefully the scars otherwise people are going to recognise her as the pink mutant with the aggressive black mutant that tried to kill the humans. Other than that, she was also known as the mysterious flying figure that lifted the Old Market Square building with only her bare hands to the looks of it from afar. The other scientists in the room were a bit startled by Venas at first. They became uneasy for a while until she suggested using Slevel for the anti-venom. The reason why they got used to her so quickly would be because they've made encounters with other mutants before. Cyris had mentioned

Lucas Lanheart, a boy roughly the same age as him and his family. But every one of them decided to keep their mouths shut and focus on their work. People in white coats rummaged past her with their busy schedules.

"We've milked a good amount of venom from the snake, will this be enough?" questioned one employee after injecting Slevel's fangs into a jar with a thin membrane lid over the course of two hours when Cyris and Atlas were in Connar's office playing with the androids whilst Venas hovered her view over the city centre.

"That should be good, we've got the horse ready for the procedure," said another.

"This snake produces a surprising amount of venom. Almost a full litre.

"Ready to inject."

Venas knew the process of making anti-venom was time-consuming, she wished that the process could be quicker but it usually takes six months to make anti-venom with normal earth snakes. What if snakes like Slevel were different? What if it took longer. And if it didn't take longer than six months, it was still a long wait.

"What am I going to do now?" Venas mumbled. She looked at her hands and her forearms and the red marks left from tugging on the building. She felt like her skin was being ripped out of her. All the people staring at her when she was holding it up to save whoever was still inside.

"You need the anti-venom to turn back don't you, I

hear it takes quite a lot of time to make, you didn't tell him did you?" Cyris coughed as he approached to join her.

"It takes six months... I didn't tell him, it's all part of keeping it a secret," she said with concerns.

"If it helps, instead of the horse, you can use me," he offered his fresh idea.

"You?"

"Yeah, I live in the forest, there's a lot of snakes there, I grew up with snake bits, I already have a strong immune system to snakes," he explained.

"But it depends on the snake, you've never been bitten by this one."

"Maybe it could work," he suggested, "otherwise, you won't be able to go home."

The decision was hard to make and the chances of turning back was uncertain but Christmas was close by and she needed to go to her Godmother's place. She's been worried sick this whole time. Now that the commotion with Slevel was over, she felt the city was safer, there was no need to worry about any more murderous snakes and flying skeleton heads on the loose apart from Slevel himself who was now locked up properly in a compact glass tank with a higher range of security to ensure that he doesn't escape and cause any more trouble. Venas wasn't so confident that Connar was capable of containing the demon and her next concern was:

"How are you guys gonna return to London?"

"We can return with you," Cyris answered.

"Can Atlas turn into a human, even if he can, it'd be

suspicious, we don't see a lot of people his size- he can be spotted easily."

"You have a point, how about we focus on how to turn you back, that seems more important at the moment."

"Since the venom killed everyone instantly after they were bitten, then how did you not die?" Atlas questioned.

"It's because I originally have immunity to poison and venom but since the venom was too strong, it started to mutate my appearance, looking like a mutant actually saved me," she answered, "all I have to do is take the venom out and hopefully, I'll b able to return to being a human again.

"Makes sense," Atlas stroked his chin. Then he had another question that wasn't related to the venom: "What... exactly are... these things, they don't smell like anything metal, how can metal be alive?" he scratched his curious head and rolled one of the androids over to observe it. It was white and blue and round. Glass eyes and stretchy arms.

"We are called androids," Cyrber announced, "unlike robots, we are programmed to learn and think for ourselves, we can socialise and solve problems by ourselves."

"Oh so artificial living beings," Cyris compared.

"Artificial intelligence," said Venas.

"That is correct, we are artificial intelligence, programmed to act like humans, I am the most humanoid android Doctor Armsward has ever created... that is, until he finishes what he's been working on for years now, I am just a prototype," Cyber walked over to the side of the office where a big plane of glass covered the wall. "This is what Doctor Armswards has been building," he switched on a button on a panel of controls next to it and the matt glass turned clear to reveal a series of mechanical appliances fixed to what looked like the inside of an unfinished human android. It was a full-sized human but all there was right now was metal wires, tubes and plates inside a silhouette of a human. It currently has no face. All the complex bits and pieces inside the shell connected to one another creating a sort of maze from its neck to its toes.

"This is incredible," said Venas.

"So you're telling me that this will look like a human when he's done," Atlas questioned.

"Yes, it will, you won't even be able to tell the difference," said Cyber.

"Are you sure you should be showing us this, it seems pretty confidential," Venas stated.

"It should be fine," Cyber assured.

Then, he pushed the button to dismiss the sight of the uncompleted android and suddenly jumped across the polished floors and beeped his way to connar's desk switching on the T.V. as it travelled from its hiding spot to the middle of the room, it displayed updates on today's highlight. The headlines of the fight between three mutants and a demon snake are not classified by the stereotypical British reporters as they believe that Slevel is a mutant too. They can not differentiate the difference between mutants and demons. Mutants are just humans, they were originally humans until some were more commonly born with an unusual source of genes and DNA that mutated their appearances and giving them supernatural powers. Over millions of years, as humans with mutations began to evolve, they were given the name "mutants" and were seen as different species of living beings as people refused to accept them as their own. Monsters and demons on the other hand have always been born with freakish features and most don't look human at all. They come from a different part of the universe, Andromeda in the Planet Ervanna and some have a natural thirst for killing mortals; this was mainly with the older generations of demons.

With that said, everyone looked up at the big screen that forced their eyes to look its way as it moved closer to the floor.

"Today we are in Nottingham Old Market Square where we witnessed an astounding performance of three mutants fighting alongside each other against the dangerous snake mutant that caused hundreds of deaths before today and it seems that he used some sort of black magic to freeze the entire city," the lady looked around at the melting ice, "... which soon explains how the Lakeside Arts was frozen on the 2nd of December when Doctor Lucy Lawson and her crew discovered the mutant Atlas Silver who is identified as a former warrior from the ancient Muman's war," the news reporter just kept talking and talking as if she was reading a script that was placed off camera but she wasn't. It felt like she was ready to cite a whole book but things became more interesting when she spoke of the devil that arrived at the scene of Market Square amongst the police cars and firetrucks. Venas could see the area from the office window where the plane of ground was good as new but the Christmas Market was still destroyed. The Oracles only repaired major damages.

"Doctor Lucy Lawson, what are your opinions on this topic now that we know it must have been the snake mutants who froze the lake, why would a mutant capture his own kind and freeze him and how old do you think he is?" Every time someone called Slevel a mere mutant, Cyris felt a tingle of rage storming through his fists.

"Hello, my name is Lucy Lawson, head of the research department of unknown creatures, we discovered Atlas Silver in the Lake of Nottingham university and thought it was strange how the lake was frozen but now you know why, once found that Atlas was here, we rushed her as soon as possible but it seems like we are a step behind," she finished her unnecessary statement of repeating things that the news lady had just said.

"And even if you were able to catch up to Atlas Silver, what would you do, he is a strong mutant, the pink mutant by his side was strong enough to repel every single bullet the police force shot, who do you think she is, have you ever seen her before and what about the blue one beside her?" she put her mic to Lawson's face.

"No, I've never seen them before, none of them showed up on our records of mutant identifications although the records are quite old, which must mean there's a chance that more mutants, a whole tribe of them must exist somewhere in the country and we are going to find them and contain them all to make our society a safer place," she planned.

A shot of rage was about to burn the T.V. into millions of spectacles until Venas caught Atlas's shot of power and dismissed it immediately. The ringing noise packed a punch into their ears as Atlas was triggered but Lawson's absurd choice of words.

"Atlas, what are you doing!?! you need to control your anger!" Venas bellowed, waiting for him to finally calm down from his heavy breaths.

"Oh right," Atlas tried to say calmly but then Cyris's head was also filled with anger, so much that he charged at the T.V with no question of the result. It was a good thing Atlas caught him by the armpits as his legs were still in the air trying to kick Lawson on the screen. He raised his fists in the air and rambled.

"That woman needs to clean her mouth, I know worm mud can go nicely on that old face of hers, you old hag!!!" Cyris commented with the same source of fury inside of his head. It wasn't hard for Atlas to keep Cyris from punching down that T.V. but he kept wiggling about.

"No, attacking the T.V. isn't gonna do anything, we can't afford to break anything here!" Venas yelled.

"What do I do then, go down to the city centre and give her a personal beating," he stopped wiggling about.

The three of them were taken by surprise when Connar Armswards butted in.

"I believe you are wrong, we need to remember that the species of mutants too evolved from us humans, it was their supernatural powers and mutated appearances that made society think they're dangerous when really, they are like us, they can communicate with us like normal living beings and they can be kind and understandable."

"Then explain why Atlas was ready to attack the police force?" Lawson argued.

"Because mutants have been treated like animals and science experiments for a long time, they feel threatened by us therefore he wouldn't have wanted to attack if the police hadn't threatened him with their weapons."

"Then he should've communicated with them," Lawson suggested.

"Do you think he will be listened to, he is still in the phase of a warzone, he was frozen in ice since the war that's exactly five hundred years," Connar made his point.

"We are still concerned about the snake mutant-" Lawson started but Connar interrupted her.

"The snake was a demon, it was no mutant, he had no traits that represent that of any mutant or human," he said.

"That Lawson is a real grumpy lady," Cyris clarified, "talking trash."

"He's defending us," Atlas realised that he was closer to the stage of giving Connar a chance to trust him, but it still wasn't safe to completely trust him in his chaotic mind. He is still holding Cyris by the armpits and finally puts him down.

Whilst Atlas and Cyris were committed to small talk about humanity, Venas screwed her eyes to the view outside. Connar's office was on the eighteenth floor therefore she was able to sight Connar very quickly although she could not see a lot of detail; there was one thing she could see very clearly. A source of dark red and black clouds running through the ground and cars, circling the people unnoticed. No one was noticing the faint ominous clouds fuming in and out of Market Square.

It looked like it was trying to track something down like a dog sniffing for clues. I stopped. And suddenly wiggled its way towards the direction of Connar's department building. Venas watched it helplessly and clueless of what it was, it disappeared amongst the buildings once it got closer and closer. She could sense an element of power from its presence. She shook her head of realisation.

It's one of the Oracles, she thought, and it's getting closer, if it's a demon then it's looking for Slevel. She jumped from the window and abused the automatic door to open it swiftly leaving Cyris and Atlas confused and dazed.

> "Where the hell is she going?" Cyris questioned.
> "It must be important, we follow her," Atlas replied.

Cyris nodded. Cyber decided to follow them too. Atlas followed her scent past the corridors of the offices of Zara, Serena and Cody who all darted their confused heads to the window sighting Venas dashing towards the stairs, then Atlas, then Cyris and Cyber who was last. They were busy watching the live news but their actions of rushing across the hallways concerned them. The corridors were long and had white walls and sea-blue carpets soon tampered on before Venas reached more double doors that led to the brightly lit stairs. She took out her amulet and it was glowing brighter now that she's learnt, her oracle glows in the presence of another, specifically an Oracle of the sword of Jade Dragon. Instead of going down the stairs like a normal human being, she leapt straight down the middle until she reached floor sixteen grabbing the railing to stop her fall and continued to rush. Swung the double doors open and made a sharp left turn. Floor sixteen was where the workers stored Slevel. Even if it was highly secure, with the power of an Oracle, almost anything is possible, including the ability to free him and restore his power. The glow got stronger. The rest of them blindly trailed after her into the storage room of Slevel where she meets the gloomy fumes of red shifting its focus from Slevel's tank to the barging doors that swung open all the way. It was already here and it was about to free him. What was that about trusting Connar to contain Slevel? She huffed and puffed under her white mask. The room was relatively dim and all the room had was the tank, a table occupied with lots of lab tech and lockers. The door closed behind her and opened again after Atlas stormed in. they all stared at the cloud of red fumes until it started to speak with what sounded like a middle-aged lady.

"Stay away from him!"

The lady ignored her at first.

"Look at you, the poor Slevel, once all-powerful and mighty, now weak and lost- locked up by humans... you even lost your Oracles to this pathetic little girl," she looked at Venas through the darkness. The clearest feature she could see was her luminous white eyes glaring at her. Venas shot a blast of power splitting the cloud in half and back again.

"Step away from the tank, he can't talk anyway so there's no point in trying," she demanded.

"My my, this one has a tone, look at those eyes, they do look delicious," she chanted.

"You eat eyes? What the heck are you?" said Cyris.

She hovered up and down in breathing motion and morphed into the gloominess of the dim lights revealing the shadow of a lady. Her appearance through the dark was mortifying to the naked eye and got worse as right pointy things started growing out of her back like the devil's wings. Eight spider legs. There was no light at all to see clearly, her face. Cyris tried to switch on the lights but the bulbs shattered before they arrived. They could hear disturbing insect noises as the lady transformed. The cloud of fumes were still lingering behind her, steaming out of her body. Slevel hissed like an innocent snake.

"Don't worry, once he turned back into a snake he's lost all his memories," she said, "he won't be of any use to me anymore... he's useless to me now," she gradually came closer, she got closer and stroked venas's chin with her long nails, she could feel her trembling. Cyris was ready to attack but Atlas stopped him, his facial expression said 'wait'.

"I did tell him to get rid of you when he found you in London two years ago but he was waiting until you had the sword of Jade Dragon, otherwise, I'd slaughter you ages ago," she circled around her. "Not to mention you already have one... very powerful gem on you, I'd kill you myself right now if it wasn't for orders."

"Order? Who's orders?" She lifted her head and tensed her shoulders.

"Oh, I must not say," she chuckled.

"What are you here for then?"

"To check up on my future opponent, of course, you're more special than you know... my name is Valdina... remember me, I'll be waiting by the embryo... for you and your Oracles."

She vanished in the air again and stormed away. Venas ran after her before she disappeared for good.

"What? Embryo? What embryo?"
"She got away?" Cyris whined.
"She looks like bad news," said Atlas.

Venas looked back at Slevel and didn't know if she could believe her when she said that he's lost his memory. She gazed at his beady reptilian eyes as he hissed. He gazed back at her and coiled up into sleep.

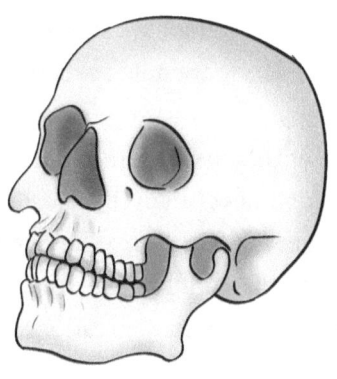

Flame 15

Goodbye

"Judging by the reactions of the horse, the anti-venom will be ready in three months," Connar estimated, "but it will not be needed during the time being so he will store it by freezing it until it is of use."

Connar didn't think that it was needed but Venas was in a rush. Three months is way too long, Christmas will be long gone by then and school would've started. She hid her disappointment but Connar could see something was up.

"That's better than usual," she commented.

"It is, it's a lot quicker than the usual process, we'll have it stored for usage in the far future- the crowd downstairs has dialled down but it still would be safe for you to head out."

"You have your company spread across England right?" Venas asked.

"That's right."

"And one of them is in London."

"Yes."

"How about you take them back home, would you be able to do that?"

"You're asking me for a favour?" he assured what he's hearing was correct.

"I know it's a long way, two hours but it'd be the easiest way for them, especially when Atlas is a mess to hide from the public- I'll get him to control himself," she promised.

"Why are you so determined to get them back to London?"

"Because that's their home, they belong there."

"And you don't, where are you going to go?"

Cyber was in the middle of their serious conversation switching his eyes back and forth between Connar and Venas as they talked.

"I... I have somewhere else to go."

Connar didn't need long to think, he took on the favour but not right now. Venas wanted to try Cyris's offer of turning her back into her original self using his blood instead of the horse since it will be a bit of a wait. She secretly took a sample of the venom from the experiments with her celestial and had Cyris inject it into his bloodstream after encountering Valdina. He's taken several doses over the course of two hours after asking Connar to take them back to London via private transport instead of the public railway service, there wouldn't be many people on the train at this time but it would still be safer to drive and keep them away from the public after what just happened today. That problem was solved followed by a phone call from her Godmother to notify her that the City will be reopened tomorrow since there will be no danger approaching in the meantime. This was earlier confirmed by Connar whilst he was on the news being verbally assaulted on live T.V. by the grumpy Lawson who showed more attitude off-camera during the evening.

"Where do you need to go?" he questioned, "I can book you a ride."

"Thank you but I can get there by myself," she replied honestly, "I need to discuss something with Cyris first before he goes," she lastly gave him a bow. It was a simple habit from living in Ervanna for so long, the manners and cultural rituals were still engraved into her mind. Everyone she sees greets and thanks, she bows to. It was a sign of good manners and respect. This meant that she was truly grateful for his help.

"What's this?" Connar was half-blood, his father was British and his mother was Korean and Venas's bow gave him a sort of Asian culture feel.

"Thank you... thank you for helping us, thank you for helping Atlas- for trying to clear his name, for having us here," she appreciated.

"The pleasure is mine," he replied with a smile.

The night sky grew gloomier after the clock struck midnight. Cyris and Atlas had to say goodbye to Venas after giving her a sample of his blood with Slevel's venom in it. It was dark outside but it wasn't hard to tell that his blood was blue. He gave her a warm hug and didn't want to let go.

"Thank you, I couldn't have got Atlas back without your help," he said.

"No problem," she replied.

"Sure you're not going to come along and meet the rest of us?"

"Maybe another time."

She turned to Atlas who cast a shadow over her standing in front of the brightly lit windows at the back entrance of the building where a white car was waiting for them. Venas wasn't sure if he wanted a hug or something because it seemed he wasn't quite sure how to express his gratitude. He was wearing a big black coat that Connar had his workers order in his size. A mutant can still get cold after all. Venas hugged him, wrapping her short arms around him. He hugged her back and thanked her for saving him.

"Thank you," he was still sorry for attacking her at first sight but she forgave him for that long ago. "Until we meet again," he said.

"You'll be good for the driver right, control yourself," she replied as he and Cyris jumped into the white car. Cody and Connar took the front seat and because of Atlas, Connar chose a much bigger car to drive instead of his usual Audi. They all waved goodbye to Venas who soon disappeared amongst the gates that automatically shut behind them as they set out.

"Get ready fellas, this is gonna be a long ride," Cody noted, "you guys can play around with the ipads under the seats, they got games."

Cody showed them how to use them and soon they were busy with lots of mini-games like children whilst Serena escorted Venas near the border of the city.

"Are you sure you don't want me to drive you any further? Where exactly are you going?" she leant over her steering wheel as Venas stepped out of the fancy car.

"It's okay, it's not far from here so I'll just walk- thank you," she said.

Serena respected her decision and started the engine before driving back to the city and calling it a day. It was midnight so everything was pitch black, lit with a few spots of street lamps. It was easy to travel around during the night. There were fewer people, less traffic and it was dark so it'd be easy for her to go unnoticed. She followed the tram tracks all the way to Toton Lane and passed the side of the motorway stepping into the woods as she leapt from tree to tree into West Park. West Park was a very big grassy area for playing sports and walking dogs but since it was midnight, the park was empty and seemed even a little bit haunted.

Once Venas arrived at her destination, she walked past the two cars parked in front of her Godmother's house and hid behind the garage door next to the garden gates. All the lights were off inside the house in Shillway Court, house number nineteen. All the curtains were pulled, everyone inside was probably asleep now that it was one a.m in the morning. She unloaded her pockets and found her bag and suitcase of which she shrunk to save herself from carrying them.

She was hopeful that Cyris's blood sample acting as antivenom would be enough to help get rid of the venom inside her body and reverse the mutation of her appearance, lastly being able to set Petal free as she has always been in her Oracle working hard to give her the strength to not be killed but the toxins. Venas popped the lid open and swirled half of it out from the test tube with her two fingers clasped together like when she performs her celestial enchantment. The substance enters her body through the skin like an injection and surprisingly enough, she was already feeling something in her arm where Phizzor bit her. She changed her clothes to a fresh white jumper with a pink logo, denim jeans and grey trainers. Before she saw changes in her body. Even though she felt a little something, there were still no visible reactions. The first ten minutes let her down since there was still no sign of her hair and skin changing colours. She touched her scars every two minutes but they remained. She slid to the ground with her back pressed against the garage wall and wiped her faint drops of tears after twenty minutes of sitting there in the dark waiting. As time grew, her eyes began to weep more, burying her head in her arms wrapped around her legs. The goal was simple but it was also very frustrating. Maybe she had to wait longer, yes that must be it. Medicine doesn't work immediately, it takes time to digest and enter the body before doing its job so she just had to wait. Just a little bit longer. She waited and waited until she felt dreary, still thinking about seeing her Godmother after these past few days of struggles and exhaustion that she had never asked for. She wished to be somewhere warm and comfy unlike the caves, all dirty and damp, some parts smelled of rotten eggs. She never wanted to be a mutant in the first place, she wished she had never been part of the danger where she nearly died like in the battle with Tao Shi, Slevel's snakes nearly killed her. When she came back to Earth, she thought that the action and adventures were going to be over because all of this was too tiring for her. Her head felt heavy, her ears sensed calming cricket calls. Her eyelids went up and down, the last thing she saw was a light snowfall. A snowflake fell on the tip of her ears and melted away. Her Oracle produced enough energy to prevent the snow from freezing her in her sleep as it fell like rain throughout the night.

Flame 16

A White Christmas

Dogs and their owners were out for walks on the snowy paths of the neighbourhood after a full night of snowfall. Children woke up with the energetic desire of playing in the snow that plastered the entire county in one night.

"Mum, look at all that snow!!!" cried a little girl who swissed the curtains to the side to reveal the gift from the sky.

She popped her warm gloves on and scooped up a handful of snow from her window ledge patting it into a ball.

The roads were salted to melt the snow but it stood 6 inches on the surface therefore people cancelled any road trips as it was too dangerous to drive on for now. Pigeons shook the branches and struggled to find any food besides the frozen red berries growing on bushes on the side of the footpath. Every leaf and green you could see were topped with a layer of white, the grass was frozen solid and the heating bills in every house were rising even though the British sun was beaming brightly from above. It glared on the snow and reflected the light back into the sky. Christmas lights, outdoor decorations and iconic Christmas character statues greeted visitors for a festive visit before Christmas day.

At ten O'clock, Venas's Godmother, Ciara Lu promptly popped on her trainers in her cosy robe to fetch something from her orange and spotted a girl sitting on the ground with her head on her arms wrapped around her knees. She approached the side of the garage and said:

"Oh my, Oh my goodness!"

Venas was still sleeping whilst sat away from the snow, her Oracle created a circle around her where the snow did not touch. She was still dry but a little bit cold from being outside the entire night. Ciara didn't notice it was her own Goddaughter until she swept away from her silky black hair and tilted her head to see her pale peach face. In shock, she quickly rushed back inside to grab a blackey and knocked her husband out of bed to help carry Venas into the house. The worried and confused looks on their faces wouldn't know how to give the news to her mother if anything were to happen to her. Instantly, she tucked her into a double bed in the bedroom that she had prepared for her since she expected her to arrive days ago.

On the bright side, Venas had already turned back into her human form and just in time before she was spotted in the daylight.

"Mum, when's Venas gonna get here? She was meant to be here like three days ago," Lily, Ciara's ten-year-old daughter questioned after strolling out of her room in her pyjamas. Before her mother closed the door, Lily peeked in and saw someone lying in the bed under the creamy-white duvet, "is that her mummy, when did she even get here, last night?" she said excitedly. Her mum put her finger to her mouth to keep her quiet as her dad went back to sleep after bringing Venas in.

"You'll see her when she wakes up, now go brush your teeth before you eat breakfast," she whispered."

"Okay," she obeyed as her mum gently closed the creaky doors and walked downstairs on the soft and fluffy carpets before.

She entered the kitchen on the left to boil the kettle and make some prompt breakfast. In this house, there was Lily, her mum, dad and her twelve-year-old brother who was also awake in his bed on his phone playing mobile games under his covers. There were four bedrooms, three toilets, a living room, kitchen and one glass warehouse at the back of the house connected to the dining room with a small chandelier. The kitchen had shiny black tiles, the walls were white apart from the corridor by the front door, they were pastel green with white tiles on the floor. The carpet upstairs was grey and the ceiling had the texture of which looked like frosted icing that hardened in the freezer. Although every single door upstairs and down was loud and creaky, the place was calm and peaceful, once the cooking was finished that is. Lily was an adorable ten-year-old girl. She had long and silky black hair like Venas although she usually has it flowing down her back rather than in a ponytail. She was up to Venas's eyes, she loved to dance and go swimming therefore was expected to grow pretty tall, probably taller than Venas when they grow up. She was slim and had long legs.

Thirty minutes later, the coldness in Venas had left her body replaced with the warmth of the radiators by the window where the bed was pushed against. Her eyelids felt replenished when she opened them to see the ceiling above her. She immediately knew where it was and bolted up to the mirror desk in front of the bed to check on her appearance. The beating of her heart plummeted wildly until she saw her reflection and pulled a face of relief as she felt her hair and her scars that disappeared along with her pink skin, white hair and glowing white eyes. All the scars on her face were no longer there anymore. She pulled up her jumper sleeve and the scratches were gone. Then she reached into the neck opening to see whether the snake bite was gone and the last drop of concerns flew out of her mind when they were no more. The blood sample worked! But she wasn't even able to tell Cyris about the great news, he didn't have a phone. He must've returned to Epping by now and she had no idea whether she was going to see them ever again. Other than thinking about Cyris and Atlas, she was also thinking about the reaction her Godmother had when she found her or was it someone else that found her? Now that she was back to normal again, she needed to check up on one more thing as a puff of clouds popped into the air, Petal appeared on the bed from her amulet. She was in good health and was overjoyed to see that Venas was alright. If only she could ask Petal how she was feeling and get a definite answer but instead she could only nod.

Through the tiny gap between the curtains, Venas saw something bright that reminded her of what she saw last night before she fell asleep on the cold pavement. She bounced onto the bed again and whipped the curtains apart to set her eyes on the amazing showcase of snow. Being further away from the equator, there was more snow here than she'd ever seen in London. But of course, this amount didn't compare to how much snow there was in Ervanna. Ervanna snowed mountains before she left. Petal leapt onto the window sill to join her on the spectacular view but it was a shame she could not come out to play with Venas as she did in Ervanna although she thought Lily would love to play with her. Speaking of which, Venas had not been here in three years, she hadn't seen Lily in two years and now that she was finally here, she was so eager to see her since they get along extremely well despite the five-year age gap. Scanning her eyes around, she noticed there was a spot on the pavement unoccupied by snow. One of the cars was missing, her Godmother must be out but there was so much ice on the road.

But the roads so slippery and full of snow, she thought. Maybe she was driving really slow to avoid slipping. After that, she saw Lily playing outside in her snug winter coat, gloves, and wellies that her mum told her to wear before she rushed outside. She was playing with two other boys that were younger than her, her cousins and they were making the iconic snowman everyone knows and loves. Lilly looked like she was having so much fun, she too noticed Venas glazed through the window and waved energetically. She rushed back into the house, took off her wellies before she did and ran upstairs to get her. Petals zoomed back into her Oracle as soon as Lily opened the door.

"Venas you're up, quick, come out and play in the snow," she said.

"But I haven't eaten breakfast yet," she climbed off the bed.

"Oh, mum left some on the table, you can eat that first," she suggested.

"Okay."

Venas brushed her teeth and carefully popped a brown contact lens one her one red eye hoping that Lily didn't notice it. She was so excited, Venas doubt that she saw it. She went downstairs, fetched some chopsticks to finish the food that was left on the table and some with still in the pan on the gas stove, still warm and very tasty. She hadn't eaten a lot in the last two days and now, she could finally feast on some home cooking.

"Have you finished?" Lily came back in, you can see her breath smoking out of her mouth.

Venas nodded, popped on her ski coat printed with blue and purple patterns, gloves and her stylish, waterproof ankle boots. She followed Lily outside to join her cousins who decided to launch snowballs at each other every ten minutes. Dog walkers that passed by were all wrapped up in warm clothing and tried keeping up with their overly enthusiastic dogs as they tugged on their leashes, jumping around in the snow. Maybe they're never seen snow before. The road was free to slide on since not a lot of people planned to drive anywhere. What a perfect place to take out a mini sledge and slide around in it. Venas doesn't really remember the last time she built a snowman but she didn't just want to build a snowman, instead, she tried something else. Some with a twitchy nose, cute beady eyes, in this case, buttons and two long ears sitting on the top of its head.

"It's a bunny!" Lily and her cousins guessed.
"But it's missing a tail," said one cousin.
"Oh… Ummm," Venas took two handfuls of snow and patted it gently to make the tail. She fixed it to its bottom.
"Luckily there's carrots in the fridge," Lily stuck a baby carrot into the bunny's mouth. She wiggled it in to make it secure.

"There, now it's complete," she said proudly, after two hours of building it.

The snow bunny was just as big as her when she sat next to it to take a picture after splashing some blue, yellow, green and pink diluted acrylic paint on the ground surrounding it to make it look more artistic. They all had their picture taken with their snowy creations when Lily's mum finally came home from visiting her friends bringing back a bunch of tasty food such as cakes, biscuits, roast duck, chicken wings and they were all homemade. Lily's mum has an endless chain of friends and plans on having some of them around on Christmas Day. She carefully parked the car into the driveway and got out to see what the children were up to, praising them for the snow bunny and snowmen they built on the grass next to the parked cars.

She was also curious about how Venas got home last night and why she didn't knock on the door when she arrived telling her to never do that ever again. It worried her so much and gave her the chills when she found her on the ground.

"I'm sorry, I got here by taxi," Venas covered up.

"From the city, that must've cost a lot, how much was it, let me give you some cash," she popped into the house to find her purse.

"No, no, it's fine, I don't need it," she stopped her from taking the money out but she took it out anyways.

"Take it, take it, I insist."

"No, really, it's fine," but knowing Chinese parents, the parent always wins when it comes to giving children money.

Venas's mother told her she can only accept money when it comes in a red envelope but her Godmother just pushed the money right into her hands and left it there with no intentions of taking it back.

After a cold morning of playing outside, it was time to come back into the house for lunch. The meals in this house were more British than it is Chinese. There was homemade pizza with corn, chicken and a bunch of vegetables, roasted chicken wings and some stir fry. The table was long so it fit more food than needed. Lily and her cousins visited the fridge for apple juice and into the cupboards for forks and plates. Venas helped take the pizza out of the oven with the blue oven mitts dangling from the handle. She had never used the oven for dinner before. There was no oven in her house for that matter so she did not expect the piping hot flame of steam that exploded into her face when she opened the oven door. The steam flew out the window before she poked the oven mittens in to retrieve the pizza and set it on the table. All the kids in the house sat in the dining room to eat before heading to the living room for games. Games on the Wii console with a game of Mario kart and Wii sports.

When Venas's turn was up, she gazed outside the window and witnessed another snowfall dropping snowflakes on top of her snow bunny. The more she looked at it, the more she was reminded of the red-eyed bunny that Markcas had got him. The bunny that she spent barely a night with. She remembered the precious moment when Markcas was holding the furball in his long slim hands when he gave it to her. His face when he said it was for her and how close they've gotten in the last three months. They were able to see each other every single day when they were in Ervanna and now, it was the complete opposite. Well, at least until school starts. The winter holidays are three weeks long but it was longer this year due to school refurbishment. A source of vibration rang into her ear from her phone. It was on the table in the dining room. She leapt from the black couch that everyone was bundled up in to see what it could be. A message on social media. She clicked on it and it was a picture from Markcas. The picture of which Erra took of them when they were with the bunny. She gazed at the photo and admired it for so long that she forgot to reply when Lily notified her that it was her go on the Wii. Venas double tapped on the message and turned the phone off instantly

"Coming," she said and took the Wii remote without replying whilst Markcas on the other side was waiting for her to say something. He laid on his bed and waited for a while now but nothing happened.

"Maybe she's busy," he thought, "but it says she read it..." then he saw the heart that she left on the message when she double-tapped it and sent him away into shyness. Markcas laid on his side to admire the photo a bit more and wondered what she was doing right now. He missed her.

Flame 17

Cleo's message

Christmas day came closer and closer as the 25th was just around the corner. Today is Christmas Eve. If this was a British household, then the Christmas tree would be sitting on top of a large mountain of wrapped gifts and bows sadly, but it wasn't. The outside of the house may look very festive but the inside had just a tree with baubles and tinsel and nothing else. At Christmas, Chinese people, and many other Asian countries don't really go all out like the British do, spending a whole load of money on each other and going Christmas shopping. Venas never understood why British family members spend so much time and money buying a load of presents for each other and especially the wrapping. Think about all the paper that is wasted. Her mother would never allow Venas to buy her gifts for any occasion because she says:

"It's a waste of money."

Whenever she gets a wrapped present, she is always careful when she opens it without tearing the paper so that she could use it for some kind of art or something. Throwing it away is just not right. The only gift-giving in this house with Chinese visitors here was food. Common fruits like apples, that symbolise good health and safety because of what the word 'apple' sounds like in mandarin or mandarin oranges and pears. The form of gift-giving that wasn't edible was going out shopping on Boxing Day, yes, the day after Christmas. That's when all the children in this household get their holiday presents. Going out to the shopping centres and picking out what everyone really wants. Usually, Christmas for Venas was just her mother having two days off from work and having a fancy seafood dinner. Speaking of which, tonight's Christmas Eve dinner was served as the stream from the food travelled all over the house. But it's not the dinner we're focused on here at the moment. It was Venas's concerning expression that's getting our attention now. Venas thought that all her worries were over with the fighting and the magic, she thought that but then she remembered Valdina and the words she said to her about waiting for Venas and her Oracles. Where exactly did Valdina expect to meet her? Venas didn't know what she even looked like since it was dark and gloomy when they encountered paths. All she saw was eight creepy legs poking out of her back, her expressive eyes and her dark red colours fuming around her.

Before dinner, she had her flute on the bed and because she hadn't used it since the attack of living corpses, it has been stored in her Oracle ever since. Today she took it out to have something to fiddle with as she liked to spin it around like a bow staff. The butterfly tassel on the end of it follows and gets messy after a while of Venas spinning it. Unexpectedly, she saw something white inside it through the holes. She took it out and it was a small piece of paper, a scroll rather, that someone had rolled up and slotted in.

"What in Ervanna is this?" She muttered.

It was tiny when she found it but after unrolling it, it wasn't so tiny after all. She scanned from top to bottom, right to left recognising the writing as Chinese seal script language.

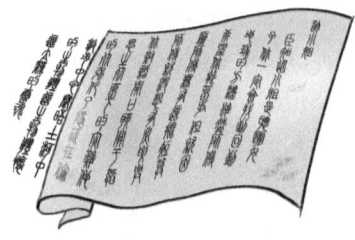

"How did this get in here?" she questioned and peeked inside the flute hole to see if there was anything else hiding in there but the scroll was all there is. She tried to read it. Translating the writing in her head, she whispered it to herself after staring at it for the longest time:

"Dear Miss Xoular, I know that you are a smart girl and you WILL find your way home to Terra eventually though Master wishes for you to stay and because he never intended for you to go, he's never opened up to tell you anything that we've been discussing since Fujimura's death. His death has caused growing concerns for the Warring States, the Land of Oracles… his death strengthened an organism hidden in the River Thames of Central London, the embryo containing the soul gathering of his older brother, Tai Shi, also known as Tai Wei… it was had just been activated not long ago and will take nine months to grow as his soul gather is complete and he grows a new body which means he'll look completely different than his former self… " Venas paused, she still hadn't mastered the art of reading and writing seal script so it took her a while to finish the letter. "… I'm telling you this so you can be prepared not to stop it now because there's currently a tight seal around it placed by his companions and right now it's invisible to the human eye... you have to take control of it when the seal is weak because Tai Wei has two of the Oracle of Jade Dragon and this is a good chance to retrieve them, to stop him from murdering any people... there is another Nevealean Monster named Slevel Fumata who is one of the demons responsible for his embryo maintenance- you have to make it there when he emerges, any time stalled will cause great danger to the city... it's also important that you don't expose yourself..."

Of course, this one tiny strip of paper isn't going to hold all this information on one side. It was a celestial message therefore more writing extended off the paper in the form of floating ink in the air. She read the last paragraph of the letter:

"... remember, it's not just him and Slevel, there are more monsters rogue on Earth, being unable to track them down from Ervanna, I'll leave the task to you, I know you are very capable and judging by how much you've improved in the last three months, you can retrieve the Oracles, kill Tai Wei and shatter his soul because immortals will have no trouble surviving anything unless their soul leaves their body and is destroyed- remember, he will have a shadow diamond- it's more powerful than dark crystal, do not destroy it before you kill Tai Wei otherwise he will not have the power to create portals to come back to Ervanna, if he stays on Earth, he will cause serious eradication to your city and any property that he touches. I know you're going to be on Earth when you read this, so good luck, your friend, Cleo."

The floating ink flew back into the paper and left her scratching her head with eyebrows wrinkled in all directions, her first reaction was:

"What?" then she said to herself, "this is from Cleo," she turned the paper around, examining it as if she was expecting something else to be on the back like a school test paper, "what on Earth is this crazy monkey talking about?" she whispered in confusion. This letter sounded like Cleo was giving her an important quest, which indeed it was. "So he wants me to kill him, and if I don't manage to kill him, I spare the shadow diamond or else he's gonna stay on Earth… but if it's the diamond that makes him so powerful then I'd need to destroy the it to kill him because then he'll be weak, monsters are weak, they don't have celestial powers… but if I don't kill him and retrieve the gems, he's gonna go back to Ervanna, " she mumbled to herself… "am I really going to face off with another demon," she put her forehead on her hand and thought about it for a moment. She never wanted to put herself in such danger. She didn't want to have a face-off with the former King of Neverlight, Akirou's father. She also wondered why Akirou is still the Crown Prince of Neverlight and not King. She doesn't know how things work in Japan's Land of Demons but in China, the son for sure takes his father's place as King immediately after he passes away. There is no delay, therefore, it was at that moment, Venas felt a spec of light switch on above her head. It was obvious

Akirou not becoming King foreshadowed Tai Wei returning hence the embryo Cleo mentioned. Why did she not see this before? But Master Ocean was already expecting this to happen, he had predicted at the very beginning that Tai Wei wasn't going to give up on his target even when he dies. If immortals are not killed in the correct manner their soul and maybe their memory will live on and enter the vessel prepared by a third party gathering the soul because it will be shattered and spread across the sky. Gathering one's soul is not as easy as it sounds. It sounds like one uses celestial to collect it like apples but it takes a lot of time. If the original body is intact, the process is a lot faster than if the body was no longer usable, to find a new body that was compatible with the soul's power. It was difficult but it looked like Tai Wei's third party had already settled it but why was it in London. London out of all places, for the river? Because the River Thames is quite a big river... but rivers are everywhere. There is plenty of water around the Island of Neverlight. The thing is, there are more people there with celestials who can destroy the plan and since Slevel is the one who was responsible for the placement of his embryo, he hid it in London and Master Ocean still managed to locate it. He located it after a long and dedicated search but how did he do it? Well, He is a professional at magic therefore, he has his ways, all this power and he still couldn't grant Venas's wish to create an all-powerful portal to go back home. They say adults have their reasons so does Master actually not know how to make portals or was he faking it? Was he pretending to avoid the question? It was quite obvious to Cleo that Master didn't want or ever intend for her to return.

Suddenly, the mortifying voice of the red lady rang in her head.

"My name is Valdina… remember me, I'll be waiting by the embryo… you and your Oracles."

She was telling Venas to meet her at the river? That must be it. The issue was: which of her two identities is she meeting her with, Venas as a human or a mutant, she must know who she is as a human.

. Since Slevel's venom is what mutated her image then if she wanted to turn back, she'd have to have a sample of it… but instead, she only has a sample of the antidote. The antivenom isn't of any use anymore.

"If Tai Wei's gonna be in a different body, will the body be of a human or a demon… wait I'm thinking about it like I'm actually gonna go deal with it…" she said to herself, "heck no, I ain't dealing with this." She grabbed her duvet and buried herself under it. This was not what she wanted to be concerned about during the holidays where she's meant to have fun and not think about life problems like these. She peeked out of the covers to have a breath of fresh air before Lily came knocking on the door to call her downstairs. Lily wanted to play some games or something before they went to sleep. It was seven p.m. and it was time for Lily's cousins to go home whilst they engaged in some drawing. HB pencil and colouring pencils scattered across the dining table. Venas didn't really know what she wanted to draw, just some characters from her imagination or maybe the ones she met from the Warring States. Prince Emerald, Master Ocean, Cleo, Lu Wei, Lee... Markcas. Well, she met Markcas on Earth before she left for Ervanna. It wasn't too long ago since it all happened. But it felt like ages for Venas, every day was intense training until the academic year started. All the long training sessions of martial arts and magic had the ability to make ten minutes feel like ten hours.

"Who you drawing?" Lily hovered over the table to see what she was doing.

"Oh, just a few people."

"From your imagination?"

"Yeah," she covered.

"I like them, they look so pretty, I'm just trying to draw a face. The eyes are tough," pencils rolled off the paper as she lifted it up to show Venas her progress. "That one looks the best, he's good looking, " Lily pointed to Markcas on Venas's paper.

"Oh, really, I guess he is," Venas continued to scramble the pencil case of colouring pencils pretending to find a certain colour as she looked at him on the paper. He wasn't even coloured. Venas was just drawing with a plain HB pencil.

She rested her head on her hand with her elbow on the table and thought about what he was doing right now. His presence continued to cross her mind all night until tomorrow when Christmas Day arrived, sending children down the stairs from their bedrooms at seven a.m. in the morning to open their presents from Santa Claus and get everything that they asked for. Venas never had that magical childhood thinking that Santa was real. All the other houses around were festive with gifts whilst Venas was still in her bed, observing the letter that Cleo left her. Everyone else in the house was still fast asleep. She could see from the window into the living rooms of the houses across the road amongst the white trees. She could hear the happiness. The kids are having a joyful morning. A white Christmas, presents, happy family and soon visitors as robins fluttered by to perch outside her window.

"Hello little bird," she gently tapped her nail on the glass. The bird chirped and chirped.

Petal came out from the bed covers to greet the bird before it flew away. Maybe it got scared. Petal has been feeling a bit lonely in her Oracle, she wanted other animals to play with but she wasn't allowed to be seen by anyone making it difficult for her to socialise.

Venas kept staring at the letter non-stop. The thin brown paper looks as though it was stained with tea bags and the writing was so neat. It was interesting how the ink can float in the air like water that soon disappeared when the door flung open.

"Merry Christmas!!!" Lily greeted.

Venas put her finger to her lips.

"Shh... we need to be quiet, everyone's still sleeping," she said quietly.

"Okay," she shrugged.

The two girls slowly crept downstairs and opened the creaky kitchen door into the brightness of the morning sun reflected from the snow outside. Shortly after, the kitchen air was occupied with steam coming from their sizzling breakfast. It was a simple breakfast with slices of bacon, sausages, milk, cereal and Venas made some congee on the side. When she was eating she decided to call her mum to say Merry Christmas and text a certain someone. She's only been at her new school for one day so Markcas was the only one she knew.

"Merry Christmas," she typed and hit send before her Godmother opened the kitchen door and said morning before she took her phone out to send greeting voicemails through to her Wechat friends and family.

It was one message after the other and she was expecting visitors at the door in a few hours. Venas opened the fridge door that stood a head taller than her to see the prepared food for Christmas dinner but this wasn't all of it. There were more coming on the way. There were dumplings in the freezer, shrimps and buns. She took a small pot of yoghurt that was buried under a bag of pak choi and closed the fridge door. Her phone was lost amongst the fruits on the table so she forgot all about it when visitors came knocking on the door when the clock struck twelve. She forgot that she texted

Markcas and he was yet to reply but when he received it on the other end, Markcas was hovering over it with his cousins and his brother, opening their presents under the tree. Once he read it, he jumped up from the carpet and went onto the sofa to text back.

"Hey, Merry Christmas," he said... "have you eaten yet?" He followed up, noting that asking people if they've eaten is a way of showing that they care about each other is what he's learned from spending so much time with Venas and Erra.

He waited but there was no reaction from the other side.
Maybe she's busy, he thought. He dropped his phone on the couch and sat back down on the carpet for his mum to hand him his gift.

"Here you go dear," she said.
"Thanks, mum."

It was a busy day today, Lily's house was packed with people by the time the clock pointed to two O'clock. Close friends and family carefully drove over and cars filled the rim outside the house. Everyone had something in their hands. Leaves hit the cars as they sat on the footpath almost touching the bushes. They still had a top coat of thick snow on the roofs and on the front. Greetings were packed at the doorways as shoes started piling into a mountain on the floor after the children rushed into the house like it was a game of chase. One of the chubby little girls who was four years old just casually toddled along the table and grabbed the treats put on the side without a word and kept eating until her mother noticed and tried to take the treat away from her tight grip. She was about to start crying but kids will always be kids. The crying and cute eyes can not be the adult's weakness. The table was still empty with just a white table mat patted on top. The food was just to come. Dinner time was only four hours away giving the adults plenty of time to chat and catch up with each other and all the kids to play. Some brought their Ipads while others just turned on the t.v. to activate the Wii. It was like a party once Ciara slid open a box of wine bottles. Fancy wine ordered from France. Lily was having so much fun on the Wii with the other children, including her two cousins, she didn't notice Venas wasn't even in the living room. She was now in her room away from the noisiness. She closed the door to cancel out some noise and jumped onto her back to reply to her text message.

"I had lunch, dinner is still a while away, wbu," she typed.

{BEEP}

Markcas heard the notification pop up and felt his phone vibrate in his pockets when he was in his room using the new guitar picks his mum got him. He put the guitar back and slouched on his gaming chair as it rolled slightly backwards.

"I just had some lunch," he sent, "what did you get for Christmas?"

Venas rests her chin on her pillow.

"I didn't get anything."

"What? U didn't get presents?"

"We don't really do Christmas like you guys do, originally, we don't even celebrate it," she answered.

"Oh."

"We're going shopping on Boxing day, that's basically our form of getting presents," she added.

"What about Christmas dinner?"

"We just have seafood and other Chinese traditions on the table, like hot pot."

"Sounds yummy, we don't really have a lot of seafood in this house."

"Ashford is close to the sea, I'm pretty sure there's good seafood there."

"Probably, when you coming back?" he asked.

"The 7th of Jan, my train ticket lasts a month and school's not gonna start until Feb so maybe longer," she estimated.

"That's fair… you heard about the mutant incident, did you see anything yourself?"

"The part when the monster wrecked the train, yeah I saw it on the news," she lied.

"So u didn't see it in person?"

"No, why?"

"No, just wondering, but how u know if he's a monster?"

"Mutants don't look like that, they have human

characteristics since they evolved from humans and the one that attacked the train was freakish, most demons don't look human," she explained.

"Oh, right, I forgot about that bit… I was reading everything on the news, the reports were saying he's a mutant so I just thought that, then Connar Armsward followed up to say he wasn't."

"You read all of it, did you see it on t.v?"

"Just a bit, it seemed interesting, it's kinda like when Fujimura attacked all the schools in Ashford."

"Kinda?"

"Okay, the same. Good thing he's dead thanks to you."

"But it was terrifying."

"But it was worth it, hehe."

"I guess," Venas didn't want to expose herself as a mutant, she wanted to keep it a secret, a secret that only Cyris, Atlas and Kasey knows. It crossed her mind and now she was thinking about where Kasey has gone. He disappeared so suddenly. Maybe he was bored and he wanted to go home. Maybe he thought he was done with his intentions and went home. But what were his intentions?

"What u planning to do for the rest of the holidays?" Markcas typed.

"Oh, probably what my Godmother has planned like visiting her friends and oddly enough for her, going to the church on Sundays", Ciara was Christian herself and tended to take her children to the church every Sunday. Not the type of church where you sit in between the wooden benches in front of a tapestry and a Father. It was a musical type of church. A more modern kind. Their form of praying was singing, singing songs that relate to Jesus, God and the Holy Spirit. Venas came from Ireland, she was born there and went to school there until she was twelve and all the things she knew about Christians was what she learned from her primary school there. She used to sit out because her mum didn't want her daughter to be Christian but that didn't stop her from listening to what the teacher was teaching. Traditional Chinese people are mainly Buddhist. She was Buddhist herself but all the songs in the church were so heartwarming to listen to. They give her shivers the first time she heard them. They were sung in a live performance by really good singers amongst the Christian society. She wondered if Markcas was Christian. But that didn't really matter.

"Oh, I'm guessin she's Christian?" Markcas asked.

"Yeah, she is but the rest of us aren't, there's a youth centre for the children to hang out, I go there with Lily," she explained to him who Lily was prior to this chat.

The Youth club had snooker, games, basketball and football and they also prayed and sang with their own band at the end before their parents called them back to the main Church area where the middle part was for the staff to set out chairs one by one in front of a stage where the band stood on. There were also doughnuts and refreshments on the side.

"Oh, that sounds cool," he replied.

"Aren't u gonna go spend some time with ur family?"

"Well they're just chatting and my bro's playin football outside with my cousins, dinner's not until six so I have a while to just chill."

"I'm in my room, it's packed downstairs, I'll go down in a bit."

"Cool, that's fine…" he texted half of what he was thinking in his head, the rest of it hid away with his face blushing.

…

There was a lingering pause between the text. On Venas's side, her phone indicated that he was typing but nothing else went through. She waited a little while. Markcas typed promptly the words 'I miss U' but quickly pushed his thumb on the back button to erase it. He didn't know how to express himself and it took a while before Venas sent something through.

"Lily's callin me, I gotta go, I'll see u round. Bye :)" she slotted her phone under the bed covers and trailed after Lily down the stairs to engage in some games.

"Oh okay, bye :)" he replied but the message wasn't left on 'seen' then he continued to type: "hav a good one."

Lily called her to play and soon it was time for the big feast set on the table. All the piping hot food plastered the dining room with smoke and luxurious steam. The gas cookers could finally take a break from working for two hours straight but it was worth it. Because the table was rather small for everyone to sit down at once and eat together, the children went first whilst adults walked around and chatted in the living room. Decorative plates of dumplings, shrimps, clams, roasted chicken wings, cooked greens, chicken soup, spicy dips and some hot pot specials laid out on the table. It was absolutely delicious. A magnificent Christmas dinner, it was a great way to end the Christmas day.

Flame 18

The First Hour

Some time has finally passed and today is the very last day of the year. It's the day when people create their new year's resolutions and only keep up with them for one week or less and give up. Things like losing weight, going to the gym regularly or eating healthy, making more money, working hard and so on. Tomorrow is what gets people motivated and inspired to improve for the new year. Where they are ready to say goodbye to 2015 and welcome 2016 claiming that this year is going to be exciting and full of thrills. New calendars were already stuck up on the wall over the old ones and the clock was ticking closer and closer to midnight. Champagne to celebrate and fireworks at the stroke of midnight were all bursting inside everyone's minds. Even though Venas was going to watch the London countdown on T.V. live, the excitement was still there circling her. It's not every day she gets to stay up past midnight, new years day is the only time she's allowed to be up until two a.m. in the morning. Although she never minded her mum not allowing her to stay up late, she has grown a habit of it by now. Her brain usually wakes up at around seven every day, even if it wasn't a school day. Lily couldn't wait for the fireworks to start tonight but it's only halfway through the day so there was still some time to spare.

Unlike the days in Ervanna, days here felt like a timelapse video and Venas enjoyed it here. She enjoyed it but that never stopped her from thinking about the embryo hidden in the waters of River Thames. She kept trying to convince herself that it was none of her business. If Tai Wei were to be reborn and kill the people of London, she wouldn't be held responsible but she feels guilt knowing about the danger before everyone else did. What about Markcas, it doesn't seem that Markcas knew Cleo, they only met at the Queen Ocean's angelversary and that was it, they've never spoken to each other so she didn't think that Cleo would've given him a letter. It was just her. It was frustrating that the concern rummaged her head for so long. She wished she had read it after the holidays because no one wants to worry about anything during the holidays.

"Why did I have to read it?" she kept asking herself but it's not like she could do anything about it since there's a seal on it preventing anyone from harming it. So it would've made no difference whether she reads the letter now or later.

Today is a Saturday, Saturday the 31st and Ciara was currently working in the Chinese takeaway that she and her husband are running. They are working on the busiest day of the week on new year's eve. There was no expectation that they were coming home early tonight. But they will definitely make it for midnight. In the meantime, Venas was at home with Lily and her brother was in the living room with the sofa up against the T.V. He slouched on the sofa whilst gaming on his Ps4. so the living room was off-limits at the moment. There was a garden in the backyard. It had a round patch of grass surrounded by a flower bed with a trampoline on the right and an old shed on the left. The grass was lush and white, the snow still lingered until now. They played with the snow out front and most of the snow in the back was used for more snowy creations. It was fun but Lily didn't have the right gloves on like Venas did, Venas wore snowboarding gloves made for being in contact with the snow for long periods of time and Lily wasn't so her hands got cold fairly quickly.

"Here, you can wear mine," Venas took her gloves off and offered them to her.
"Thanks."

There wasn't much snow left but it was fun whilst it lasted. After thirty minutes in the backyard, things got a little bit boring when there was no one in the house besides the two girls and Lily's brother. What to do now?

"Well, I have all this," Lily dug into her box of fun things that she bought online with her mum's credit card, "there's kinetic sand, bracelet kits, nail stuff, sticker maker, slime kits, loom bands… and…" she rummaged, "… play dough."

"Kinetic sand?"

"Yeah, kinetic sand, there's also sand that gets all weird in the water and dries instantly after you take it out," she expressed and took out her box of sand that looked rather new.

"It's so colourful…" Venas thought she saw something wiggling sound on the ground outside the glass doors of the warehouse but it must've been her imagination.

"There's blue, purple, green… and pink, look," Lily took some out of the packet and moulded it before stretching it to watch the effects.

It was interesting, Venas didn't think it'd be all that amazing despite all the ads she's seen for it but again, she saw a tiny glimpse of something out the window. It didn't seem usual. She got up and watched out the window for a closer look but there was nothing.

"What you looking at?" Lily called from the dining table.

"Oh, nothing, it's nothing" she took a second look and sat back down, wrinkling her eyebrows in suspicion. It looked like a spider but… it was white. Could it be Kasey?

No, Kasey has black spiders. Since when were spiders white. Then again, it could just be her imagination. There are lots of things going on in her head, she wouldn't be surprised by now if she saw a flying pig... although, that wouldn't shock her. After entering the world of martial arts and magic, not a lot of things surprise her. It was normal to see things move by themselves and it was almost normal to hear animals talking to you like Cleo for example, it surprised her when she heard actual words flying out of that monkey's mouth. There still isn't an explanation for how Cleo is able to talk as if he were human himself. She looked back at the moments, the first time she met him after falling on the floorboards of Master's library.

"Ah, there you are." cheered an unfamiliar voice.
"Talking monkey!!!" she remembered grabbing the closest book, raising it up in the air as a source of useless defence.
"Yes, that is correct, I am indeed a talking monkey- very nice to meet you, I am JingFei. Jing of gold, Fei of fly but please, call me Cleo."

Her first reaction was hitting the monkey out hoping that this so-called dream would end sooner and then saying in her head that he looks like a child... but furrier. The monkey even gave himself an English name though he knows no English.

There's no such thing as talking monkeys, she thought. Well, now there is such a thing. She laughed at herself, she laughed at her past self when she first landed in Ervanna. It was a bit embarrassing actually. Everyone's embarrassed by their past but it was fun to look back on it. She recalled the time when she met Markcas at school when he was late to class. They sat on opposite ends of the classroom because the seating plan was set to alphabetical order.

The first person she met after landing in Ervanna was Prince Emerald when he found her amongst the Court garden bushes was not how she expected she'd meet a prince.

"You're awake, here, have some water," he handed her a warm cup.
"Who're you?" she remembered her reply.
"I thought your clothes looked untidy from the mud so I asked one of our Palace maids to change it."
"Palace maids?"

He was so kind and gentle but he was also strong. His strength was never exposed until he stood up to defeat the evil artificial blood elf that Tao Shi created. Then meeting Kayne who threatened her with his sword and his cold eyes at first sight, what was his problem?

"How'd you want her, your Highness? Dungeons for being insolent to you or punishment planks, also -for being insolent to you," said Kayne who stared coldly at her.
"Kayne, what are you doing, - Put that down," Emerald ordered.

Kayne had the same stare as Kasey; he was nowhere as scary as Kasey was. She remembered her first encounter with

Erra Stone outside his family's restaurant and being locked up in the dungeons with him. Getting to know him after waking up amongst the hay. She encountered Master Ocean after landing in his library from Celo's rescue. All this was three months ago? Why does it feel like it was years ago? She felt she's gotten so close to Erra and her relationship with Cleo was pretty cute, she loves that monkey. Cleo may be old but he's as energetic as a child. Her connection with Kayne was very confusing, she still thinks that he hated her ever since the moment she stepped foot on Ervanna. Prince Emerald is the reason why Kayne is nice to her... almost.

The Lake of Past crossed her mind before Akirou appeared in her visions. The son of Tai Wei. It doesn't matter how corrupt Tai Wei was, she still accepts Akirou as a friend. He's a shy boy, he is kind and helpful or is it because Venas saved him from the waters after Kayne left them there. He's an eel demon but he acts nothing like one. An electric eel-like him isn't supposed to touch others when he's in the water unless he wishes to kill them, he can actually survive in the water so when Kayne knocked him into the lake, he didn't panic to save himself. He just wanted to relax and hide away. He didn't expect someone, especially a mortal to come save him. He appreciated Venas for her kindness and diversity. He wanted to be friends with her. Venas was his first mortal friend and after returning to Nevelight Island, he's always missed her, he saw her as his big sister. But he didn't know that Venas is now back on Earth, she wasn't in Ervanna anymore.

If he's an eel descendant, then his father was an eel? Or

his mother could've been an eel. If Tao Shi was a lizard then it would be likely that he was a cold-blooded creature too. Something like a komodo dragon? A komodo dragon is very deadly and Venas has seen one before in London zoo. They have extremely poisonous venom and can kill a person with one nasty bit within hours. The Komodo dragons on Earth are already so deadly, she could imagine how strong Tai Wei's venom is, it could be five times stronger than Slevels. But now, he's going to be a completely different creature once he's reborn. Would it be a creature unfamiliar to the knowledge of Earth humans, some kind of demon from the Neverlights? Anything would be bad if it were to be altered and slotted into an embryo gathering the soul of a destructive demon. It can't get any worse than that but what was she to do? All this thought whilst Venas played around with the kinetic sand. She then thinks about her more recent encounters in Ervanna. Starting her training at Ninchanted Academy, the training wasn't intense like with Master Ocean but she quite liked it there. Getting to meet Lee's younger brother and Lu Kai, whose name reminded her of Lu Kai Yuan, Kyle who was one of Prince Emerald's personal guards. She could never put down the horror of witnessing his fall, how he left the world from Tao Shi's slaughter. Seeing people die in front of her was the most taunting thing she has ever experienced and she couldn't help but think she was next. The look in Kyle's eyes when he said goodbye like he knew he was going before it even happened. He knew that without a celestial, it was hard to survive in this world.

Demons like Tao Shi showed no mercy for people like him,

someone he sees as a weakling. The weak get turned into the undead, slow but vicious. Those strong with Oracles become more advanced living corpses that fly across they cross the atmosphere at top speed and thrasher spirits, the dead with Oracle but no longer have a sustainable body. What's left of them is their skeletons. They're not like zombies. Zombies infect and turn humans they bite into the dead These are rather puppets, they're controlled and manipulated, they don't bite but they fight. They fight and they snarl. They're tongue-tied to prevent them from giving speech. They are the most morbid creatures she has ever set her eyes on. Venas never really has nightmares but sometimes she couldn't help but vision them during the dark hours and tries to think of something more cute and fluffy to fill her head with. Happy things like puppies and kittens or bunnies and hamsters. Like the red-eyed bunnies at the marketplace in the Empire city. Sometimes, she even thinks about going back, maybe there's still a way to make portals and travel between the two planets whenever she wants... but as Kasey said, it's merely possible to make portals as a mortal without the help of a superior element like the dark crystal and the shadow diamond. The shadow diamond was a new one. Out of all the books she's read about shadow arts, there wasn't a lot about the shadow diamond. She read it briefly, one of the first books she read about shadow arts was about the shadow diamond. Just like the dark crystal, they are made from killing people with Oracles and killing people who don't have Oracles does not affect its power. However, the shadow diamond is a little bit different. It takes in the power of slaughtered Oracle holders and sucks the energy from those who don't therefore, everyone killed increases the strength of the diamond. Making it way more powerful than dark crystal. That was all she knew. Any more information in the book was ripped out. It was a very tattered book and worn out but it seemed like someone tore the page out on purpose. It wasn't burnt or soaked. But it didn't matter now. Shadow diamond or not, she was helpless and to think that the red lady is expecting her when the time comes. With her around, how is she even going to sleep soundly every night without thinking about her? This is Earth and yet, Venas still doesn't feel safe. She hoped that the lady doesn't know her identity as a human; that would make her more relieved and less anxious. If she didn't know, then she wouldn't need to be concerned as much. It's better to keep human life separate from the mutant life that she's lived for three days. Or maybe she knows already. That would be terrible. Every night would be exhausting if she were to find out where Venas lived.

A gust of shivers rushed down her spine just imagining what could happen. Being here isn't safe anymore.

"Are you okay?" Lily interrupted her thought process.
"What, oh- yeah I'm fine," she fiddled with the sand.
"We can play games on our ipads- mum's gonna bring us some lunch later," she said.
"Sure, I'll go get mine," Venas left the dining room and trotted upstairs to fetch her iPad from her bag and came across the anti-venom she kept on the side of her bag.

It would be useful to keep it around. It was amazing how it got rid of all her scars along with her mutated appearance.

But it will only work with Slevel's breed of snakes. And they've all gone except Slevel himself, what if he does remember everything and escapes. Valdina must be lying. It's hard to believe what she says… or any demon on her side.

As time went on, things were still the same, the adults still weren't back yet and the upstairs was dead silent whilst downstairs got a little bit noisy from the music of the games. Lily got caught up in an intense game of jetpack where her brother, Kris came to join them in a casual and friendly contest of who can go the furthest. Chatter rose between the three of them and it killed the time too. Kris was two years younger than Venas but one year below her in school, his birthday is a few days off from Lily's birthday which is the 4th of January. He and Venas have met when they were toddlers but none of them remembered that moment. The only way Venas knew was when her mum gave her a photo from the time. three-year-old Venas with her chubby belly holding a breading stick while Kris was wriggling about in his stroller. Venas recalled a lot of moments from when she was little but this, she did not.

"What I got 3572!" He bellowed after losing first.
"Oh, I'm still going," she said. Kris won most of them, he was more flexible when it comes to games.

The winter night fell quickly after what seemed like a few games but yes, New Year's Day is just half an hour away. The sofa was now back to its original space, a bit further away from the T.V. in front of the grand piano. The ones you see at a piano concert were smaller and coated with a shiny black polish reflecting the crystal chandelier that dangled from the ceiling. Lily mum came home first at eleven O'clock, she scurried through her to-do list and got Kris to switch on the BBC channel to have it ready for the countdown that everyone's been waiting for. Even though it was just watching some fireworks on live T.V. but it was with family. And that's all that matters. Soon, Lily's dad came back home at forty minutes past, he made it to sit down with the children after having some midnight snacks but on the way, he got changed and took a quick shower. The kitchen in a takeaway does not let you exit without making you smell like grease and chips.

"Quicker dad, you're gonna miss it," Lily rushed when it was fifteen minutes past.

"Don't worry, there's still time," he said.

Venas was currently sitting at the dining table drinking some apple juice to relieve her thirst and saw Lily had poured out some more for the family. She handed them the juice to drink before snuggling on the sofa with their cushions. Lily bounced up and down on the cushions waiting for her mum to finally come and sit. There were three tight minutes left until all the camera panning of Central London came to a halt to focus on the London eye instead of the traffic of humans down below. The city was crowded like usual, every year it's chaotic but there's no need to worry because there are hundreds of police officers on duty. A blister of light sparked from the London Eye and caught everyone's full attention.

"It's starting," said Lily.

This year is about to end, and London Eye's amusement is going to brighten up the new day like it was the last night of their lives. Why wouldn't it? Hundreds and hundreds of fireworks were about to go off and launched into the sky like sprinklers. Venas thought about all the money that it must cost for the procedure. A number that she could not imagine but that wasn't the point of tonight, the point is when the last minute finally arrives in preparation to celebrate the first hour of 2016. Heartbeats pumped fast in everyone's blood as they all watched the small hand pointing at twelve and the bog hand ticking second by second from thirty to thirty-five. From thirty-five to forty. The tension of the New Year feels slowly bursts into an exciting and energetic countdown, all eyes on Big Ben. It was time to say goodbye to 2015 everyone.

10... 9... 8... 7...

But along with everyone counting down at full volume. Venas mouthed the numbers as she couldn't help but think something wasn't quite right. The thing she saw early, it feels like it was here again and it was watching her. She couldn't hear its heartbeats but that's mainly because of how loud everyone is. Well, she didn't hear its beats before.

... 6... 5... 4...

It got closer and closer to the front door behind the living window.

... 3... 2... 1 !!!

DING! DONG! DING!

Happy New Year!!!

The moment those fireworks began, the crowd sparked glory and joy and welcomed the new year with a raging hip and hooray feasting their eyes on the explosion of colour and sparks illustrating art in the sky and crackling as it evaporated in mid-air. One by one in an endless loop, colours spread across the sky.

BANG!!!

Instantly after the firework display, the room fell into silence. The T.V. kept playing but everyone in the room fell into peace. Venas was taken by surprise by the sudden drop in human activity in the house. The volume went from ten to zero within the flash of a millisecond.

"I suddenly feel really... really tired," Lily rubbed her eyes and dropped on the cushions.
"Lily?" she shook.

She popped her cushion down to wake everyone up.

Everyone was sound asleep, propped on top of one another, all cosy and warm.

"What in the world... why- hey, wake up, they're fast asleep," she shook them again, "why so sudden," she looked around, zooming her eyes from the darkness of the room past the brightness of the T.V. "Don't- don't scare me like this," she panicked.

She took in a sharp gasp, all she could hear was her own breathing. A spec of light whizzed past the window, the light shone through the blinds and disappeared. She stumbled towards the window and pulled them up to see what was outside but all that's there is snow. Partially melted snow and her partially melted snow bunny with its eyes on the grass. She released the blinds and stormed a view towards the dining room door that leads to the kitchen. The gloominess of the first hour of the new year turned out to be quite daunting given there's a sound coming from the kitchen but nothing was there. It was some sort of tapping noise. Or was it just the sink water dripping? Slowly, she creaked the door open and switched on the lights...

"What, I could've sworn the lights worked perfectly two minutes ago," she said as another tapping attraction hit her direction. It came from outside?!?
"Who's there!?!" her right-eye contact slipped out of her eye with a blink and glared a red glow as she stared out the window through the darkness.

BEEP   BEEP   BEEP

Taking deep breaths, she bravely moved closer to the door into the glass warehouse. Her eyes and head moved around vigorously to the beeping noise, trickling of gravel and the rustling of the wind.

There's definitely something there, she thought. But it's moving and it doesn't have a heartbeat. She still couldn't hear a single thump. Could it be a living corpse- no, corpses don't beep. They growl and snarl. For some reason, she felt anxious, the trembling brought her back to her midnight wander in the academy library with Markcas. Everything she felt at the time, she was feeling now. Her heart throbbing, her hands shaking and the terror, the fear of seeing the face of another living corpse. She told herself: it better not be a living corpse. She mentally prepared herself for anything that was about to happen, gripping the window ledge behind her, preparing her right hand to speed right the Chinese character 'open' in the air with light energy and slashed it at the warehouse door leading to the garden. The character was absorbed into the glass door and swung open. She stormed out to attack but it was no living corpse.

A hand grabbed her and nearly swung her over the fence to the neighbour's backyard but she stopped herself in time to press all four limbs on the brick walls before bouncing back on the ground like some kind of animal. She remained in her squatting stance on the ground like a monkey with her back to the house and the mysterious figure standing in front of her. He was a person but his beats. He didn't have any. Then she looked closer and noticed a familiar structure to his figure. Amongst the dim moonlight seeping through the clouds, a source of white metallic material reflected into her eyes. The blue and the white with black bits that camouflaged with the darkness the rest stood out from the snowy background of the garden. His human form, the steel and iron coating and the buttons on his arms. He looked down at her. His silhouette stood out from the moonlight.

"You're..." her eyes widened in astonishment, "Astron!"
"Hello, do you know who I am?" he said.
"Of course I know who you are, I just said it, it's Astron," she repeated.
"No, do you know my identity?" he asked again.
"What? No, I don't," she answered with no hesitation, her ability to lie in situations like this was getting better.

Connar could see no tell on her face when she answered or maybe that was because it's dark outside. Nothing gave her away. Not a single movement of shakiness but he knew why he was here.

"What else do you want me to say? Iron man? You're Astron, icon of robotics and society protection and defence," she made her answer more detailed.
"That's true but you know who I am under the helmet."
"What you talking about, I've said it already, everyone knows who you are, you're in magazines, the T.V. social

media, you're everywhere but I don't know who you are under the helmet," she remained on the ground and looked up at him.

"I know you know my name is Connar."

What, it's him, why would he tell me that? His suit, it blocks out the sound of his heartbeats. She thought. Her hands and feet pressed on the ground with nothing to grip. She refrained from fidgeting with her clothes to show how nervous she was when Connar kept questioning her.

"Let me reintroduce myself, I am Connar Armsward, head of Arms String Department of Robotics and AI Technology," he said.

"Are you expecting me to tell you my name?"

"Your name's Venas Xoular," he said.

How the heck does he know?

"Yes, that's me, is there any reason why you're trespassing our property?" she tried to ask politely.

"I'm here because I believe you're the pink mutant... you're human now I see," he justified.

"Now? I've always been human," she attempted to cover but somehow, those words hit like a bullet.

"So you're telling me you're not the mutant I was talking to in my office, the one that refused to give me her name?" he squatted down to the same level as her.

"I'm not quite sure where you're going with this but no, I think you have the wrong person, if you're hunting a mutant, I don't think hassling a human like me will do anything for you."

"I see, so you're not who I'm looking for? That means you have to keep my identity secret now that I've told you."

"Why did you tell me in the first place?"

Connar leapt back onto the grass sending snow into the air from his force as orbs spun past him, darting towards her. A staggering gust of wind flattened the grass as the sudden shock in Venas's eyes sensed the orbs of steel fly past her head when she dodged them one after the other. They hit the ground and when she had her back against Connar, he boosted a ball at her. The red in her eye sparked and she caught it without even looking at it.

BANG!!!

The ball was heavy and made of metal and she caught it. She gasped as an explosion of fireworks invaded the night sky. The neighbours were all outside. Did they hear them? No, they're all too busy celebrating. Venas couldn't help but think Connar had exposed her. He knew all along that she was human ever since he met her or maybe a bit later than that; when did he find out.

Damit, he already knows, she thought.

You can't see it but Connar was smiling under his helmet.

"You're a bright one I have to say, you're fast and your reflexes are effective," he praised. Venas heard him despite being so far apart, hearing him pass the banging and crackling of the fireworks.

"Thank you," she kept her guard up but that seems to be the reason she was exposed.

"You caught the ball pretty fast… and without looking as well, that's impressive…," he looked at the house," may I?" he invited himself into the house with Lily and her family still sleeping on the couch.

Connar removed his helmet and clicked a button to free himself from the warm suit. He made himself comfy at the dining table. Venas asked him politely and nervously if he wished for some drinks. He replied with tea. Once she made the tea, she sat opposite to him. He took a sip, Venas clenched her hands and waited for him to talk or for the right time to ask:

"You did something to them," she implied.

Connar grinned.

"Don't worry, they'll be up and running in the morning," he assured her.
"Oh, what did you do though?"
"Sleeping pills, it's as simple as that."
"But how did y…" she briefly pointed behind her for some apparent reason. She thought back and recalled the strange thing she's been seeing in the corner of her eye all day, "That was you? You've been lurking around all day!"

"Not me, it was one of my androids," he sipped his tea calmly as a spider-like android crawled out of his suit and onto the dining table. It was cute and he was a piece of AI equipment that Connar brings with him wherever he goes. Though he is kept hidden.

"So basically it was you, do you want to tell me why you're here, you know who I am now, is that a reason to seek me at this hour?"

"Yes, you're the pink mutant, do you have a name for your mutant identity or were you serious when you said you don't have a name?"

"I was serious about that."

"Why is that?"

She waited a while to answer his question. Is it a good idea to pitch him the story of how she got bitten by Slevel's snakes and turned into a mutant only a few days ago therefore not having much thought of naming herself when she was busy taking care of Slevel. She told him why in the end. It was a long story short kind of explanation and he understood everything. He understood why she suggested using Slevel to create anti-venom, but since it takes so long to make it, she didn't wait for the result.

"But in the end, you turned back."

Venas nodded and showed him the serum she used. She too started drinking... a glass of water instead of the contaminated apple juice.

"You're telling me that Cyris's blood turned you back?" he observed the tube.

"He grew up getting bitten by snakes, it helped."

"That's understandable, it's impressive," he put the blood back on the table, "but this isn't the reason why I'm here."

"Really? I couldn't tell," she said with sarcasm.

"Yes, you seem to be waiting for something," he chuckled and suddenly became serious and focused on what he was about to say. "I'd like to offer you a role in the Society Protection and Defence programme."

Water shot down her throat the wrong way and she started to choke from the surprise of Connar's choice of speech.

"Are you okay?"

"I'm fine - I'm fine, you want me to apply for England's society protection?" she repeated with a question mark.

"Not apply, you don't even need the interview, I've already seen your abilities. You're flexible, fast and strong, I'd like to give you the opportunity to work with me."

"Work FOR you?"

"No, work WITH me."

"Uh... I'm not sure if that's a good idea, sir."

"Why not?" he inquired.

"Because... I don't live in Nottingham, I'm not gonna be here for long so there's really no point in hiring me, I live way too far away," she said.

"Well, where do you live?"

"Southeast England," she prompts.

"Then you can be based in the London department," he solved the problem that Venas never wanted solved thinking that this was the cliche moment the hero gets an astounding offer but turns it down. She understood why. All the danger that she's faced.

She didn't want to go through it again, not again. At least this time, she didn't lose any of her friends to the God of death. She couldn't help but still have visions of Kyle dying in her arms and all the blood he left on her clothes, all the blood stains were pianted in her mind. If she was part of some kind of protection programme then she'd have to be responsible for every human being in the county of London, their death and lives. With Tai Wei in the River Thames and Valdina loose on the run, her job as a protector will be stressful. London isn't exactly a small city. Valdina could be anywhere. She's probably out attacking innocent victims right now at this very moment. No, Venas needs to think of it a different way. If she becomes part of the protection programme, she can protect them, she can do more than what Connar and his team can do, she has an aurora, she has a celestial. She is more capable of defeating demons than they were. Without guns and devices, they'd be defenceless against them. Gadgets and devices are limited. Connar can help her hide her identity and the idea of preventing innocent people from getting hurt and getting killed for one's greed is growing in her head. Is she about to say yes?

"That's not the problem anymore," she said nervously.
"What's the problem then?"

"The problem is..." she started. She dug in a bit deeper with the thought and intentions, her concerns for London and its people. Connors' offer still hovered over the table. Venas couldn't make an excuse anymore. Like Master Ocean offering her to be his first disciple, she rejected it at first but in the end. She became his disciple and trained with him for two and a half months until she landed back on Earth. It was the thought process. She stared out the window with the noise of sparklers and fireworks still banging in the air. It was final. "I have one condition," she said.

"Oh, what is it?" Connar was caught off guard.

...

"Slevel isn't the only monster loose in the UK, there's more like him lurking around the country, specifically, the city of London- Slevel only went to Nottingham because her was after me and the what was in the caves."

"So you're saying...?"

"I know I'm..." she moved her hands around to express herself, " in no position to tell how to do your job but you need to keep your guard up because they will keep attacking the city like they have for the last few years," she warned and explained briefly, and her condition is: "you let me and the mutants deal with the monsters."

Connar took a little while to digest the speech bubble that she shot into his ears. He didn't think he was serious but he looked in her eyes and saw the focus she put into her words.

This girl, he thought.

"You're not serious are you?"

"I'm serious about this, you've seen what they can do, they have powerful orbs called dark crystals and shadow diamonds and the reason why I destroyed it is because I can't beat them as long as they have them let alone humans with no powers. The next monster we're able to deal with is three times stronger than Slevel, everyone's gonna get killed," she explained.

"I understand your concerns it's our job to protect the city."

"You can't protect the city from something you can't even fight, guns are not gonna work this time," she stated.

"We can improve our technology, make them stronger," he suggested.

"I don't think it's gonna help, devices aren't enough to beat them, I'm suggesting that you leave it to us, we can fight them," she stood up and pressed her palms on the table. The chair squeaked across the black floor tiles, "you're gonna get killed," she repeated, "not hurt... killed, they're not mutants, they have no heart, they won't show humans any mercy because killing people is what makes the shadow diamond power which gives THEM power, the fewer people they kill, the more of a chance we have to defeat him, I don't want to witness another murder scene Armsward," her eyes shook when those words came out of her mouth. Like she was ready to cry but she wasn't crying, she was holding it in. She's right, it's too much risk for humans with no power to deal with demons like Tai Wei and Valdina. "They're after me," she added.

"What do you mean they're after you?" he felt her words.

"They couldn't care less about the city," she said sorrowfully, "they're just using it as a safe place to raise the embryo so that no one can destroy it, I can't do it alone, it's too strong," then she thought: if it was on Ervanna then everyone's power combined would be more than capable of destroying it but no, it's on Earth, a place Andromedians find difficult to travel to.

"There's no need to force it out, if you're this concerned about the situation then I'll take your condition," he accepted sincerely, "whatever it takes to keep the city safe."

Connar wasn't possibly going to leave the city to Venas and the mutants, but this means that they can prove themselves. It can be a way of unveiling their potential towards humanity.

"Say what now?" she said.
"I'd like to have you on the team," he grinned.

Venas stared at him. He's acting like he's just won something.

"That's... that's great, I guess," she said, "what's next? You want me to sign something?"
"Yes, there are some papers, you also get a badge."
"Like a plastic one?"

"Platinum... of the team logo."

"Plat- platinum? Are you sure about that, I can do with a plastic one, I can't carry that around with me," she insisted.

"You're not changing my mind, I'm giving you platinum and you're to carry it with you all the time," he demanded.

"But, I'm gonna lose it."

Connar stared dead into her eyes to reveal that he did not want any more excuses.

"I - I'll be quiet now," she shut her mouth. She sat back down

"From now on, we'll be in contact when any danger approaches the city and for anything, I may need you to do..." he stated.

Wait, am I getting paid for this? She thought.

"If you're not confident in being an official member of our team, then you can take on an internship, you will keep your identity a secret like myself, Serena, Zara and Cody, there are only four of us, with you that makes five," he continued.

Does that mean I'm gonna get a suit like them? She glanced at his suit laid across the table and thought: ain't no way I'm wearing that. An iron and steel suit does seem pretty heavy to wear around.

"Being part of the team means you do not mention it to anyone for your safety and the safety of your family and friends, it important that we keep ourselves confidential, amongst Armsward String AI, not a lot of employees know who Neon, Echo and Bult are but only a few know that Astron is me, they are under a contract to not spill anything and science no one in the company has seen you in human form, it's easy to hide you," he justified.

Right, this doesn't seem familiar at all, she thought sarcastically. She went backwards in time to when Master performed his ritual of claiming her as his new disciple. When Kayne was in charge of doing the speech.

"I Kayne Wen, hereby enrol Miss Venas Xoular as the first official disciple of Master Hai LoonFei, Miss Xoular must adhere to three rules: firstly, you must respect your Master and his wishes on the subject of your training as well as the respect of your own health and safety, secondly, you must not use any of your teachings to offend or negatively take advantage of others, therefore think carefully on how you portray yourself as a disciple and thirdly, you must not expose yourself as the first disciple of Master Ocean to anyone, your friends, peers or anyone else who questions you, who you are enrolled to, only the members of the royal family and close Palace employees are to know of your relation to Master Ocean, this ensures your safety as well as the safety of your Master."

She was still Master Ocean's disciple. Nothing was done to announce that she was no longer therefore, her position was still valid but what good would that do if she wasn't able to see him. She never thought of going back to Ervanna for one, she isn't capable of going back anyways. Over all this thought, Connar asked:

"Is there any name you prefer to go by?"

"Name? I'm not quite sure."

"Whilst you're thinking, let me go through some important factors, I have these papers here about all you need to know about the company and London's Society Protection Programme, make sure you keep them somewhere safe, you still have school so you will keep that at priority but in emergency's you will need to make some time for this role, it is expected that there isn't much you need to do besides anything practical and paperwork, a few tasks you can take on whilst getting started and finally, the role of defending the city. There's been plenty of unsolved murder cases since now, as you said if it's the monsters you're expecting to fight, you and the mutants will handle it, I know a few mutants living in the city, Lucas Lanheart and his family as Cyris has mentioned before, during the summer you'll be able to meet them, now you must adhere to signing some forms, a contract and your internship, this will end once you've turned sixteen- that is when you are legally able to work in the UK, you will get some new updated forms to sign, do you understand?"

"I- I understand," she said confidently.

"I'm giving you this watch, it's a form of communication," along with the paperwork, Connar slides a white mechanical watch across the table. It had plenty of buttons and functions on it.

"Thank you, I'd be happy to meet them, you just need to remember, nothing is to get close to the bottom of the

River Thames and nothing is to die near the city otherwise it gives the embryo power, it absorbs lost souls and that's what makes it stronger, it takes nine months to release the vessel that the demons are using, you must be aware of the demons are hosting the embryo because they're the ones on the loose apart from that, I have nothing much I need to say," she stated. She felt her heart racing from the pressure of talking all of a sudden, she was nervous so she talked pretty fast. Talking at a fast pace is something venas tends to do when she gets nervous. Connar can't tell but she is internally excited about the role he had just offered her despite her concerns and 21 questions.

"And how would you like to be addressed?"

The lights were still switched off so all Connar could see was her two-toned eyes slightly glowing amongst the darkness and the dust particles that slowly floated around within the rays of the moonlight shining in from the midnight sky. The sudden silence was broken by a wild burst of fireworks and it clicked. The name to cover her identity, she announced:

"Wildfire."

THE END
THANK YOU FOR READING

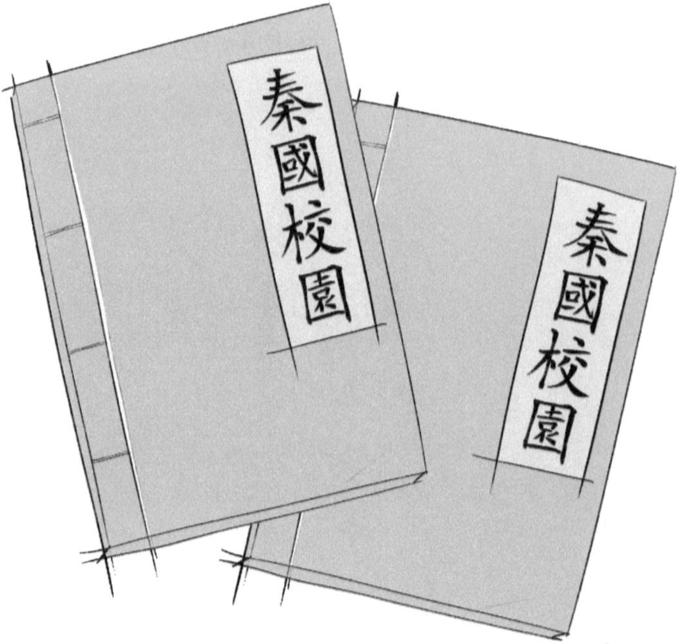

SEE YOU ON OUR NEXT ADVENTURE IN

TO BE CONTINU...

www.ingramcontent.com/pod-product-compliance
Lightning Source LLC
LaVergne TN
LVHW091529060526
838200LV00036B/541